# The Summer You Were Mine

Andrea K. Goss

Published by Gypsy GoGo Creative
Oakland, Maryland, USA / Rancho Cucamonga, California, USA
www.gypsygogo.com

ISBN: 979-8-218-47680-9  (Paperback)
ISBN: 979-8-218-48439-2  (eBook)
Library of Congress Control Number: 2024916719

First Edition 2024

Editor: Marie Beswick-Arthur
Proofreader:  John Wisse
Cover designer: Kaitlin Goss, Joy Media Designs / www.joymediadesigns.com
Interior designer: Paul Baillie-Lane /www.ingenious-books.com

For more information or inquiries, visit the author's website at www.andreakgoss.com
Facebook: Andrea K. Goss – Author
Instagram: andreakgoss_author
Email: author@andreakgoss.com

# Dedication

**For ScottyMac**
Not many people in a lifetime get to ride a
perfect wave like that—boy, did we.

~

**For Summer**
I carry you with me.

~

**For my family: Scott, Kolten, Karina,
Mom (Jane), Dad (Terry), Damon, and Angie**
You are my roots, wings, and heart. You are home, wherever I am.

~

**For those doing the hard work of healing from loss and grief**
'Weeping may endure for a night, but joy comes in the morning.'
Psalm 30:5

*Here, I say, we have lived, we have been happy.*
*This has been ours, however brief the time.*

~ Daphne du Maurier, *Rebecca*

*If I should meet thee after long years,*
*How should I greet thee?*
*With silence and tears.*

~ Lord Byron, *When We Two Parted*

# *Prologue*

AND SO WE MEET AGAIN

SEPTEMBER 2022

September in Ocean City, Maryland, 1,676 miles away. My heart called, so I followed.

It's Saturday night. My red kitten heels soak in water from the rain as I run from my car to the door. I don't care. It's nice to feel pretty again. As I enter the elegant wine bar atop the new hotel by the bay, I take a deep breath to calm my racing heart. I hope he's already here.

This place is beautiful; he always did know the places to go, though we couldn't afford most of them back then. It's classy, upscale, and without any nostalgic ties.

The amber lights cast a soft glow from the brushed gold, candle-style chandeliers and the colorful array of bottles lit from above and behind the bar. The European décor is a nice change from most of the beach-themed bars that dot this coastal town. A mix of dark and light wood contrasts well with Old World brick walls and arches; the floor-to-ceiling windows beckon my gaze to the bay beyond. Soft

1

piano music plays as I walk to the circular bar with more hope than confidence.

I have always followed my heart. Sometimes this is wise. Sometimes it isn't. This time, I've come full circle to a place and a person I have loved for so long. The romance that he and I shared in the summer of 1986 was like something out of a movie; coming back here to see him is bittersweet. After all this time, and so much change, the love I feel remains the same.

For so long, and for many reasons, I kept my love for him buried deep within my heart. I've lived a good life, but one spent mostly in a fog. Some big things happened to shake that up, and the need to see him has become greater than the need to keep what we had in the past. I recently looked him up on social media—a profile containing scenic views of the ocean and old pictures of him—and after working up the nerve, sent a message.

> *Hi Sam,*
>
> *Hello from the past. I hate to be that cliché ex-girlfriend who divebombs back into your life out of the blue after all this time, but I have the nerve to ask a favor. I'm sorry about the way things ended long ago. I regret that, but I've never regretted a moment with you. The summer you were mine and I was yours was pure magic; that has never changed.*
>
> *Could we meet in person? I've written an article that a magazine wants to publish. It's about us—and about a secret I never told you but should have. I don't want it to go public without you hearing it first; after all, it's your story, too. It may help you understand why things ended the way they did. You never knew. It's personal. I would prefer to tell you face to face.*
>
> *Why now? After the unexpected deaths of three people I loved, all within two years, grief has shattered me, and some painful things from the past have poured out of dark areas*

*to demand light. Writing about it was part of a long-needed healing. I'd like to share that with you.*

*I don't want to step on any toes if you're married. I heard that you're separated, so I hope it's okay to reach out. I'm divorced, but don't have an ulterior motive to rekindle a romance. I simply want to share the rest of our story because you deserve to know.*

*I live in Texas now but will visit Ocean City in September. Do you still live near there? Can we meet? You always said you can't say no to me. I hope it's still true.*

*What salutation should I put here? ("Sincerely" is too formal; "Yours truly" too honest),*

*Kristin*

His name is Shayne, but I've always called him Sam. I was terrified to hit send, but I did. Would he mind my use of that intimate name for him? Would he mind me reaching out? Would he write back? Would he be open to meeting? It could go either way. On the fourth day, as I was about to give up hope, he responded.

*Hi Kit,*
*I still remember you sitting at the bus stop in front of*
*The Greene Turtle—and everything else after that. I'm intrigued—and apparently still can't say no to you. Let's meet. I live about an hour away from OCMD. You give me the day and time; I'll give you the place.*

*Not sure this is all real, but it's a helluva prank if it's not. My instinct says yes, it's real. It was always real. Let's go with that.*

*(A writer who can't think of a clever salutation? Slacker.)*
*Curious,*
*Sam*
*p.s. There is no instinct like that of the heart. ~ Lord Byron*

I smile at his use of his nickname for me, his quote from one of my favorite poets, and the warmth and humor of his response. I don't deserve it, yet he wants to make me feel at ease. He has never been unkind to me or let me down, even though I had let him down grievously.

From that first exchange, we'd made plans to meet in Ocean City in September.

Then I told my best friend Annie, who also knew him in '86.

"This has to be the dumbest thing you've ever done. And you know how low of a bar that is," she'd said.

I had laughed. She's like a sister to me; she can get away with saying things like that. We've been friends from birth, and she loves me even when she doesn't approve of what I do. She offered to come along with me for support, but I have to do this myself.

I've learned the hard way that life is short, that people we love die or leave, and that we don't always have another time to say things we need to say. I've learned to process difficult things sooner rather than later, or good people suffer. I've learned that the sting of truth is not as painful as the rot of holding secrets. I've learned many things too late, but better late than never.

After all this time, I'm going tell him the secret I've kept for too long, and maybe redo a bad goodbye from so long ago. Is there such a thing as a good goodbye? Is there a way to make amends for a wrong done to someone? I don't know, but I'm going to try.

Annie, of course, doesn't think so. She knew him and liked him, but she shut down the concept of re-opening doors to the past.

"Most goodbyes are shitty," she'd said. "They're supposed to be, so you stay away from each other. And secrets are supposed to stay hidden. He doesn't need to know."

"I should've told him long ago," I'd said. "And since then, I never thought it was right to interrupt his life to tell him. But he may read the article when it's published. Doubtful, but he'll know it's about him. I don't want to blindside him."

"Of course you should've told him back then," Annie had said. "And you should've told me back then instead of just a few weeks ago. I still can't believe you didn't."

"I didn't tell anybody. But now you know. And he should, too."

"I guess. It's just usually best to let the past alone. I don't want you to get hurt or expect some storybook reunion. That's for fairy-tales, not reality."

That summer was like a fairytale, except for the ending. I'm not the girl who gets those endings. I do sometimes daydream, though, about living by the bay in Ocean City and walking barefoot onto the back deck to sit beside him. I would hand him a Stoli Gimlet, and I'd have a cherry cola. We'd watch the sun set over the water, his hand in mine, and then make love under the moon like we used to. The reality is, I'm here just hoping he shows up. I'm nervous to see him again. I need to make things right after all this time, to share something that's been hidden for so long, to set part of me free and, hopefully, do the same for him.

I'm grateful to be here, especially after two years of pandemic iso-lation. Thankful to be in this town that holds so many great memo-ries. It's the last place I felt like my true self. I haven't been here since that summer with him, before cell phones, the internet, and social media, when life here was like the Wild West, with crazy antics but no lasting evidence.

I wonder if we'll recognize each other after all this time. I don't even recognize myself anymore. I've gained weight, wrinkles, and wisdom over the years. I guess most people do. I'm certain, though, that no matter what Sam looks like now, I will see my golden Adonis from that summer. I could never forget him; my heart is too sticky.

So much time has passed. Time enough to know about betrayals, loss, harsh realities, and stubborn hope. Time enough to have withered inside by the secret I kept, weakened by a toxic marriage with a good man who wasn't safe when he was angry, and regretful for passions I never pursued—until now. Time enough to know that in a world where so much is fake, my heart remembers what is true. What I had with Sam was true. Tonight, he deserves the truth.

I wonder if he will be warm or cold to me. Will he be disappointed in the middle-age me instead of the young woman he remembers? What if he doesn't show up at all?

Meeting somewhere new to both of us was a good idea. I look around. I like this place. Muted music and laughter mix with the rhythm of the rain. A string of lights sways outside over the deck as candlelight dances on the wood tables inside. Patrons talk in hushed tones.

I don't see Sam, so I go into the restroom to apply a light coat of courage in the form of red lipstick. The mirror reminds me I'm not the nineteen-year-old I was with him, but I'm also no longer the dispirited middle-aged woman I had become. I've been doing the work for healing and growth. Finally. I'm forgiving myself for mistakes I've made, admitting hard truths, and opening up from being closed, like a flower slowly welcoming the sun—and the rain—to bloom.

Deep grief was the catalyst for a monumental change in me. I went from feeling nothing to feeling everything, and remembering everything that I had tried so hard to forget. Grief gutted me and, oddly enough, jolted me to life again. Decades of captive, stifled feelings poured out: pain, love, loss. I wrote an article about it all. That's what has brought me here to him.

I know I can't get back what was lost, but it feels good to feel again, even if it is painful. I still have so much love in my heart for Sam, and it's freeing to let it flow again, even if he can't receive it or return it now. At least he will know it's still his.

I smile at myself in encouragement. Whether this night goes well, or not, I will be okay.

I walk back into the bar area and suddenly stop. I feel him before I see him.

This is nothing new. Any time I was ever in the same room with him, there was an electric charge in the air, and a magnetic pull. Even now. Even now.

I turn in the direction of my instincts; there he is, sitting at the bar, the light reflecting off his faded golden hair like the sun used to all those years ago. I would know him anywhere. The familiar curve of his lips. The chiseled jaw. The high cheekbones. His perfect nose. The proud strength of his profile. The way he holds his beer, delicately almost, with an easy elegance. The sound of his laughter: hearty, deep, and true.

My heart leaps at the sight of him as he chats with the bartender, laughing without a care. Typical Sam. He could get along with anyone, anywhere. His laughter transports me back in time, and I know I am safe with him, no matter how much I may have hurt him. I have to trust that the goodness in him is as timeless as the love I still hold for him.

Before I can talk myself out of it, I walk over to him and put my hand on his broad shoulder. "Sam," I whisper.

He slowly turns. We lock eyes. His gorgeous, cobalt-blue gaze rests on me, guarded but kind. I feel like myself again, lost in his eyes and the soul behind them.

We stare at each other, so much unsaid but felt in one glance. Time doesn't matter. I am his and he is mine, and whatever happened between then and now is irrelevant in this moment. Some things never change. Our connection is still deep and true. To be in his presence one more time is worth all I went through to get here.

We embrace. The feel of him is like coming home.

"It's been a minute," I say.

"I've thought of you often in that minute," he says.

We step back and take each other in. The softness of his voice, his sincerity, and the way he looks at me makes me feel young and beautiful and his again.

"You still know how to charm me," I say. I remind myself internally to pull back from a flirtatious mode. That's not what I'm here for. He is no longer mine.

"Let's go somewhere more private to talk." He gently takes my elbow and leads me to a table for two by the bay window. We sit and automatically lean in toward each other.

"From your Facebook profile, I see you're a college swim coach," I say. "Good fit."

"And you're a writer. Like you always wanted. I'm proud of you."

My breath catches at his words of affirmation. When we were together, he constantly uplifted me with encouraging words I didn't know I needed to hear until they fluttered like a feather from his mouth to my heart. He filled so many spaces I didn't even know were empty.

For a moment I feel like that young woman again, at the beginning of our story so long ago. I want to slap her and hug her. She was so unequipped for everything back then. So naïve and stubborn. So ready for the love that was to come. So unprepared for what happened next. Who was she before the destruction? I briefly close my eyes to try to find her again.

When I open them, my eyes inadvertently wander to where the top button of his shirt meets the hair of his chest—one of my favorite parts of him. I desire him, instinctually, and have to wrestle my mind from that direction. It's been a while since I've been intimate with anyone; it's good to feel desire again. I glance up. He's smiles, having caught me. I blush and smile back.

"So, Kit." His husky voice still hypnotizes me. "I'm curious. What's this secret I should know about? Where do we begin?"

*A dreamer, I walked enchanted,*
*and nothing held me back.*

~ Daphne du Maurier, *Rebecca*

## TRUST ISSUES

APRIL 1986

"Shit or get off the pot," Mom says. She loads the orange dishwasher while I grab the car keys and try to sneak past her. "Lifeguard at the town pool again, or work at the mini mart or the factory? Those are your choices."

"None of those," I say. "I told you two weeks ago that Annie and I are going to live and work in Ocean City this summer. Why do you pretend you don't know?"

"Because the beach is not an option."

"I'll be twenty in four months. I'm old enough to do what I want."

She gives me the death stare. I glare back. Two months ago, my best friend Annie and I hatched our plans to spend the summer at the beach, far from our Pennsylvania hometowns.

"We should do something crazy," I had said to her at our college place when we were lamenting the summer ahead with dread instead of anticipation.

"Like what?" Annie had appeared bored—knew I wasn't the crazy type.

"A girl in my Mass Media class is going to live at Wildwood, New Jersey, for the summer with her sister. Let's do that but at Ocean City, Maryland. Wouldn't that be fun?"

I hadn't expected Annie to take me seriously. She was quiet for a minute.

"Our moms would never go for it," she said.

"Not in a million years," I said.

Annie smiled. "Let's do it."

I thought she was joking until she came to me with a whole plan of when we should tell our parents, when we would go on a scouting trip to line up jobs and a place to live, when we would move there, and when we would return at the end of the summer for band camp.

Mom's resistance is not surprising. We knew our parents wouldn't want us to go. That won't stop us. This feels right, and I'm going to do it. I've learned the only one I can trust in life is me. I've always been the obedient, compliant girl who did what I was told and blindly trusted guidance of people who said they loved me, but that hasn't always worked out for me.

My trust issues started when I started dating my first sort-of boyfriend. I had been an overweight, mousy-haired middle schooler until puberty visited and I lost weight, gained breasts, and traded what my sister called my bug eyeglasses for contacts. By the time I was almost fourteen, I was visible. I didn't know how to handle attention after being invisible for so long.

That's when Ben asked me out. He was seventeen, and the first boy to notice me and tell me I was pretty. He went to school in another district; we met at my dad's company picnic. I was shocked when Mom and Dad said it was okay if he took me to a movie. Like, a date.

I was confused. I had so many questions. Why were Mom and Dad letting me go out with him? Wasn't I too young? Wasn't he too old? Shouldn't we be chaperoned or something? Mom had said that he seemed like such a nice boy. They trusted him, so I trusted him.

Not long after our first date, Ben said he loved me and then tried to have sex with me in the back seat of his black Dodge Charger; I was only thirteen. Thirteen! When he tried to force me, despite my saying no, I kneed him in the crotch and said I never wanted to see him again. And I never did.

My parents were wrong about Ben. After my experience with him, I stayed clear of boys until I started dating Jake when I was fifteen; we didn't go all the way until I was seventeen. That probably was still too young, but I believed I was ready and in love. Trust took another hit when Jake started cheating on me early on in the relationship, and often.

In high school, I had told my parents and guidance counselor that I wanted to go to college for advertising. I trusted them when they said I should go to a two-year trade school to learn to be a legal secretary, instead, because it was "more sensible." It only took one semester there for me to realize my mistake and transfer to the same college as Annie to major in English.

I trusted the adults in my life who led me in directions that weren't true to myself. Even though I expressed what I wanted, they didn't listen. They didn't *hear* me. I began to doubt who I was and what I wanted; all I could hear was their voices and not my own.

Now, headed into this summer of possibilities, I'm trusting myself, trusting my gut and what feels right to me. I don't quite know what I want, but I know what I don't want. I don't want to stay in my suffocating small town. I don't want to work in that dark, dreary factory.

I do want to do something memorable and exciting with Annie this summer before my junior year of college. Ocean City is a great choice because our families have vacationed there together since Annie and I were kids. It's the perfect mix of adventure and familiarity.

Mom has the opposite opinion, with no room for mine.

It's almost the middle of April, and Annie and I are home from college for the weekend to let our parents know our beach summer is a plan, not a possibility. Final exams are early next month, and then Annie and I will go. I need this conversation out of the way.

After the mutual death stare with Mom, she resumes loading the dishes, banging them with great theatrics to show that she's for real mad. She continues her resistance.

"Old enough to do what you want, yet Dad and I pay your bills," she says.

Dad is watching a *Bonanza* rerun in the living room nearby, collapsed on the floral couch that he had burned a cigarette hole in one night as he dozed off after a late shift at the steel mill. I cup my hand over my ear because the TV is so loud.

"Denny, turn the TV down!" Mom yells.

The whinny of horses and gunshots decrease. I take a step closer to the back door.

"I pay for a lot of my own things," I say. "And I never ask for money."

"That's because we make sure you have it. You have no idea how much it all costs. Your part time college job and summer work put a dent in it, which is why you need to work at the factory—it pays well. You need money for books, clothes, and gas money."

"I'd rather eat my fingernails than work there."

"I didn't raise you to be such a snob," she says. "Every college student wants that summer job, and I can get you in."

"I know all that. I'll save money working at the beach."

"Not once you pay all your bills there. Your dad and I can't afford for you to learn this lesson the hard way. You're not going."

Smidge, our black cat, has been watching us like we're playing ping pong; he stretches out on the floor between us like the net.

I head to the door, desperate to leave.

"I am," I say. "You and Dad can stop paying for college, the car, whatever else. Annie and I are going to scope out apartments and jobs there at the end of this month. We've saved a little from our part-time jobs for a security deposit and our initial expenses. We'll move there by Memorial Day weekend and stay for the summer, whether you and Aunt Sue like it or not."

Our moms have been best friends since they were kids. Annie and I have always called them aunt. Both moms rule their roosts. Her family lives in a town a half an hour away, so we weren't in the same school when we were younger, but our families often went on vacations together and we saw each other most weekends growing up.

"This is Annie's wild idea, isn't it? You always follow her like a puppy."

"What? No. We both want to go. Geez, Mom, I just want to go away for the summer, not join the circus."

Mom jams a dish into the dishwasher. I notice her hand shake a little. "It's not safe, and you're not ready for something like that. Neither is she. What's gotten into you both?"

My hand slides around the door handle. I should've said I was going to be a stripper. This desire to live and work at the beach for a summer is apparently a bigger sin.

Going against my mom is new territory. Annie isn't used to going against her mom, either. It's terrifying. But today, Mom seems unsure of herself. For the first time, it's like I'm speaking with her woman to woman. She doesn't have my blind obedience anymore; neither of us knows how to handle that.

I'm not used to seeing vulnerability in her steely strength. She has a beauty, elegance, and intelligence to her that is out of step with our surroundings. The rural town where we live, with its one blinking light, can't hold me anymore, and it should never have held her.

Mom once said that when she was a teenager, she wanted to move to Philadelphia after high school to be a stewardess. That was before she got pregnant and married Dad. My sister Sarah was born six months later. I came along seven years after that. Whatever dreams of flight she had were grounded by family and her job as a secretary at the local factory. I had once asked her if she ever regretted it. She had told me that family always comes first.

I respect and love her, but this is my life. I'm not going to budge. I half open the door.

"Annie and I will look out for each other," I say. "I just want a fun summer before I graduate and get a real job for the rest of my life. I want to get away from here and from Jake. See what else is out there in the world. I'll go back to college in the fall. No big deal."

Mom stops shuffling dishes and lights up a cigarette. "It is a big deal. I don't want you to struggle like Dad and I do. You need money for college so you can graduate and get a good job that gives you freedom and security. And you don't need to live at the beach to untangle yourself from Jake. Just stay away from him. Have some self-respect for once."

I hold my breath and bite my tongue from releasing harsh words that are forming there.

"That's low," I say.

Mom's unsympathetic, blue-grey eyes sear into me. She's intimidating, despite being five feet tall and built like a tiny bird. I have her eyes and weird nose—that's about it. I'm five foot five, and slim but curvy. Mom and I can't be more different, physically or emotionally. I need to dial this down, and fast.

"I know you want what's best for me," I say. "And this is best. I work hard. Always have. I'll make the money I need. And this isn't just about Jake."

"Then why did you mention him? Didn't you break up with him at Christmas because he was cheating again? Why do you still see him when he calls?"

I sigh. She registers her scored point by taking a long drag on her cigarette.

"Yes, we broke up. And, yes, when we were both home from college, I saw him sometimes. That was stupid of me, but I'm done. You should be glad about that."

"I hope it's true," she says. "Why buy the cow when you get the milk for free?"

I can't stand another cliché. It's time to go. Even Smidge gives up and saunters away.

"I'm going to Annie's to plan our scouting trip. We've already advertised for two beach roommates in the classifieds of the college paper. This is happening. It'll work out fine."

There, I've said it. I take a breath. She scowls.

"Seems like you two have been plotting for quite a while," she says.

"Planning, not plotting," I say. "I'll be home by ten. Please don't be a bitch about this."

I practically run to the carport. Saying bitch to her isn't my style. I don't know why I said it, except I'm finally willing to face her wrath for doing what I really want to do.

I'm going to Ocean City for the summer. There's no turning back. Annie and I have responses to the ads we put in the college paper and on bulletin boards. Two girls have said they'll put down deposits when we find a place.

I go out to the driveway and open the door to my old Chevy Celebrity when Jake's white Mercury Cougar pulls up. What's he doing here? He isn't supposed to be back from Penn State until June, after Annie and I have gone. I want the no goodbye option with him.

Jake Jasco is my kryptonite, or at least he was. A hard habit to break. My first love. My only love. The only guy I've seriously dated and been completely stupid for. I don't trust myself to see him before leaving for the summer, since he's the only one who can probably talk me out of it. I have to cut ties with him for good, any way I can.

He walks over to me and shuts the door to my car. I guess I'm not getting in it anytime soon. His tall frame and broad shoulders fill all the space around us with electric energy. I feel like I'm fifteen again, at the start of my sophomore year of high school when he first spoke to me—awkward, dazzled, and gobsmacked. I hate that he still has that effect on me.

When he had approached me that day, I thought it was a prank. He was a popular senior, the football team's quarterback, and gorgeous.

Muscled, a megawatt smile, feathered light brown hair, blue-green eyes that looked a little sleepy. He could have any girl he wanted. Why me?

Even after morphing into someone who got asked out by cute guys, I couldn't shake who I felt like inside. At my foundation, I was a geeky loner bookworm. Attention from someone who looked like him was unfathomable. I had grown up quiet and plain—not ugly enough to be made fun of, and not pretty enough to notice. After the Ben thing, I'd ignored attention and rarely said yes to date invitations. Jake was different. We shared a chemistry I didn't understand.

He'd walked up to me as I was putting books in my locker. "Hi." His dazzling grin and mesmerizing eyes put a spell on me. "I'm Jake Jasco."

I'd looked up at him, scowled, and said, "Congratulations. I'm Bo Derek." Then I'd slammed my locker shut and walked away.

I'm sure he wasn't used to that reaction from girls. He must've thought I was a bitch. I was pissed because I was sure he was just messing with me. Nothing else made sense.

He called me two days later to ask me out. There are only so many Spaides in the phone book; it's a small town.

I caved. Who says no to a date with Jake Jasco, prank or not?

He showed up the next Saturday night in faded jeans and a tan button-down shirt. I opened the door to his irresistible smile. "You ready, Bo?" he asked. I was hooked.

He opened the car door for me and took me roller skating. He bought me ice cream. Took me home. Gave me a soft peck on the cheek before he left.

Thankfully, the date was not a joke. It was like a dream. We've dated on and off since then, with many ups and downs. He's always been more than good looks. He's smart, funny, nice, and a hard worker. Unfortunately, he's also a serial cheater. I'm not. No matter how much fun we had, he would cheat. I'd break up and date other guys who didn't measure up. Jake would apologize and swear it wouldn't happen again. I'd take him back. Rinse and repeat.

I'm exhausted. I can't do it anymore.

When we broke up in January, it didn't even hurt, I was so used to it. The occasional weekends we saw each other after that were like habit, not love. I'm done. This summer away is my perfect getaway. The plan was to leave and let him figure out I was gone. After all, we aren't together anymore. I don't owe him anything.

"Hi," I say. He inches closer to me. "What are you doing here?"

He puts his arms around my waist and leans down to kiss me. I turn my head and step away from him. His eyes widen in surprise. Neither of us are used to this.

"I heard you and Annie are going to Ocean City for the summer," he says, "but that can't be true. You wouldn't do that to me."

"It has nothing to do with you."

"When are you leaving?"

"Soon."

"For the whole summer? What about us?"

"There is no us," I say. "Not since January, remember? It's just that now I won't be a periodic pit stop for you. It's over for good this time."

He shakes his head. "With us, it's never over for good." He has the audacity to smile.

The light in the sky is fading, and the sunset peers through the maple and pine trees. The lightning bugs start blinking, and the humidity has made his hair wavy. It isn't fair that this setting is pure romance. I wonder if the neighbors are looking out their windows at the Jake and Kristin soap opera, now starting season five, tuning in to see what happens next.

He gently brushes a wisp of hair from my face. "We'll see about that." He leans over to kiss me. I don't resist this time. Such a good kisser. We are great together that way.

I never smoked, drank, or did drugs; I never wanted or needed to. Jake has always been my drug of choice. He's a gravitational pull that consumes me. I've been told, too often by too many people, that I should've quit him long ago. They're right.

I've given Jake way too many chances, and we both know it. Maybe he's been irresistible to me because I think I don't deserve him. The truth is, he doesn't deserve me. My summer plans with Annie feel like a turning point. I'm ready to turn around and face new days without him.

"Stay," he says. "I'll come home every other weekend. We'll go to some concerts. Annie can find another roommate for the summer. I can't find another you. I love you."

His words have always sounded sincere. He's good at that.

He doesn't say he wants to get back together. He doesn't say he wants to commit to me. He doesn't say anything meaningful except his familiar, empty, I love you—bait for a hook I've been caught on too many times before.

I shake my head. What a fool I've been. I step back.

"Is this a game to you?" I ask. "To hurt me on repeat? To not care about what may be best for me? You use me like a toy."

"That's not true," he says. "I keep coming back to you, don't I? There's a reason."

"Yeah, you can't stay away, but you can never stay, either. Do you know how much it hurts that I'm not ever enough? Great sex, but you can get that anywhere. And you do. I don't. For me, it's always been only you. But for you, I'm just an easy yes."

"You're more than that, and you know it," he says.

"Your actions say otherwise. Goodbye, Jake."

"You'll come back to me."

"I won't."

"I'll visit you at the beach."

"Don't."

I've stood up to Mom. I'm standing up to Jake. Who am I?

We stand in my driveway at the exact spot where he first kissed me under the full moon what seems like ages ago, as the same stars wink like a secret floating in the air. I'm ready for life to take a dramatic turn. The sunset is a fitting end to the day, and to the relationship.

I stand up on my toes and kiss him softly on the cheek.

"I love you, but I want to be enough for somebody. And that's not you."

I turn and get into my car.

I'm sure he thinks it will be like all the other times when a little time will pass, and he'll wag his finger and I'll run back. He's wrong. I can no longer tolerate his disrespect.

I drive the twenty minutes to Annie's house. Not one tear shed. I'm finally finding some dignity buried beneath my bad decisions. Of all the trust issues I have, I've realized that I can be the most untrustworthy of all when it comes to Jake. I can't let myself down this time.

For once, I'm the one leaving Jake behind, not the other way around. I'm choosing my next steps, not Mom or my guidance counselor. I'm listening to myself instead of fitting in with everyone else's needs, wants, and expectations. I'm taking a new road to the one place I always find peace: the beach. I trust my instincts. It feels good. I'm ready to finally choose myself.

Filled with renewed confidence, I go to Annie's and confirm our plans. The next morning, I deliver a conciliatory smile—and a compromise—for Mom at the kitchen table. I tell her that I'll work at the factory next summer if she'll let me work at the beach this summer without any more fuss. I don't intend to follow through with it, but it does the trick because Mom knows I'll go either way; this lets her feel like she got some sort of win.

Annie and I return to college. A week later, after two long phone calls, Mom and Aunt Sue reluctantly agree to help us with our summer beach plans, probably because they know we're going to go no matter what. That includes them going with us on the scouting trip to find a place to live and line up jobs. Annie and I will drive home from college that weekend so we can all go to Ocean City together. I can't say it will be fun, but it sure will be interesting.

*Afoot and light-hearted I take to the open road,*
*Healthy, free, the world before me,*
*The long brown path before me leading wherever I choose.*
~ Walt Whitman, *Song of the Open Road*

# Chapter 2

## FLYING THE NEST

### APRIL / MAY 1986

April flies by. All I can think about is the scouting trip that will lead to the move, and then to the summer of freedom. Thankfully, the two girls who responded to our ad, Bianca and Marion, remain interested.

As planned, on the last weekend of April, Annie and I drive home from college and hop in the back seat of Aunt Sue's blue Monte Carlo. The dads have to work, so they aren't going. Aunt Sue drives as Mom navigates from the passenger seat and manages the snacks. Annie and I giggle and gab in the back seat like we did when we were kids.

We've already been briefed by the moms that, although the only area Annie and I can probably afford is by the inlet and the boardwalk, they will worry if we live there. Mom has made an appointment at the real estate office where she's always booked our vacation rentals. She wants us to find a nice place to rent uptown, in North Ocean City. "North is nice, midtown is moderate, and south is sketchy," Mom says. Probably not true, but she thinks it is.

I'm sure we'd be fine anywhere, but we won't turn down a nicer place. Once we're in Ocean City and filled up on gas and food, Aunt Sue pulls up to the midtown real estate office. Mom puts on lipstick—she's now in charge. We go into the office and watch as she flirts with agent Ronaldo 'Ron' Domenico, who has dark slicked back hair and a cheesy mustache.

We are soon following his BMW down Coastal Highway to see a few condos for rent. He shows us several that the moms veto because they're either in an area that's too unsafe, or too pricey, or not nice enough. You'd think Mom and Aunt Sue are used to country clubs and caviar instead of diners and tuna casserole.

The fourth place, in a residential condo complex tucked back toward the bay off of 139th Street, is the winner. Ocean City's dual appeal of ocean and bay is divided by Coastal Highway. One side is the Atlantic Ocean; the other is the bay, with an array of hotels, motels, condos, small houses, townhouses, and single-family homes on both sides. Either side is great; Annie and I can walk to the water either way. This place, though, is particularly nice. And pricey.

The second floor, two-bedroom condo is in a quiet neighborhood; the complex has an outdoor pool. There's a bus stop a few blocks away, so I won't have to bum a ride from Annie all the time, since we're taking her car and leaving mine at home. It's kind of far from the action of midtown and south by the boardwalk where most college kids live for the summer, but we like the thought of a quiet place to return to after work and parties.

Ron goes downstairs for a cigarette to let us discuss the condo without the pressure of his presence. Mom, Aunt Sue, Annie, and I gather in the small white and brown kitchen.

"This place is nice, but out of our league," I say. "Annie and I planned to get something south of here, where it's more affordable and there are more people our age. Let's go see some of those places. It's not as bad as you think, Mom."

"Yeah, this would be really tight for us," Annie says. "We don't have enough for the security deposit. We'll be fine somewhere cheaper."

"Well, we won't," Aunt Sue says. "We'd worry too much."

"With two more roommates, you should be able to make rent," Mom says.

"Barely," I say.

"I can help with the security deposit," Mom says. "This is a safe neighborhood, and if you insist on being in Ocean City, I insist on you being here."

Annie and I nod at each other. Resistance is futile. We'll make it work. Once we all agree this is the one, we drive back to the real estate office, where Ron requires the security deposit. Annie and I offer what we'd put aside, and then Mom pulls out her checkbook and fills in the difference. It's Mom and Ron who shake hands—we are still the children. Ron hands Annie and me a set of keys. My heart skips a beat. We are doing this!

The moms stroll down vacation memory lane as we eat dinner at a cheap buffet. We head to the inexpensive but clean hotel that Mom booked and, in the morning, Annie and I follow up on classified ads we see for waitress and hostess jobs; we don't want to work retail.

We line up jobs before the afternoon is over. Annie has serving experience, so she gets hired as a waitress at an upscale restaurant a few blocks from our condo; they hire me as a hostess. It's a nice place with a beach-chic interior and a massive outdoor deck that overlooks the bay. Annie will make good tips. My position won't pay as much, but I can pick up a second job once we move there.

Things are falling into place so smoothly that I have to pinch myself. Mom has always said that when things are meant to be, they happen easily; they never have to be forced.

Before we head back home, we drive by the condo where we'll be living and stare at the summer that is to come. I'm so excited, I can't stop smiling during the drive back home and then back to college. Neither can Annie.

We confirm with the beach roommates that we have a place. They're as excited as we are, and they get their deposits to us within days.

"What happens if they back out?" I ask Annie.

"There are lots of ads in the Ocean City paper looking for rooms to rent," Annie says. "If they bail, we'll replace them. The condo is gorgeous. Who wouldn't want to live there?"

Studying for finals is worthless; I can't concentrate. Thankfully, most of my classes don't have cumulative tests as finals. Annie isn't worried about hers; she's good at tests. Once we finish finals the week of May fifth, we have two weeks to pack, plan, and be on our way.

Jake calls me several times at college fishing for information on where I'll be living and working at the beach. I don't tell him, and I stop taking his calls.

"I'm proud of you for finally giving him the boot," Annie says. She's been pushing for that for years. "I know it's hard, but it's best for you. You deserve better."

"You know what, Annie? I finally know that's true."

She hugs me and takes my hand. "Promise me that once we get to the beach, you won't talk about Jake or pine over him. Ocean City is a great place to casually date—nobody wants to get serious there. You've been with him so long, and he's hurt you so much, I'd love to see you just date around and have fun. Promise?"

"Date around. Casual. Fun. Check."

Jeff, Annie's boyfriend of two years, broke up with her six months ago. She handled it like a champ. If she can move on from someone special, I can, too.

Once finals are over, we quickly close up the college rental house for the summer and head back to our hometowns. The two weeks we have to pack and plan logistics go by quickly, and it's soon time to leave for our great adventure.

Saturday, May 24, is here before we know it, and I can't wait to get on the road to the beach. My heart is full. Annie shows up with her car loaded with luggage; she left a little space for my stuff. Aunt Sue and Uncle Al arrive separately to join Mom and Dad in seeing us off. Mom and Aunt Sue run in and out of the house getting snacks and drinks for our road trip.

Dad and Uncle Al look over Annie's 1980 mustard-colored Dodge Omni—Annie calls it gold, I say it's mustard—to make sure the tires are good, the oil is full, and everything is in working order so that it has a good chance of making it from Pennsylvania to the Maryland coast. They joke around like they always do to lighten the mood and take the edge off the moms.

The humidity is already sticking to everything. Smidge peers through the big bay window of our small, single-story house. The weeping willow in the side yard rustles in the breeze like it's waving goodbye for now, goodbye for the first summer I'll be spending away from home. The modest house, with the light green siding, cute carport, and small front porch, has been all I've ever known. I just might miss it.

My suitcase slips perfectly into the remaining spot in the trunk. While everyone fusses with something, Dad comes over to me and leans against Annie's car. From photos I've seen, and from Mom's bragging, he looked like Elvis back in the day. He's still handsome, but with a small belly paunch and some gray peeking through the dark hair at his temples. He slides his hands in his pockets.

He never says much and isn't very affectionate or bold. He works a lot, so I rarely get to spend time with him. When I do, we watch TV westerns together, play Wiffle ball, or just sit out on the carport some evenings listening to the radio as he smokes Marlboros and the bug zapper violently kills flies and God knows what else. He rarely tells me he loves me, but he shows it. He always makes sure I have what I need for school and works overtime for vacations and other "extra" things, like a used car for me when I went off to college.

"Hey, Dad. Thanks for looking over Annie's car," I say.

"Still got some life in her. Wouldn't let you drive to Ocean City if I didn't think it would see you through."

"You're the best."

"If it causes you trouble, call and I'll come get ya."

He straightens up, looks over his shoulder, and then pulls out a Hershey's chocolate bar. It's a covert operation, one that takes place every time I return to college from a weekend at home. One of his calloused hands returns to his pocket and retrieves something else. He slides a wad of cash into my hand.

"Don't tell your mom." He winks.

I feel the bulk of the cash. "Dad, this is too much. I can't take it." Usually he slips me twenty dollars; this time it's more than a hundred.

I know how far he and mom make a dollar stretch. I know how many hours he has to work at the steel mill to make this much money. The overtime must have been on the sly so as not to dent Mom's strict budget. It isn't the kind of extra money he typically has.

"Sure, you can." He kisses me on the cheek and gives me a quick hug. "I'll feel better if you have something to fall back on. You be safe and call us to check in."

I tear up. It's the most he's said to me in ages. "Thanks Dad. Love you."

He walks away, then mutters. "You, too."

Mom knows he gives me a stash of goodies now and then; she's made the occasional comment. If she knows about this one, she has uncharacteristically let it slide. As if on cue, she comes out of the house with a few bottles of lotion in her hand. "Did you pack sunscreen?"

She stuffs the lotion into a beach bag full of towels that also holds my stuffed turtle named Amara that I've slept with every night since I was four when I went to the hospital to get tubes in my ears. It's the only present I remember getting directly from Dad.

"I've got enough for us both, Aunt Jeannie, don't worry," Annie says. Of course, Annie has remembered to pack sunscreen. She does all the practical things, while I pack posters for the wall and feather clips for my hair.

Annie is like a big sister in a way my own sister, Sarah, has never been. To be fair, Sarah is seven years older than me—a big gap. She's always had her own life, friends, and interests. I felt like an only child once I got into middle school and Sarah was at college. When she did visit, the most I got was an affectionate tap on the head. I don't see her much anymore; she's an accountant living an hour away near Harrisburg with her nerdy but nice fiancé Gary.

Annie, on the other hand, is only a year older than me. We're different in many ways, but we balance each other out. I'm the dreamer; she's the doer. She's athletic; I'm artsy. She's tough; I'm sensitive. She's the glue; I'm the glitter. When I had the crazy idea of living at the beach for the summer, she took action to make it happen.

What started as a pipedream has materialized. Somewhere in our luggage are the rules our moms have created that we will pretend to follow.

1.  The parents will not contribute one dime toward our rent and bills.
2.  We will call our parents at least once a week to check in.
3.  No guys will stay overnight at the condo.
4.  No Alcohol. No Drugs.

I agree with the no drugs rule, but we all know there will be some alcohol consumption, even if it's just wine coolers. Fortunately, the moms will be far away and not know. Surely the no guys overnight rule is a joke.

Rule number one would be easier if we had gotten a cheaper apartment, like we wanted to begin with, but we won't ever ask them for money. Mom's help with the security deposit to get us in here was nice, but that's it; I hope it doesn't come at a cost.

The money Dad slipped me will help me to get a local phone number set up, plus a local bank account, a bus pass, and lots of other things I need to pay for before I get a paycheck.

Finally, the car is packed to the max. Final hugs are exchanged. Annie settles in the driver's seat. I buckle up as her passenger and prime navigator. Mom, Dad, Aunt Sue, and Uncle Al wave from the front yard.

I've been waiting for this moment for what seems like forever. Now, leaving feels weird. Mom and Dad have always been my safety net. They're only an hour away from college, close enough to come and help me if I need it. I'm not really ever on my own. Annie and I share a room in an old, three-bedroom house near college that we rent with four other girls. Someone is always there.

Mom and Dad will be five hours from Ocean City—too far for an emergency trip. It's both scary and exhilarating. Annie and I have each other, though. I'm not alone.

The air is charged with excitement on the long drive. We roll down the windows, mainly because the air conditioning doesn't work anymore in her car—has it ever?—but also because the hot wind on our faces feels like freedom.

We blast the radio and sing loudly out the windows at Whitney Houston's "Greatest Love of All," Janet Jackson's "What Have You Done For Me Lately," Madonna's "Live to Tell," and everything in between. We are hoarse by hour three.

"I can't believe this is real." I scream it for the twentieth time.

"It's actually happening," Annie screams.

"We're going to live at the beach!" We laugh when we say the same thing at the same time. We carry on like crazy fans at a Van Halen concert. We headbang at rock songs. We make weird voices with punk songs. We stick our arms out the window and pull in a downward motion when truckers pass by to get them to honk. They always do.

Annie pulls over for a bathroom break and we buy sodas and Snickers bars. We restart the adventure and laugh as we say, "Cheers."

"I can't believe how easy it was to find roommates," I say. "I mean, what's the catch?"

Annie shakes her head. "Don't overthink everything. No catch. Just meant to be."

"I hope we'll all get along well, or at least that they'll pay their part of the rent and utility bills on time each month," I say. "They couldn't be more opposite."

"Go with the flow," Annie says. "They do seem so different, but it'll work out."

I think back to when we met them, after they responded to our ads. We met up with Bianca Esposito at an off-campus pub. She's Italian, the daughter of a Pittsburgh judge, and blunt. Mom would say that she's full of piss and vinegar. I liked her brashness and confidence right away. She'd said that she was spoiled and got what she wanted, and that what she wanted was to live at the beach for the summer. She'd also said that her family may or may not have mob ties, and how it helped with getting out of speeding tickets and into sold-out concerts.

"I also can get quality fake IDs if you need them, with the friend's discount," she had bragged. Annie and I didn't know whether to be impressed or afraid about the mob ties. I would need a fake ID, though; Annie just turned twenty-one, so she didn't need one.

When we signed for the condo and let Bianca know about it, she brought her part of the security deposit and the first month's rent to us right away. No way she is backing out.

We had met Marion Cannon in the dining hall one day after classes. She had seen the classified ad and called us the next day. She's a devout Catholic who doesn't drink or party, and she frowns on what she calls "slutty behavior." She wears crop tops, short skirts, and Madonna-like jewelry. Her dark blonde, curly hair is cut in what can only be described as a long mullet. Somehow, she carries it off and gives "don't mess with me" vibes.

The plan has always been for Annie and me to arrive at the condo first. We'll share the master bedroom that has its own bathroom. Marion and Bianca will join us two days later and share the smaller bedroom, which has two twin beds; the main bathroom is theirs.

The drive is long, but we make it fun. I can't wait to get there. The air is full of promise. For once in my life, I feel carefree. This is our summer. We want to make it memorable.

The ocean has always felt like home to me, especially this one. Years of family vacations at Ocean City are baked into me; I love it. As we drive through Lancaster, Pennsylvania, then through Delaware, and then enter the city limits with its familiar salty air and sea breeze, I scream with joy. This summer, I'm a local, not a tourist.

Annie drives past the turnoff to the street where our condo is and instead heads down Coastal Highway all the way south to the boardwalk. We pass condo row, and then the mix of budget motels and cottages of midtown, and then arrive at the grittier southern tip where the boardwalk meets the inlet and is alive with energy. We can't stop smiling.

Annie turns around and heads back north.

"How many times have we played mini golf there?" I ask Annie as I point to the one with the big pirate ship.

"Or eaten at Phillips?" asks Annie.

All along the strip, I see pockets of good memories. When I was little, Mom and Dad would stuff their green Volkswagen full of suitcases, beach towels, and drinks to drive here without knowing where we were staying. Dad would pull up to one small mom-and-pop motel after another on the south end, where things were cheaper—and still are—until they found a vacancy. We'd spend a week swimming, walking the boardwalk, and having fun together. Mom and I would often read on the beach, while Dad and Sarah body surfed in the ocean.

As I got older, Mom and Dad splurged on nicer places. Mom would go into ultra-frugal mode and save a little bit of each paycheck throughout the year so she could book a nice condo in North Ocean City that people like us usually couldn't afford, like at the Sea Watch.

Its indoor and outdoor pools, game room, tennis courts, and ocean-front balconies filled me with wonder. Mom would walk in like a queen, regal, like she owned the place. Some summers we vacationed with Annie's family and shared expenses; it was the highlight of the year for all of us.

Annie and I reminisce as we drive along Coastal Highway, where east and west promise stunning sunrises and sunsets along the ocean and bay, and where adventure awaits in every direction. We stop to eat at Dumser's, a family favorite ice cream place that also serves casual lunch and dinner food, and then head to our condo.

As we turn onto 139th Street, the surroundings change from commercial to residential. We pass townhomes, houses with cute front porches, and upscale condo complexes. Ours is tucked about five blocks back from the highway, and about two blocks from the bay. It's even better than we remember. We park, grab some suitcases, race to the entrance, leap over the threshold, and drop our stuff in our sea-green bedroom. We run around like kids at a carnival.

"It's perfect," I scream.

We hug and collapse on the living room couch. We can't stop laughing. There's no joke, just joy. Who knew freedom had the same effect as a good comedy act?

"I'm glad we've got a couple nights to ourselves before our roomies arrive," I say.

We eventually return to the car, unpack, and make up the king bed with the sheets we've brought from home. It's a little after eight o'clock, just enough time to walk to the bay to watch the beautiful pink and purple sunset. It's a beautiful welcome to the promising summer.

"It's a whole new world," Annie says. I agree.

We sleep well and look forward to a little time together before our roommates arrive, and before we start work. We're ready for it. We're ready for it all.

~ Ralph Waldo Emerson, *Merlin's Song*

# Chapter 3

THE NEW WORLD


MAY / JUNE 1986


Annie and I are glad to have two days to ourselves before our roomies arrive. We shop and stock the fridge and cupboards with basics, put toilet paper in the bathrooms, buy bus passes, and get some ice cream. When that's all done, we lounge by the pool and then lie out on the sand by the ocean to get a start on our tans. There's nothing like the sound of the waves and the feel of the salty breeze on the skin. We agree we'll set up bank accounts on Monday.

Memorial Day weekend is a week away; we'll start our jobs on Wednesday in time for some training before the rush of tourists on the holiday weekend. Annie and I are glad we aren't tourists this summer; we get to stay and enjoy it all for three whole months.

Two days pass quickly. Bianca bursts into the condo as we're eating a lunch of turkey sandwiches on the tan, brown, and orange striped couch in the living room.

"Honey, I'm hoooooooome!" she yells. She's a firecracker. We greet her with hugs and help her bring in a lot of luggage.

She's short and pretty, with shoulder-length, thick brown hair, mischievous brown eyes, and a killer body. I know she'll get any guy or any job she wants. She's fun and fierce—I can learn a lot from her. She finds her room and plops her things on a bed.

"A twin bed, huh? Small but mighty, like me," Bianca says. "Good closet space, though. I won't be here much, anyway. It's a great home base. Not like some of the dumps I've seen."

Marion arrives mid-afternoon while Annie and I are at the beach. When we get back, she is settling into the room she and Bianca share. Bianca sips wine and watches television in the living room as Marion unpacks in the bedroom—so much for our no alcohol in the condo rule.

We order pizza for dinner and, as planned, meet in the living room to discuss the house rules so we can all reconfirm our commitment to each other.

Annie lays it out: "First, this needs to be our peaceful place away from work and play. We'll get kicked out if we're loud, so no parties here—go somewhere else for that. No drugs, no pets, no boyfriends living here, and keep the place clean. We need to schedule out of town guests staying over so we don't have a million people here at once. No surprises. Agreed?"

"I'm gonna be out a lot, so I'm good having this as a place for some downtime and quiet," Bianca says. "If I bring a guy home, we won't be too loud."

"No guys in our room. And be quiet if it's late," Marion says.

Bianca smiles slyly. "No promises."

Marion gives Bianca a cold stare that could rival Mom's. There already seems to be tension between them; I hope this doesn't spell trouble.

"If we're all respectful, we'll have a great summer," Annie says.

I wonder if it will play out that way. I hope so. Annie has handled it so well. She's such a peacemaker. What would I do without her?

Mom was right. Living here is going to be more expensive that I thought. The groceries we picked up the first night were basics, but pricey. Then there's rent and utilities. I'll want to eat out once in a while, too. When I write it all down, the figures show me it'll take nearly every penny I'll make to pay all my monthly expenses.

I'll have to get a second part-time job, and probably still won't save much money. I won't tell Mom she's right; I can figure out school expenses in the fall.

I start my hostess job on Wednesday; they barely provide any training. After the first few hours I'm overwhelmed and feel beaten up; the waiters and waitresses haven't given me any grace on the learning curve as I either sit too many customers at one station, or not enough. I don't like everyone being mad at me all the time.

On Saturday, I quit. It's just not for me. I still have my lifeguard certification from when I guarded at the town pool last summer and am quickly hired as a lifeguard at the indoor pool of the Carousel Hotel, a nice high-rise resort on condo row. Jobs come and go fast around here.

Annie quits her restaurant job soon after I do because she doesn't like the stress, so she takes a job as the Kids Club coordinator at the same hotel where I work. She supplements that by working a few mornings a week at a breakfast diner in midtown.

Since I don't have full-time hours, I get a part-time waitress job at a small café in an oceanfront condo complex just a few blocks from the Carousel Hotel for breakfast and lunch shifts. I don't have any serving experience, but the owners are nice and give me a chance.

Marion finds a job as a banquet server for a catering company. Most of their business is at the convention center. When she's not working, she's on the beach or attending Mass. She's already made it clear that she will be minding her own business, no matter how much I try to make conversation or invite her out. She's polite but aloof.

Bianca is a fun badass on all fronts. Only days into her stay and she's made friends. She makes the most money and works the least number of hours. When she found out that bartenders make more money than waitresses, she bought a book on mixology and lied about her experience to get a bartending job at a popular high-end restaurant. Bianca could sell eggs to a chicken.

Within our first week there, Bianca supplies me with a fake ID for cheap so that I'll be able to go out to the clubs and bars with Annie and the friends we're making at work.

The first weekend in June, Annie and I decide to try it out at a club. It works. We dance. We have fun. Between the two of us, we'll have a full schedule with our jobs, clubbing, and catching rays on the beach. Sometimes our days off will align. We soon settle into flexible routines and love every minute of it. We feel like we belong in Ocean City.

On one of our days off together, Annie and I swim in the pool at the condo complex, and then go upstairs to have some lemonade on our balcony. We talk about work, our roommates, and guys—we've each already had a date.

"How was your date with what's his name you met at the club? Mike?" Annie asks.

I shrug. "Okay for a casual Sunday date. He's nice and cute enough, but after we got some burgers and took a walk on the beach, he made a big move too soon."

Most people my age who work at the beach for the summer are into casual flings. I'm not built for casual sex, but I thought I might give it a try to see what all the fuss is about. I tried to relax when Mike and I started making out on a blanket on the beach. He was gentle and good with his hands. I thought I could go all the way with him, but I couldn't. I need love to do that. I think I'm going to just flirt and have fun with friends this summer.

"I'm proud of you for saying yes to a date for once," she says.

"I don't know if I'm picky or if I just compare everyone to Jake, but nobody has really interested me. I'm having a good time working and hanging out with you and the other girls."

She lifts her glass and taps it with mine. "Me, too. Cheers! We don't need guys."

I'm glad that she isn't going to pressure me to date more than I want to.

"Do you miss Jake?" she asks.

"Not really, surprisingly."

"I'm so stoked about that. You seem to be doing great without him."

"It feels good. Do you miss Jeff?"

"Sometimes. But I'm good just casually dating for now. It's all my heart can take."

"I know what you mean." I really did.

"Any scoop with Derrick?" she asks. "He's really hot. And we both know he likes you."

Derrick is on the summer maintenance crew at the Carousel Hotel. Since day one of my lifeguard job, he finds reasons to fix things that don't need to be fixed at the pool. He's tall and lanky, with thick brown hair, nice muscles, and unique amber eyes.

"He hasn't asked me out yet," I say.

"A matter of time," Annie says. "It's only been a week. Would you say yes?"

"Absolutely."

Derrick and I have chemistry, though he isn't great at conversation. He's the first one to catch my interest, but I'm not going to make the first move on anyone. Truthfully, I don't care if he or anyone else asks me out or not. Being single feels good. Being without Jake feels right. He was never really mine; I was always wondering if he was with another girl when he wasn't with me, and most of the time I was right. I don't know why I lived with that so long. Plus, I feel at peace at the beach. I know I'm at the right place at the right time.

A little later, on the weekly call with Mom, she tells me that Jake has called a few times.

"He's asking for your number at the beach. I haven't given it to him, of course. I told him to stop calling. He sure is persistent."

"Funny how he only cares so much now that I'm moving on for real. He's not used to me not running back when he snaps his fingers."

"I'm glad to see you doing good without him. You deserve better."

I almost drop the phone at words that might be a compliment from her. "I agree," I say. "And hey, nobody back home besides you guys and Annie's family know where I work or have my number. I don't want anyone else to know."

"Got it. Have you and Annie settled in? How do you like it?"

"Mom, I love it here."

I tell her about my work schedule and life here. I work some mornings at the café, and most afternoons and some evenings at the pool at the Carousel Hotel, including Saturdays. My days off vary each week. The bus goes anywhere I need to go when I'm not going to the same place as Annie—she has her car, but she usually also takes the bus because parking is a nightmare. I'm making friends at work, on the bus, and even on the beach. It's a friendly town.

The café is a great introduction to waitressing. Most tables are out on the deck overlooking the ocean, so I get some sun. The café owners, Marty and Serena, are nice, and the customers are a mix of tourists renting the upstairs condos, or condo owners themselves. They come in to get coffee or breakfast before they start their day, or lunch before or after some time on the beach. Many of the customers I serve are wealthy and tip well.

I like my schedule. After my shift at the cafe, I usually go to the Carousel, change into my bathing suit, then cover it up with the hotel uniform of khaki shorts and a maroon polo shirt with the hotel's logo. The indoor pool area is hot and sticky, but it's a pretty easy job. My boss, Russ, is chill, and the other guards are fun and friendly. Seeing Derrick is also a bonus.

I work as many hours as I can. At night, if Annie wants to go out, I'm all for it. Whether we go out to a club, or to a home party of a new friend, we take Annie's car or the bus. We don't drink much, or at all. We always dance.

Although I get into clubs using my fake ID, I usually order a Roy Rogers. I don't like the taste of alcohol, plus I don't want to make a fool of myself, or throw up, or have a bad hangover in the morning like so many others do. I also worry that I'd be slutty if I had too much to drink; I don't want to go there. When I go out, I have fun—I don't need anything to loosen me up.

Annie drinks in moderation. I don't know about Marion, because she doesn't go out with us. We hardly see her. Bianca is a party machine—she can drink anyone under the table. She's fun anywhere, anytime, sober or drunk, and never seems to have any consequences from alcohol.

That's her luck. It might not be mine. I'm not taking any chances.

My life centers around uptown and condo row for sleeping and working. We find out quickly that most of the clubs and home parties are midtown or further south by the boardwalk. The culture is a fun, frantic mix of college kids like me who are here for the summer mixed with sunburnt tourists and salty locals. There's always something to do. And it's always done with that beautiful backdrop of the ocean and the bay. In my rare down time, I swim, read, walk on the beach, play tennis, and relax. Life is good; I don't miss my hometown or college at all.

When our phone rings, it's fun to guess who the call will be for. It's usually a guy calling for Bianca, but Annie and I also get calls inviting us out to dance or to a party.

We've gathered recommendations from co-workers and new friends for where to go each night of the week. I think we'll be extremely busy this summer.

*Monday:* Harpoon Hannah's 2-for-1 drinks (cute bartender,
   Tony)
*Tuesday:* Taco Tuesday at The Green Turtle
*Wednesday:* Ladies' Night just about everywhere
*Thursday:* Wherever there are half-price margaritas
*Friday:* Scandals and home parties
*Saturday:* Varied:  Samantha's, Playpen, Big Kahuna, or a
   home party
*Sunday:* Designated day to rest and swim (if not working)

There's also Angler's Reggae Night, riding the horse at Libby's, and live music at Trader Lee's. Bianca already is often out at the hottest places. Marion is rarely home, yet we don't see her out at clubs, either. Sometimes I wonder if she's a figment of our imagination.

We quickly find our groove. Bianca convinces Annie and me to join her in a Best Body on the Beach contest at the Sheraton. It's hosted by the popular disc jockey, DJ Batman. I go along but chicken out at the last minute, because no matter how far gone I am from my pudgy pre-teen days, I'm too self-conscious for a competition. Bianca gets third place, and Annie gets fourth out of twelve girls. First place goes to a blonde, busty girl named Natasha who looks like a Playboy supermodel. We're told she enters most of these contests and usually wins.

When Annie and I go out, it's to dance. It's fun and freeing. We don't care about guys, drinking, or anything else, and we usually don't have to pay for drinks. There's always some guy (or guys) who wants to buy us drinks, even though we tell them we aren't going home with them.

Annie had said it would be a whole new world, and it is—one that welcomes me with open arms. Living in Ocean City for the summer is the best decision I've ever made. I'm having a great time with the girls, working to earn my own keep, breathing the ocean

air, and going to the beach any time I want to when I'm not working. I feel free. Life is good. I don't think it can get any better—and
then it does.

*I cannot fix on the hour, or the spot, or the look, or the words, which laid the foundation. It is too long ago. I was in the middle before I knew that I had begun.*

~ Jane Austen, *Pride and Prejudice*

# Chapter 4

## THE INVITATION

### JUNE 1986

Marion is a mystery. Our work schedules are opposite, and she isn't interested in spending time with any of us. The only thing I know she does is go to the beach to fry her lily-white skin into dark brown submission. She puts more oil on herself than my dad puts in the pan for his famous fried haddock and crunchy fries. She's polite but doesn't socialize with us.

It's late afternoon on Wednesday, my day off. I'm on the balcony reading *Rebecca* for the second time, when Marion pops her head out the sliding door and asks me if I'll go out with her. I almost fall off my chair. Then she tells me she needs to go to 46th Street to see a guy named Dave at one of those places that rents umbrellas and beach chairs on the beach.

"They close around sunset. I'd like to catch him before he gets off work because I don't know how to contact him otherwise." She says she met Dave on the bus the day before; he'd asked her to stop by to see him sometime. "If I go alone, I'll look desperate," she says.

I don't feel like going, but since she's never asked me to do any-thing, I say yes. Plus, a girl's gotta help a friend when it comes to matters of the heart.

We take the bus to midtown. It's strange to see Marion nervous; she's usually aloof and quietly confident. By the time we get to the umbrella stand, she's so unlike herself I want to shake her. She's chatty and giggly, and then sullen and snappy. By the time we find where this Dave guy is, I've had enough.

"Chill, Marion. You're giggling like a first grader, and I'm not even being funny."

Marion has never giggled since I've met her; she's the most seri-ous person I know.

I see two guys gathering umbrellas and chairs from sunburned tourists. She points out Dave. He's lean with surfer blonde hair that falls in his eyes; there's something cute about his crooked smile and the way his copper brown eyes shine when he sees Marion.

"Hey," he says. "Marion! Glad you stopped by."

Her face softens, and her eyes light up. "Hi," she says.

I'm a third wheel. "I'm going down to the water. Be right back."

I walk down to the ocean, spellbound as always by the sight and sound of the waves crashing on the shore. It never gets old. I sit on the sand and enjoy some alone time. When I return to the umbrella stand, Dave is gone. Marion is beaming.

"You're beautiful, Marion. Especially when you smile. You should do it more often."

"He asked for my number. Wants to take me to Fager's on Satur-day. I said yes."

Fager's is the go-to date place. It's on the bay and has a pier that leads to a romantic white gazebo on the water. Sunsets are like a postcard. He could've been more creative, but whatever. I wouldn't turn down a dinner date at Fager's.

"Don't you work Saturday night?"

"I'm going to call in sick and hope nobody from work goes there."

"You, breaking the rules? You must really like him." Is Marion blushing? I've seen it all.

I like that we're having this girl time together; I see a softer side of her. We decide to walk on the beach for a while before catching the bus. I've never been to the midtown beaches, so it's nice to see the different hotels and restaurants that face the ocean in a different part of town.

It's just after six o'clock, the perfect time to be on the beach. In about two hours the sun will set over the bay on the other side of Coastal Highway, but for now the sky over the ocean reflects soft remnants of color from the low sun. The lifeguards are off duty, and most of the tourists have returned to their hotel rooms and condo rentals to prepare to inundate the cheap buffets and overpriced seafood restaurants. We take off our shoes and walk in easy silence.

The beach has a sense of calm about it after its daytime swarm of summer tourists. The sun also isn't scorching hot anymore. I need to come out here more often this time of day.

"Dave seems nice. He's cute. What do you like about him?" I ask Marion as we walk.

She thinks for a moment. "He's funny and polite," she says. "Not arrogant like most guys here. Mainly he seems like a good person. Also, his smile makes my stomach flip."

"That's a good sign," I say.

As we pass a few people fishing at the shoreline, she tells me she had a bad experience with a boyfriend a few years ago. After that, she hadn't wanted to date anyone else for a while.

"I feel ready to take a chance again. Dinner with Dave seems like a good first step."

I hope it's a good first step toward her opening up to all of us more.

As we talk, we walk in front of the Ocean Club on 48th Street, where two lifeguards are sitting together laughing and joking around on a lifeguard stand. Beach guards get off work at five-thirty, so it's odd that they're still here. They wear red swim shorts and red t-shirts with the letters OCBP on the front. I know it stands for Ocean City Beach Patrol because I've seen those shirts on beach guards here almost every summer of my life.

One guy is tall with thick, wavy, brunette hair tinged with highlights from the sun. The other has pale blond hair and is average height; he's built more like a boxer. Both have dark tans, broad shoulders, sculpted bodies, and shiny smiles. Easy on the eyes.

"Hey, hi there." The brunette stands to show his tall, lean frame and muscular legs. He reminds me of Jake with his magnetic looks and bold confidence.

"Is he talking to us?" I ask Marion.

"Seems like it. But who cares?" she says. "The girls at work say to stay away from lifeguards; most of them are arrogant jerks."

"That's a pretty broad brushstroke. They can't all be like that." I say.

"Enough to have a reputation," she says.

"Hey!" The tall guard calls again, looks right at us. The blonde one waves.

I look behind us. Nobody else is here. Their workday is done; maybe they're just bored and flirting for something to do. We walk closer to them. These are exactly the kinds of guys Marion doesn't like; it shows on her surly face. I smile and wave back like a dork.

"Are you the late shift?" I ask. "For bad girls like us who might swim in the ocean after hours when we're not supposed to?"

I can't believe I said that. Is this me, trying but failing to flirt with these guys way out of my league? I laugh at myself. They laugh, too. I wonder if Marion is going to kill me.

"You're not good at this," she says.

"Tell me about it."

The tall guy says, "Well, we're not opposed to bad girls." He turns to his golden friend. "Am I right?" Golden Guy smiles and nods.

He's wearing Vuarnet sunglasses; his head is angled toward Marion, who looks pretty in jean shorts and a green halter top that matches her eyes.

Marion isn't having any of it. "Kristin, seriously? Let's go."

"Nah, no late shift," Tall Guy says. "We're just unwinding. Too lazy to leave. I'm Kurt with a K, by the way. And this is my ugly friend, Shayne with a y."

"I'm Kristin, also with a K," I say. "This is Marion, with the conventional M."

Everyone laughs except Marion.

Kurt elbows Shayne, who finally stands and speaks.

"Are you here on vacation?" Shayne asks.

Marion is stubbornly silent. I speak for both of us. "Living and working here for the summer. We're from Pennsylvania."

"We'll forgive you for that," Kurt says.

I know from being a tourist for many years that Pennsylvanians are known in these parts to be the worst drivers. Locals make it known.

"We've gotta go." Marion starts to walk away.

"Hey, wait." There's urgency now in Kurt's voice. "We're having a guard party this Friday night on Jamestown Road at Shayne's place. Nine o'clock. Why don't you both stop by?"

Marion stops and turns toward them.

"We're not guards," Marion says. She starts to walk away again; I tug her elbow to stay.

"I'm a lifeguard, if pool guards count," I say.

"For you that counts," Kurt says. "It's for guards and guests. Say you'll come."

I'm flattered that these guys are talking with us, and even more so that they're inviting us to a lifeguard party. The younger, invisible me would never believe that this could happen.

I give Marion the side-eye. She shrugs. It's better than a no, so I'm relieved.

Shayne smiles. "Free beer, loud music, and lots of bad jokes. It'll be fun."

I know that doesn't sound fun to Marion. I'm not even sure it sounds fun to me.

"So. You'll stop by?" Kurt makes prayer hands.

This guy is so much like Jake. Hot, charming, and charismatic. Shayne is a looker, too, but it's hard to tell with the sunglasses. He clearly has a nice body, but I'm not into blonde guys.

"Maybe," I say. I can't commit when I know it's a hard 'no' from Marion.

Marion starts to lead me away.

"That's a start," Kurt says behind us. "A really good start, right, Shay?"

"We'll take it," Shayne says.

Kurt shouts the address. "See you there."

"Do not look back again," Marion says as we walk away.

"I know, play it cool," I say. "Why are you in such a hurry to go?"

"I'm totally into Dave," she says. "Plus, I told you, we should stay away from beach guards. They're players. And, before today, I would've said not your type, either."

"Fair enough, but they seem nice, and I've never been to a life-guard party. Not beach guard parties, anyway. I really want to go. Go with me?"

"Not my thing. Drinking, probably drugs, sex, and arrogant hot-shots. Absolutely not going. Annie will probably go with you, though."

"I'm pretty sure she works Friday evening," I say. "Come on, come with me. Just for a half hour. There's no way I'll go alone, but I really want to go."

"I hate parties like that. And people like that," Marion says.

"People like what? They save lives, Marion. Rescue people from drowning in the ocean. If I did that all day, I'd need to let off steam after work, too. They seem nice."

"All guys are nice when they want to get in your pants."

I laugh and then resort to begging. "Please?"

"Okay," she says. "If Annie says no, then maybe I'll go. Maybe."

I know she won't, but Annie will if it's important to me. Just like I would with her.

"Shayne was checking you out," I say. "The blonde one. He likes you, so that's probably why they asked. I'm just the friend they have to ask so you'll go."

"Kristin, you're so naïve. Don't you know how pretty you are? Never mind. You don't."

"You're being nice. But thank you." I hug her. Surprisingly, she receives it.

We walk a little more, and then hop on the bus where we each get lost in our thoughts.

By the next morning, Marion is off the hook. Annie says she'll go when she gets off work because it's important to me. Annie also likes athletes, so I know that's also part of it. If Shayne and Kurt are going to be disappointed that Marion isn't there, so be it. They invited me, too.

I didn't used to be the girl who gets noticed by beach lifeguards. Or gets invited to their parties. College parties are plentiful, but this is different. The big leagues. It may be the only time I'm ever invited to go. I'm not going to miss it.

~ F. Scott Fitzgerald, *The Great Gatsby*

# Chapter 5

## FEELS LIKE MAGIC

I can barely concentrate at work the next two days. I know how important it is to focus on watching the pool for swimmers in trouble, but it's challenging. All I can think about is Kurt and Shayne, and the party, and what to wear, and…

"Kristin!" My boss, Russ, jolts me out of my reverie.

I look up, startled. "Yeah?" I hadn't even noticed he had come up beside me.

His lips barely move beneath his thick brown mustache. "Daydream all you want off the clock. Believe it or not, people drown in pools, and you have to notice and rescue them. That's your job. I usually don't have this problem with you, so let's not have this talk again."

He's right. I change up my pool routine. Usually, I sit in the chair by the door to check guest passes while watching the pool, but now I stand up and walk around to keep myself more alert. I pay attention to the scene around me: children laughing and screaming in the round pool, parent's wrangling their kids, old folks trying to swim tiny laps, and teenagers running on the wet cement. "Walk!" I remind them for the thousandth time.

I don't need thoughts of the upcoming party to distract me. The job is pretty boring, so I'm easily distracted, but I can't be. Russ is right. Lifeguarding is an important job, and one moment of being distracted is literally the difference between life and death.

I wish I'd applied for a job lifeguarding at an outdoor pool. I took this one because it's at a nice resort hotel and I don't have to worry about getting a sunburn. It's weird that it doesn't have an outdoor pool, because many people are like me—I like to be at the ocean, but I prefer to swim in a pool where I can see what's in the water. I don't have to worry about sharks chomping me, and the water isn't going to pull me out to sea and drag me under.

Because the indoor pool is hot and muggy, I leave the pool area on my breaks to go to the beach, the on-site restaurant, or the hotel's gift shop. Sometimes I watch people skate on the indoor ice-skating rink in the atrium, or I stop by the Kids Club room to see if Annie is there. She's usually either indoors or out at the playground with the kids and her co-worker Tina.

Lifeguarding is a lot of nothing until there's something. Then, saving a life is a big deal. Most of the time, I scan the pool for people struggling, make sure the swimmers are hotel guests, replace used towels with clean ones, and make sure the chemical levels are good in the water. It isn't difficult, and that's okay. I don't want a stressful summer. The most stress I have here is from back-talking teenagers, and from guys trying to hit on me while I work.

The only exciting times are when Derrick stops in and we exchange flirty glances, smiles, and hellos. There's chemistry between us, but he's taking too long to make a move, and I'm not going to chase any guy. I wonder why he hasn't asked me out yet, but I'm starting not to care.

After an uneventful Friday shift, I get off work at six and run to the bus stop. The party is three hours away. Though I know it won't be cool to get there right on time, I want to be ready by nine so when Annie gets home and changes her clothes, we can go and get there by ten.

I wait at the bus stop in front of The Green Turtle at 118th Street, across from the Carousel. The bus isn't due for another five minutes, so I pull my classic poetry book out of my backpack to pass time. I look up from reading as a dirt bike turns into the bike lane and stops in front of me. It's Kurt, with Shayne sitting behind him, barely fitting on the seat made for one. Both wear Vuarnets and big smiles.

Of all the places they could be, they're right here in front of me.

"Well, hi, again," Kurt says.

"Kristin, right?" Shayne asks.

I nod. They remember my name. Did I give them my name? I must have.

"Fancy meeting you here," I say, and immediately regret it. Did I just say fancy?

"Small world," Kurt says. "We're on the way back from picking up our radios and saw you. You hang out here often?"

"I work across the street. I'm headed home. Well, I need to go south first to pick up the paycheck from my other job, but then home." I'm rambling, nervous.

"You work at the Carousel?" Shayne asks.

"I'm a lifeguard at their pool. I don't do the heaving lifting for guarding the ocean like you guys do, but I do my part with screaming toddlers who pee in the pool."

They laugh. I mean, they're the real lifeguards, and we all know it.

"Are you and your friend coming to the party tonight?" Shayne asks, his hair shining white-gold in the hot sun.

"Chances are about eighty percent," I say.

"Let's make it a hundred," Shayne says.

"I'll see what I can do." The banter with them is easy and fun.

"What are you reading?" Shayne asks.

I blush, realizing how nerdy I must look sitting at a bus stop with a book. I hold it up.

Kurt leans forward to see the title.

"Let's see, *Lord Byron: The Complete Poetical Works, Volume One*," he says.

I put the book in my backpack. I feel like such a dork.

Kurt laughs and turns to Shayne. "Not only does she read, she reads classic poetry. From a lord no less. She's too smart for you, Holiday."

"I guess I need to add that to my library list," Shayne says.

"You wouldn't know the library if we crashed into it," Kurt says. He sees the bus coming and turns back to me. "Hey, we gotta run – it's been fun. See? I rhyme. I can do poetry, too. Be at the party for more!"

The bus pulls in behind them. "See you tonight, I hope," Shayne yells as they drive away.

I get on the bus in a daze. What are the odds they'd drive by when I'm at this bus stop—and recognize me, and stop to chat? They're probably flirty with a million other girls, but I'm going to take it personally and make sure I'm worth the invite. I don't have many nice clothes, but I'm going to dress to kill with whatever I have, and make sure they're glad I'm there.

When I get home, Bianca lets me borrow some of her clothes, which are always stylish, and they're high-quality brands. The result is a simple and cute: white capris and a bold blue crop top that has large buttons down the front. I pair it with white sandals, my white watch with the pretty floral face, and a small white handbag to hold essentials.

When Annie gets home, she's tired from work but pulls herself together to go out with me. She tries to be cheerful, but I can tell she's faking it. We take the bus since she's too tired to drive; she nearly falls asleep on the ride. I elbow her awake when we're getting close to the stop where we need to get off.

"I know you're tired, but please be awake and fun for the party," I plead.

She straightens up. "I'm your wingman, baby. I gotcha. Just give me a minute to transition. Those kids at work are cute, but they wipe me out."

I start to overthink things. What if Kurt and Shayne are disappointed that Marion isn't with us? What if I make a fool of myself? What if…

"Kristin, stop it," Annie says.

"What? What did I do?"

"You're shaking your leg and biting your lip. What are you nervous about?"

"Not fitting in. Doing or saying something dumb."

"Why? You go to frat parties, football parties, band parties; you mix it up with book clubs and church retreats. You fit in with all sorts of people and places. Why is this different?"

"This feels more out of my league, I guess."

"Nothing is out of your league. This is probably just like any other party, but probably more people get laid."

"I don't want to get laid. I just want to fit in and have fun."

"Oh, relax. You fit in anywhere, and you always have fun. These are just regular people who swim better than us and have better tans. Just because they're super-hot and save lives doesn't mean they're any more special than anyone else. Okay, maybe it does."

We break out laughing.

"Seriously, though," she says, "I know inside you still feel like the pudgy girl with the big glasses who only had books and me as her friends. But you're way beyond that now. Be like your mom, walk into any room like you own it. She's good at that. It works."

Annie sits up straight; she's awakened herself with her own pep talk.

"Thanks for the reminder. Thanks for coming with me, I know you're tired."

"I'm always here for you, but let's not stay long—maybe an hour? And then if you want to go to one of their parties another night, I'll go with you when I'm not working that day. That way I'll be up for stealing some of your prospects."

I side hug her. "Deal. One hour. I won't put up a fuss to leave."

"You look amazing, by the way. You're going to have to fight them off, I'm telling you. You didn't get that from Kmart, that's for sure."

I don't usually dress up. I'm a t-shirt and shorts, not-much-makeup kind of girl with a limited budget. Bianca has dressed me well. The crop top is just low enough to show cleavage, and just high enough above my belly button to be sexy but tasteful. Mascara and a touch of pink lipstick top it off. My hair has caught enough sun to be more honey blonde than light brown; I've sprayed enough Aqua Net on it to be full without being sky high like some other girls wear it.

"Not too much, but enough," Bianca had said. "My sister always says be a lady in public, a cook in the kitchen, and a whore in bed." Bianca is full of carnal wisdom.

Annie didn't try to doll herself up much, yet she looks great, as always. Her short, sandy blonde hair is spiked with a little gel. Her tan has deepened her pale skin to a respectable local's tone. She has on jean shorts and a light blue sweatshirt with white tennis shoes. Small gold hoop earrings dress it up just enough. Casual, sporty, and just right.

We get off the bus and walk quite a few blocks on Jamestown Road to a small row of townhouses that back up to Assawoman Bay. We know we're at the right place because of the loud music and all the sun-kissed, buff people spilling onto the street holding red party cups.

"How do these people stay in shape with so much drinking?" I ask Annie.

We enter the crowded townhouse, and I wince at the smell of beer and sweat. We float in with the crowd to the small living room sparsely furnished with a faded brown couch, some mis-matched tables, an old television, and surfboards leaning against a wall. A trash can overflows with red cups. Someone is throwing up behind a door that I hope is a bathroom.

"Hey, Kristin, right?"

I turn to match the deep voice to a face. Kurt stands at the center of a crowd of pretty girls and boisterous guys. "Glad you made it."

He wears a buttoned-down peach shirt paired with teal OP shorts. His electric energy lights up the room, and he has a circle of people around him.

"Hi. Thanks for inviting us," I shout above the noisy crowd and rock music. "This is my friend Annie; Marion couldn't make it."

"Welcome, Annie. Get some drinks and make yourself at home," he says. I'm glad to see him, and realize that although he's incredibly attractive, I'm not really attracted to him. I feel more of a friend vibe with him, like he's a big brother type.

It's just as well, because just then a girl with long blonde-hair steps up to him and wraps her arms around him. She might as well be a model out of a Guess ad.

"This is my girlfriend Ingrid," he says. She tugs at him to go.

"Hey, Kristin," Kurt continues. "Shay's in the kitchen on bar duty— go say hi to him. He'll wanna know you're here."

"Will he be disappointed Marion isn't here?" I ask.

"Huh? Hell, no. He'll be very glad to see you. Trust me." He waves as he walks away.

"I'm not surprised he has a girlfriend," I say to Annie. "Shayne probably does, too."

"Guys invite pretty girls to parties, whether they have girlfriends or not. It attracts more people. I'm sure these guys like to have options. Probably lots of single guys here, too."

On cue, three guys came over to talk to us. They're varying degrees of Ken doll cute. "Hey, haven't seen you around before," one says. "I'm Brad. This is Stretch, and this is Tubbs."

Annie and I say hello. Brad looks like a Brad, all preppy and blonde. Stretch is short, and Tubbs is tall and lanky. Clearly, they've had fun with their nicknames.

"Hey, you're empty-handed," Stretch says. "Let me get you a drink." He hands his drink to me, and I hand it to Annie. I don't like beer. Annie tolerates it.

"Hey, let's make a deal," Tubbs says. "We give you drinks, and you give us your phone numbers. What do you say?"

Annie gives me the get-me-out-of-here look, but I don't want to be rude. The guys are cute and nice, and I can't blame them for trying. It would be fun to stay and flirt, but none of them really catches my interest. Besides, Annie comes first.

I give the guys my biggest smile. "We're just on our way to the kitchen to see Shayne."

"I'm one of his roommates," Tubbs says, "Take a number."

"Awww, Holiday strikes again," Stretch says. "He needs to share once in a while."

On the way to the kitchen, I slip into the now empty bathroom, freshen up my lipstick, and wash my hands. The big towel hanging on the door hook looks dirty, so I shake my hands to dry them. I spy a small, monogrammed towel on top of a cabinet and unfold it. The letters S, A, and M are neatly hand embroidered at the end. It's too nice to use, so I don't.

On the way to the kitchen, I wrestle with competing thoughts. Although it's nice to be invited to a party like this, it's not really my scene. It's basically a frat party at the beach. Square peg, round hole. I don't think I'm a prude, but maybe I have more in common with Marion than I want to. She wouldn't have liked it; I'm glad she didn't come.

Annie and I make our way through the raucous crowd. "I'm going to say a hi-goodbye to Shayne, and then we're outta here," I say. Instantly, her shoulders relax.

Annie holds up her red cup. "Cheers to that."

In the kitchen, I see Shayne busy serving up beer from a keg, some sort of red punch from a big bowl, and smooth conversation. He wears a pale blue Izod shirt with light gray Jimmy Z shorts that accentuate his dark tan. When he looks in our direction, his smile grows wide.

Since he isn't wearing sunglasses, I finally see his eyes, and I can't look away. They're cobalt blue, like a perfect summer sky, and are framed with long golden lashes. His hair is butter yellow like the sun, and he has an air of calm authority about him. I feel drawn to him.

He waves us over. It's weird, because as I make my way to him, it's as if I'm seeing him for the first time, and he's seeing me for the first time. Everything and everyone else fades away, and it's just me looking into a deep, beautiful sea. He looks at me like I'm the only girl in the room; I have goosebumps. Finally, we get close enough that I can see the sweat on his brow and the way his hair curls at the ends on his neck. We both smile dumbly at each other.

"Hi," I say.

"Glad you could make it," he says to me with a look that sizzles. "What can I get you?"

I thought he was interested in Marion before, but maybe I'm wrong. The way we look at each other has an electric kind of heat and familiarity. What is happening to me? I've never felt this kind of strong chemical connection to someone before.

"A cola with grenadine, if you have it," I say.

"Hey, Mac, put your eyes back in their sockets and pour me a cold one." The order comes from some big muscle guy who pats Shayne on the back. "Though I can't say I blame ya."

"Just a minute," Shayne tells the guy. He turns to me. "For you, I'll find grenadine." He pivots and heads to the pantry, and then returns with my drink. "You look beautiful," he says.

I believe it when he says it. I feel beautiful with him.

"Thank you," I say. "You look pretty good yourself. Hey, I have a question."

"What's that?" he asks as he hands out another beer.

"That guy called you Mac. Kurt and some of the guys here call you Shay and Holiday, and the monogramed towels in your bathroom spell SAM. What should I call you?"

He laughs. "You can call me anything you want. Everyone here has a few nicknames."

"Do you have a preference?"

"Well, my name is Shayne MacCabe, so any variation will do. Holiday is from—well, that's a long story. Don't call me that. My grandma made the monogram towels with my initials. She's my favorite person in the world. Most people call me Shay or Mac."

I smile flirtatiously. "Well, I'm not most people."

"You most certainly are not," he says.

"Can I call you Sam? From the monogram on the towels. I like that you honor your grandma by using them."

"Sam. That's a new one," he says. "Sure, but only you can call me that. Sam I am."

"From my favorite Dr. Seuss book," I say.

More people begin crowding us to get drinks.

"Sorry, I'm the bartender right now, but my buddy will relieve me soon. Talk later?"

I nod before the crowd separates us.

"Hey, Shayne," Annie calls out. "Got a girlfriend?"

"He's got quite a few," a nearby guard says.

Sam shakes his head. "No girlfriend." He smiles at me. "Not yet, anyway."

Annie nudges me and raises her eyebrows as we flow away with the crowd. "I'm going to catch on fire with all that heat. What was that about?"

"I don't know. I'm definitely feeling something with Shayne.

Shay. Mac. Whatever his name is. I'm calling him Sam. I mean, I had goosebumps, Annie. And you know I don't usually go for blonde guys. Or party guys. This is like crazy attraction."

"I'm glad to see this," she says. "And he's easy on the eyes for sure. But he's definitely a party guy, so proceed with caution."

Annie and I chat while I watch him. He moves with an easy confidence and has a masculine vibe I really like. He's one of the few people here besides Annie and me who isn't drunk or close to it. It's his party and he has it, and himself, under control. I like that.

"Do you mind if we stay just a little longer, until his break?" I ask Annie.

Annie nods. She'll do anything for me. And vice versa.

We make our way to the back of the townhouse onto a balcony overlooking the bay. What a relief it is to go from the stuffy air inside to the cool breeze outside. The view is spectacular, with the glow of the distant city lights on the bay. We hang out there for a while, meet a few people, and get caught up on each other's work stories. Half an hour passes.

"I know Shayne is the host and all, but we have fifteen minutes to catch the next bus," she says. "Let's bounce. We can make it if we hurry."

I'm disappointed, but I had promised her that we'd go when she wanted to go.

"He hasn't come around yet, and the party is no big deal," I say. "Except I really like him. One more stop at the kitchen so I can say a quick goodbye?" Annie nods reluctantly.

Sam isn't in the kitchen anymore. Annie is getting impatient, though, so I have to leave without saying goodbye to him. I'm bummed. Even if I never see him again, it's nice to know that I can feel an attraction that powerful for someone other than Jake, even if it's momentary.

We're out the door and almost past the crowd when I feel someone touch my arm and a sort of a spark. Like an actual current. I know it's him.

I turn around, and there he is. Like before, everyone else fades away.

"Hey, leaving so soon?" he asks. "I just got off bar duty."

"It's my fault," Annie says. "I worked a long shift and need to get to bed."

He glances at her and smiles, and then is laser-focused on me, as I am on him.

His face is perfectly sculpted, with high cheekbones and blonde, slightly arched brows. He has a straight nose, a strong jawline, and soft-looking lips that I desperately want to kiss. The way he looks at me makes me melt, and not with lust like Jake always did, but with a kind of shy appreciation. I feel like I'm in a dream. There's magic in the air.

Not knowing what to say or do, my manners take over and I extend my hand for a handshake. "Thank you for inviting us," I say. "It's a lovely party."

Annie shakes her head. "Geez, we're not at a country club," she whispers.

I can't believe I've invited a handshake and said the word lovely.

"You're something else, you know that?" he says. "In a good way."

He takes my hand, shakes it, and then lifts it to his mouth and softly kisses it. "You're like Cinderella running off." His voice is low and husky. "Don't make me go door to door with a shoe to find you. Can I have your number?"

Annie breaks the spell. "Listen, Prince Charming, she lifeguards at the Carousel pool most days, so you can find her there. For now, we gotta run to catch the bus."

"I can drive you home," he says.

Annie grabs my hand. "We don't know you well enough yet. We're taking the bus."

"Thanks again. Good night," I yell as Annie drags me toward Coastal Highway. We get to the bus stop just as it's pulling up; we climb onboard.

"Why did you do that? I want to see him again. He needs my number!" I say.

"If he wants to see you, he'll find you," she says as we plop down in our seats.

"But—"

"No buts. Men like the chase. Some mystery. Remember, he's probably a player. Don't get your hopes up. But I have to say, I like seeing you this way: unreserved and a little crazy."

All the way home I can only think of Sam, and how his blonde hair curls at the nape of his neck, and the way he says my name, and the intense deep blue of his eyes, and how much I hope he will find me so that I can see him again. Soon.

*Her heart did whisper that he had done it for her.*
~ Jane Austen, *Pride and Prejudice*

# Chapter 6

## RETURN TO ME

The day after the party, I work at the café and fill in for another guard who called off sick at the Carousel pool. My focus is even worse than before the party. Why didn't I give Sam my number? Why didn't I ask him what guard stand he works at? Asking another guard would be so tacky. I know where he lives, but I also know how desperate I would look to just show up there.

After work, I take the bus to 48th Street and walk to the beach where Marion and I first met Sam and Kurt. A random lifeguard sits there. Maybe this isn't Sam's stand. I don't dare ask.

Back at home, Annie shuts me down when I ask her for a ride to drive past his place.

"You are not a stalker. Or at least I won't let you be."

"Chances are he won't even be there."

"So why go?"

"Just let me be a little obsessed for a moment," I say. "Maybe I'll see him."

"Then what? Then you jump out of the car and say, 'Hey, I'm the girl from the party. Don't mind that I'm a weirdo stalker, but I just can't wait for you to come to me.' Is that it?"

"You're right," I say. "But I like that I like him so much."

"I'm glad you do, too, but you'll scare him away doing stupid stuff. If it's meant to be, it'll be. He knows where you work. If he doesn't make a move, it's honestly his loss."

"Why would he? He probably has his choice of girls. I should've given him my number."

"To make it easy for him? If he doesn't show up, others will. Lots of cute guys here."

"It's not just his looks. It's everything. He has a light about him. And—"

"Yeah, yeah. He's all that and a bag of chips. But guards have a reputation for changing girls more often than underwear. I'm sure he charms and sleeps with lots of girls. Not, as you would say, your cup of tea. He'd probably hurt you. Probably better not to go down that road."

"You're right." I've heard it all before. He flirts with me like he probably flirts with all the other girls, and who am I to think I'm anything special? Too bad the one guy I'm finally interested in is someone who is probably even more of a player than Jake.

"Hey, DJ Batman is at the Big Kahuna tonight. Let's go."

We do go. Batman makes everything fun and plays great music. I dance a little. I drink a little. I flirt with guys. None have Sam's easy conversation, electric connection, intense blue eyes, or slow, sexy smile, but I still have a good time. I can't stop thinking about him, though. Sam, Sam, Sam—in my mind he's no longer Shayne or Shay or Holiday. He's only Sam.

When we get home, I thank Annie for distracting me, and I go to bed. Whether anything comes of this or not, it feels good to feel giddy about someone. To feel excited and hopeful. To be looked at as a prize, and not as a runner-up. It's nice to feel like the sun is shining on my face instead of being in the shadows with someone. I go to sleep smiling.

Annie and I have Sunday off. We make it a proper beach day: reading, relaxing, tanning, and walking along the shoreline. We eat a light dinner at the condo, and then walk to the bay to watch the sun fade from the sky. I wonder if Sam stopped by the Carousel today to see me, but there's no way to know. If Sam doesn't pursue me, I have to forget about him. Pining over someone who isn't interested in me is a waste of time.

I work at the cafe Monday morning and then head to the Carousel for my Monday afternoon shift. I can't help but watch for him. I can't help but hope. He doesn't show.

Tuesday comes and goes. By Wednesday I'm back to my normal flow. My hope level has waned, and I chalk up flirting with Sam to a good time. I want to believe something is there, but I have to protect myself because he could've stopped by Monday or Tuesday, but he didn't. As I close out my shift, I open the pool door to the hotel's atrium area— and there he is.

He's leaning against a wall by the ice-skating rink, his hands casually tucked in the pockets of his shorts. I do a double take. It's him all right. His eyes light up when he sees me. He's gorgeous; I have to force myself not to stare.

He walks over to me and brushes a sweaty strand of hair out of my face. Our eyes never leave each other.

"Hey," he says.

"Hey." I'm at a loss for words. I feel shy around him.

"I found you," he says.

"Was I lost?"

"Just missing. I guess you didn't work the weekend, because I stopped by Saturday and Sunday. I suppose I shouldn't be so eager to see you, but I am."

"You did? I worked Saturday, but apparently not the time that you stopped by."

He smiles. "I guess not. Or maybe you're playing hard to get."

I shake my head. "I don't want to play games with you."

We stare at each other. No need for words, really. Is anyone else even here?

"Thank you for finding me," I finally say. "I give you an A for effort."

"What do I need to do to get a A-plus?" He asks this in such a sensual way that I want him to take me into the broom closet and have his way with me, even though I barely know him.

"I'm sure I can think of something," I say.

"I'm sure I can, too," he says.

I like our easy banter.

"My work hours are a little weird," I say. "I'm glad you kept trying."

"Me, too. I came here Monday and Tuesday, too. My stand is in front of the Golden Sands, so by the time I got off at five-thirty, put my gear away, and ran here, you were gone. Today is my day off, so I came earlier. My lucky day, I guess."

He ran all that way on the sand to see me. The Golden Sands is about eight buildings south of the Carousel along condo row. I can barely walk to the ocean on the sand.

"I can't make things terribly easy for you, can I?"

He steps closer to me. "Well, you could, but then maybe it wouldn't be as fun."

I want to touch his long, golden lashes. I could stare into his eyes forever. We're in a bubble. Is he going to kiss me? I hope so, because it doesn't matter. Nothing else matters.

Some obnoxious kids scream past us and break the spell.

"Walk out to the beach with me," he says. A statement, but a question in his eyes. "I have to work my other job soon. I'm a bouncer at Tio Gringo's two nights a week. I need to shower and change for my shift, but I'd like to ask you something away from all this noise."

Noise? What noise? I look around. People going to and from wherever—who cares? The ice-skating rink is filled with skaters, and Annie is leading her group of Kids Club children outside to the playground. She catches my eye and gives a thumbs up.

I follow him through the back doors, past the beach bar, and down onto the sand. The crowds have thinned; it seems the beach is just his and mine.

We make small talk. I learn that this is his third summer as a guard, and that he's a crew chief and a competitive swimmer. I ask him what a crew chief is; he says he's the leader of a crew of six or seven guards spanning five stands. There are fifteen crews along Ocean City's ten miles of beach, divided into south, middle, and north, which is where his crew is.

"I'm surprised you have time for a part-time job," I say.

"Guarding is the greatest job in the world, but it doesn't pay well, so most of us have something else part-time at night after work. I work two nights a week from nine to two, so it's doable. Forty dollars cash plus meals is a pretty good side gig."

We walk down to the shoreline and chat comfortably, like we've known each other a long time. He stops and hands a card to me.

"Oh. Is it my birthday?"

He laughs. "I hope not, because I'd do something much more special than this."

"Good, I'll look forward to that in September," I tease. "Should I open it now?"

"No. Wait until later. It's no big deal. I was just thinking of you."

Everything in the air feels charged with him, and yet also so comfortable. We seem pretty different, but clearly have chemistry—deeper than merely sexual from the start.

I can't ignore the sexual part, though. He looks good no matter how undressed or dressed he is. He's wearing a white polo shirt that makes his tan seem even darker, paired with pale blue OP corduroy shorts. I bet I look like Casper the Friendly Ghost next to him. No matter how long I'm in the sun, my tan is always more olive than dark. I'm wearing my boring maroon work shirt and khaki shorts. I feel beautiful, though, just from the way he looks at me.

Sam's blonde hair blows in the breeze and his eyes sparkle. He's about a head taller than me, and I want to tuck my shoulder under his arm and curl into him.

I put the card into my pocket. "Thank you," I say.

I can't imagine a more perfect day. It's like a movie set, with the fading pale pink sky, the ocean as a backdrop, and this handsome, charming man in front of me.

"Perfect weather," I say. Did I just talk about the weather? I wanted to say 'perfect moment,' but 'weather' came out instead? I want to slap myself.

"Perfect everything," he says.

"What did you want to talk to me about?" Suddenly I'm nervous, because maybe this is about Marion. I'd hate to be wrong about his interest in me.

"I want to invite you somewhere," he says. "I hope you don't mind, but I need to ask how old you are first. I don't want to ask you out if you're underage."

"Well, I'm under drinking age if that's what you mean. I'm nineteen." I respect that he asked the question. "I'll be twenty in a few months, though. Do I need to be twenty-one to go to wherever you want to invite me to? I have a pretty good fake ID."

"No, no. It's just—I don't date anyone under eighteen. Lots of girls who are younger than eighteen look a lot older than that. I wanted to be sure."

"How old are you?" I ask.

"I'm twenty-four; twenty-five next month. You good with that?"

He's older than I thought, but not too old. "I'm very good with that," I say.

"I know it's short notice, but on Saturday night, my roommates and I are hosting a crab feast at my place. We pick and eat two bushels of crabs, tell tall tales, and drink a lot of beer. A keg of Michelob, to be exact. We charge a small entry fee to cover costs, but of course no charge for you. Will you be my guest?"

A million things run through my mind, so I hesitate, trying to process it all.

My hesitation seems to unnerve him. "You probably have other plans," he says. "I just thought maybe I'd get lucky, and you might be available."

My hesitation may have come across as a lack of interest. I'm embarrassed to tell the truth but, for him, I do.

"I'd really like to come. It's just that I–" I take a deep breath. "I'm from a small town with one blinking red light. No restaurant for fifteen miles. No ocean. The only crab I've ever had is a crab cake here on vacation; I don't even know what it means to pick a crab, so I won't know what to do. I don't want to embarrass myself. Or you."

He laughs. "Is that all? Oh, don't worry about that. I'll show you what to do. You could never embarrass me. Believe me, I do enough things to embarrass myself."

I look down at my feet.

"What else? You have a boyfriend. Of course you do. I should've asked about that first."

"No, no," I say. "I mean, I did, but we broke up back in January so, no."

"Oh, man. I'm on a lucky streak. What else then? You're making me work for this."

"I'm just wondering, is this like a date, or a party where I come with a friend like last time? Are you inviting me so I'll bring Marion? Because you seemed to like her when we met at the beach. I just want to know so I don't make a fool of myself, because I like you. Unless I'm too late and I've already made a fool of myself."

He takes my hand. It's warm, soothing, and fits just right.

"I love your honesty, and the way you think, and how you put it all out there," he says.

"Well, I do want to go," I say. "I did have plans, but I'll break them. But if you're asking me so that I'll bring Marion, then no. I like her, but I don't want to be used to get to her."

He smiles even broader than before.

"I'm happy that I think your answer is yes. So, let me be crystal clear.

I'm asking you. I admit that first time we all met on the beach, I was drawn to both of you. You're both gorgeous."

"I knew it," I say.

He squeezes my hand. "Then when I saw you at the bus stop, I was wowed. That was fate. And then at the party, I was mesmerized by you. It's you I want to spend time with. You I want to get to know. It's your eyes I want to stare into and wonder if they're more grey or blue. It's you I can't stop thinking about. And it's you I want with me on Saturday. Not her. Okay?"

I nod. I'm so relieved.

"Good," he says. "It's a casual 'plus one' thing. Not quite a date, because when I take you on a date, it will be a real date, and you'll know it. Plus, it won't involve picking crabs, drinking bad beer, and being surrounded by a lot of drunk people."

I smile. "*When* you take me on a date, huh?"

He nods. "Yes. Which I hope will be soon. Anyway, it starts at seven. That means people will start arriving at seven-thirty. Dress super casual. It'll be messy and sticky and fun."

"I'd love to do messy, sticky, fun things with you." I surprise myself with my audacity.

He chuckles. "Oh really? Believe me, we're on the same page there."

"Thanks for inviting me, though I don't know if I can keep up with you. You may be too wild for me, and I may be too tame for you. We'll have to see how it goes."

"I see the wild in you," he says. "I think you just may bring out the tame in me."

I smile and shrug. "I guess we'll have to see."

He looks at his watch. "There's no place I'd rather be than here, but I have to run. I'm not leaving without your phone number this time, though." He pulls out a pen and paper from his backpack. "I'll call you with details of when I'll pick you up on Saturday."

I write out my number, and hand the pen and paper back to him.

"I'm looking forward to Saturday," he says.

"Me, too."

He drops my hand and runs off.

Blissfully dazed, I walk back to the Carousel deck and find a seat. I open the envelope from Sam and pull out a card with the illustration of a kitten on it and the words: Thinking of you. The inside of the card is typeset with 'Have a purr-fect day,' along with a handwritten note.

*Kristin,*
*Thanks for coming to the party. You made my night. Hope to*
*see you much more often.*
*Sam I am.*

*p.s. She walks in beauty, like the night of cloudless climes and starry skies; and all that's best of dark and bright meet in her aspect and her eyes. ~ Lord Byron*

Underneath is his phone number and address, along with a drawing of a smiling sun.

I can't stop smiling like that sun. He came to see me. He wants to see me again. He wrote a poetry quote to me. I'm sure he doesn't know Lord Byron from the man on the moon, so that means he put effort into tracking down his writings. He must've found the town's library, after all. For me.

I hold the card close to my chest. For such a masculine guy, this was pretty damn sweet.

In a happy daze, I make my way to the bus, and then back to the condo. Nobody is home. I'm glad. I put his card by the mirror on my bedroom dresser, go out to the pool for a swim, and think about Sam and the possibilities of Saturday night and beyond.

*It must be very improper that a young lady should dream of a gentleman before the gentleman is first known to have dreamt of her.*

~ Jane Austen, *Northanger Abbey*

# Chapter 7

MR. SUNSHINE'S HAPPY PUNCH

For the first time since the day we moved into the condo, we four roommates sit together in a circle in the living room and gab like sorority sisters. It's a rare evening for us to all be off work and not have other plans. Even Bianca and Marion are friendly to each other as we talk about our love lives and guys.

Marion says her Fager's date with Dave went well, and they've seen each other a few times since then. "He's so down to earth," she says. "His parents own a construction company, so he doesn't have to worry about money. He works because he wants to. Must be nice." That's all she's willing to share. It's nice but strange to see her happy.

"Money isn't everything, but it sure is a lot of things," Bianca says. "Let him treat you to nice things. Enjoy every moment."

Marion nods. "It's nice to be served good food at a nice place instead of doing the serving. I could get used to that. What about you, Bianca? Anyone special?"

Bianca had vowed to date around all summer without getting serious with anyone, but she's crushing on a French waiter named Alain at the restaurant where she bartends. "He's not the hottest guy I've ever dated, but his French accent totally turns me to mush. Plus, he doesn't take my shit. I like that. I'll bring him by sometime so you can meet him."

"Ooo la la," Annie says. "Bianca is bringing a guy home? It must be loooove."

"Or at least lust," I say.

"Oh, that's for sure," Bianca says. "Speaking of lust, did my lucky outfit serve you well for that party, Kristin?"

I blush. "You could say that."

"I knew you'd rope him in with that outfit and those tits."

I shriek. "Bianca!" I throw a tissue box at her.

Everyone laughs. Annie jumps right in. "She sure got his attention. He tracked her down at work and asked her out for Saturday."

"Is it one of the guys we met on the beach?" Marion asks. "The tall one?"

"The blonde," I say. "Shayne, but I call him Sam. The other one we met, the tall one, has a girlfriend. I wasn't vibing with him that way, anyway. Big time vibe with Sam, though."

"Big time," Annie says.

Bianca demands that I describe him.

"He's sort of a mix between Robert Redford and Tom Cruise. The coloring, build, and masculinity of Redford with the intensity of Cruise. But so much more."

Annie chuckles. "Maybe if you squint your eyes and take a couple of shots. A bit of a stretch, but fair enough, I guess."

"I can second that since I briefly met him on the beach. If I wasn't so into Dave and so not into party guys, I may have fought you for him," Marion says.

"It's a really weird mix of chemistry, looks, and personality," I say. "I admit to lust. I want to rub my hands over his chest endlessly. I'm a little obsessed."

"That's why I love swimmers," Bianca says. "The chest, muscles, and endurance."

I tell my roommates about the upcoming crab feast, Sam's visit to my work, and the card he gave to me.

They each run into their rooms and emerge with bits and pieces for me to wear Saturday. A denim Calvin Klein miniskirt with two thin belts and a black Bolero jacket from Bianca to go with my white Blondie t-shirt. Bangle bracelets from Marion. Annie's gold hoop earrings. Bianca titles the ensemble 'casual punk get laid glam.'

"We know you're too much of a prude to get laid yet, but we're gonna make him want it really bad," Bianca says.

We try to get guy talk out of Annie. If she's met someone special, she would've told me. I know she's still recovering from her breakup with Jeff, but also know she's having fun casually dating. She isn't one to sleep around, either. She seems happy just to listen to our stories.

We end the evening watching TV and eating popcorn and chocolate. It's one of the best evenings yet—I'm glad it's with the girls.

Sam calls Friday night with details about Saturday. We talk for two hours about everything and nothing until Marion gets mad and tells me to get off the phone because she's waiting for a call from Dave. I signal to her several times that I'll be off in two minutes.

"You quoted Byron in the card. Thank you, that was a nice surprise," I say.

"I'm just getting to know him. I want to, since he seems kind of important to you."

"He and some of his peers are amazing writers. Maybe you can meet Jane Austen one of these days, too, though she may bore you," I say.

"She may, but you don't. You're good inspiration for me to get acquainted with the Ocean City library," he says. "I signed out a few classic poetry and literary books. They were covered in dust. The guys can't see me with them, though, or I'll never live it down."

I've never dated anyone who asked about my interest in classic poetry and literature, or why I like it. It's nice to talk about it and have someone be interested in my answers. Eventually, I tell him that I need to get off the phone, but that later I'd like to know more about how he got involved in swimming, how he got started guarding, what kind of documentaries and history shows he likes, and other get-to-know-you things. I want to know everything about him.

He doesn't call or stop by Saturday during the day, but that's okay. I like that he's not needy. I don't trust guys who are too eager too quickly. I'm excited to see him again. I get off work from the Carousel early enough to take my time getting ready. I can't believe it's the third week of June already. I love being here. I can't go back. This feels like home.

Annie insists dropping me off at his place instead of having Sam pick me up at the condo. She thinks I don't know him well enough yet to give him my address.

"I know how much you already like him, but please try to keep it casual. These guys are known for shuffling girls like cards."

"Is that so? You haven't mentioned that before," I say.

"It bears repeating," she says. "I'll drop you off, and you can decide as the night goes on if you want me to pick you up, take the bus, or have him to bring you home."

"I think you're more nervous that I am," I say.

"I want you to have fun, but not get hurt. Can you do that?"

I stop fussing with my hair and turn to look at her. Her pretty hazel eyes are full of love and concern.

"I'm taking a risk to get hurt whenever I put myself out there," I say. "So are you. We have to decide if it's worth trying. Hopefully, we'll get more rewards than hard knocks for that. I'm willing to go for the ride, and I'm glad you're with me for it. I love you."

We hug, and then go off into the night to the pumpkin carriage. She's my fairy godmother, and her mustard-colored car might as well be from a children's story. She delivers me to the crab-fest ball, the fish feast, the seafood soiree—we come up with all sorts of silly names on the ride to Jamestown Road.

I'm taken aback when she parks instead of idles nearby. She gets out of the car.

"Are you chaperoning me? This is a bit much. I'm an adult, you know."

"I'm not leaving you here with a bunch of strangers. We'll find him, then I'll go."

I know better than to argue with her. I adjust my bra and shirt so there's just enough cleavage to show off the girls, yet not quite enough to forget modesty.

The street is swarming with beautiful people mingling and laughing. I fidget some more.

Annie abruptly stops, turns toward me, and grabs my shoulders.

"What's wrong?" I ask. "Do I have something on my face? Is my lip gloss—"

"You look scared. You're doing that nervous thing where you pick at your clothes and bite your lip. Don't make me have the pep talk with you again. You have a hot guy here who's into you, who wants you to be here. Rock what you got, and what you've got is a lot."

"Okay, I can do this." I attempt a smile.

"Yes, you can. Let me see it, then."

I hold my head up, put on my dazzle smile, and sway my hips to add a little sizzle to my walk. We move confidently through the crowd. Annie blends in; she looks like one of the sporty girl guards. Though there aren't a lot of them, the ones I've seen are confident and fit.

I finally see Sam, and he sees me. Our eyes lock, and everything is suddenly all right. He comes over and hugs me.

"So glad you're here," he says, drinking me in with those captivating eyes. He turns to Annie. "Hi again, Annie. Thanks for bringing her. Can you stay?"

"No, but thanks," she says. "Have her home by midnight."

"What?" We say it in unison.

"Just kidding. Have fun!" Annie laughs at our response, and then turns to go.

Like before, there are so many people all around us, yet all I see is Sam. With him, I really do feel like I belong.

"Annie seems protective of you," he says.

"That's an understatement. She can be tough, but she loves me."

"I'm glad you have a friend like that."

"Me, too."

"Let's get you something to drink and I'll introduce you around," he says. "Everyone is curious about you. I don't usually bring dates to these things."

I raise my eyebrow and smile. "I thought this wasn't a date."

"Correction. I don't usually bring a plus-one to these things. Want a drink?"

"Do you have any Coke or Pepsi? With grenadine, like last time? I don't drink much alcohol."

He raises his eyebrows. "Don't drink much alcohol. I don't hear that around here much."

"I just don't like the taste, but I can have a good time without it."

"Let's find some." He grabs my hand and guides me through the crowd, introducing me to so many people I'll never remember their names. Everyone is nice and welcomes me.

I decline the free-flowing beer. One of Sam's friends hands a big red cup of punch to me. "No beer? Then you gotta have some famous Mr. Sunshine's Happy Punch," he says.

I eye it suspiciously.

"Punch? So, this doesn't have any alcohol in it?" I check with Sam.

He laughs. "Of course not."

I take a sip. It's delicious—sweet and fruity. He leads me inside to the empty kitchen—everyone is outside with the food, beer, punch, and Bartles and Jaymes wine coolers.

"I'm going to make myself a Stoli Gimlet; I don't have enough for everyone."

He reaches for the vodka from the cabinet above the fridge, and then adds lime juice, syrup, and a sliced lime. "You asked me about history. My dad drank this, and his dad, too. It has an interesting history, but that may bore you. Do you want one?"

I shake my head. "No thanks, but it has a cute name. And I'd love to hear about it. I like history. But, like classic poetry, I know it bores most people."

He raises his eyebrows and smiles. "It's unusual to find someone who likes history like I do. The short version is that the gimlet dates back to the nineteenth century as an effort to combat scurvy—part of providing British sailors with daily lime juice rations."

"Combining it with liquor is brilliant," I say.

"I'll tell you the whole story another time. Gotta make your drink and get back outside before they send a search party."

"No, that's okay," I say. "This punch is really good."

I sit on the counter and watch him move as he finishes making his drink and wipes the counter. He's a born athlete, but moves gracefully like a dancer, with hands that seem to be good at everything he touches. I think about them touching me.

In the middle of whatever he's doing and whatever he's talking about, he stops, comes over to me, and puts his hands gently on my face. We're eye to eye, and I notice that his pale eyelashes shine beneath the kitchen light like glitter.

"Let's get this out of the way," he whispers.

He gently kisses me.

His lips are soft. Time stands still. He pulls away, smiles slowly as he sees me smile, and resumes making his drink as though that intoxicating kiss didn't just happen. It's the perfect thing to do to both relax our sexual tension and ignite it. His kiss is respectful, yet sensual. I want more. I like that he isn't pushy or assertive. He knows how to handle me.

He returns to the counter and, even though I've said I'm good with the fruit punch, he pours a glass of soda for me and drops a little grenadine in it. A couple of people wander in. He holds my hand, grabs his cocktail, and leads me outside. I snag the cup of punch, leaving the cherry-flavored soda behind.

Outside, I begin to feel tipsy. I wonder if it's the kiss, but my gut says no—I've only felt this way once before, when I had two glasses of wine. I pull Sam to the side of the townhouse.

"The food is the other way," he says.

"Tell me what's in Mr. Sunshine's Happy Punch," I say.

"The punch? Hawaiian Punch, ginger ale, pineapple juice, orange juice, and vodka."

My heart sinks. "Vodka?"

He nods, seemingly oblivious to how this is a problem.

"I'm going home now. I'll take the bus."

As I turn to walk away, I pour the rest of the punch from my cup onto the ground.

"Wait, Kristin, please. What's wrong?"

I turn back to him, my body pulsating from hurt and anger.

"I told you I don't drink. I asked you specifically if the punch had alcohol in it, and you said no. In case you didn't notice, you don't have to trick me into drinking to get close to me. That's really shitty. I didn't think you were that kind of guy."

His eyes widen as if aliens have just landed behind me. "I'm not. Ask anyone." He takes a deep breath. "I'm sorry. This is a total misunderstanding."

"Oh? How so?" I ask. "You lied to me about the alcohol in the punch."

"Completely my fault. The punch is famous around here. Everyone knows it has vodka in it. I thought you knew and were joking around, bantering like we have been. So when I said 'no, of course not,' I was joking in a sarcastic way. I thought you knew I was kidding."

"I'm not from around here. How would I know what everyone else knows?"

"You wouldn't. I wasn't thinking. I'm really sorry. I thought you knew and wanted to try some, because you said you didn't drink *much* alcohol, not *no* alcohol. Then I got a soda for you, even though you said you liked the punch. I promise I wasn't trying to trick you into anything. I'd lay into any son of a bitch who tried to do that to a girl."

I see the sincerity in his eyes. "Fair enough," I say. "Sorry. I do drink a little, and what you say makes sense. It's just that last year, some guy at a frat party put something in my drink and took me to his room.  He locked the door, and tried to force me to—"

"Oh no."

"It's okay. I managed to get away. But I'm pretty sensitive about it. I'm fun without drinking, and I don't want to be tricked into it."

His eyes close for a few seconds, and he bites his lip. His hands form into fists. "I'm sorry that happened. I'd love to pound that guy. I need to know you know I wasn't tricking you."

"I do believe you. I'm sorry I got weird."

"I don't care if you drink or not. It's kinda nice that you don't because the decisions you make are sober ones. Plus, it's gonna make you a cheap date."

I smile. We move closer together.

"Funny as it is, and I do have a sense of humor," I say, "people have made fun of me in the past for the things I don't do or call me a prude. I don't really care, but I want someone to like me for who I am. I won't pretend to be someone I'm not."

"Good," he says. "I like that."

"Listen, I might as well put it all out there," I say. "I don't drink much. I don't smoke or do drugs at all, and I don't have casual sex. If we go any further, you need to be okay with that."

He takes my hand and kisses it. "I am. I respect that. I respect you. I have to admit, I want to do more than kiss you, but that will be entirely on your terms and timeline, if at all."

I grin. "More than kissing sounds nice. Eventually."

"For the record, I don't smoke or do drugs, either," he says. "They're deal breakers for me. I drink, but not too much. Except for bar golf a couple times a summer on payday."

"Bar golf? What's that?"

"Long story. I'll explain later. I admit to having casual sex in the past, but that's certainly not what I have in mind for you. I don't feel anything casual about you."

I'm relieved. I want him to be a good guy, and I don't want this to end when it's just beginning. I'm glad we're getting this out of the way.

"Anything else?" he asks.

"I don't like Old Bay," I say with a straight face.

Marylanders put Old Bay seasoning on everything. And way too much of it.

"Oh no," he says. Equally serious. "Now that could be a problem."

"You'll have to get over it." I kiss him on the cheek. "Now, let's go pick some crabs."

He takes my hand and leads me back into the crowd.

The rest of evening is wonderful. The light, warm breeze complements the balmy night, the stars are out, music blares from a boombox, the food is delicious, and laughter fills the air. I can't believe how comfortable I am with Sam. It's as if I've known him all my life.

Our conversation is easy and natural, and despite all of the pretty girls there, I feel like the most beautiful girl in the world with him. It's a pretty perfect night.

Although he's one of the hosts, I discover he's asked his buddies to man the keg, bring the crabs out, and make sure the punch keeps flowing so he can be with me. He's done a lot of setup work. Picnic tables fill the driveway in front of the townhouse. They're covered with brown craft paper, paper towels, mallets, knives, paper plates, crabs, and lots of butter. A big side table holds grilled hot dogs and hamburgers, plus some side dishes that others brought.

Drinks flow freely, and everyone digs into the crabs like pros. Except me. He quickly discovers I'm not a stellar crab picker. Even though he shows me several times how to do it, I just can't. It's gross, especially removing the lungs and the mustard, which I'm told is a digestive organ. I don't have the patience or stomach for it. I chow down on a hamburger and cantaloupe while he expertly picks crabs and gives me half of the meat.

A sassy brunette smirks at Sam. "Your new girl can't handle it, huh?"

"She can handle me," he says. "That's all she needs to know." He hands another big chunk of crab meat to me. It's delicious.

Most of the people are encouraging.

"It took me two summers to get it right." A girl named Crystal smiles at me. "I'm from Ohio, so this was all new to me, too. Stick with it, and you'll nail it."

Maybe I can, but I don't want to. I don't like it enough to put that much work into it. I'm happy just to be with Sam, and to see how much fun he's having with his friends. They tell stories of rescues, parties, and bar golf, whatever that is. Closely bonded, they tease each other about everything from girls to hangovers and lost underwear.

"Seems like great friends you have here, Sam," I say.

"We're a family. We don't all get along, but we've got each other's backs."

"The party is amazing, but how do you afford all this? You mentioned guards don't make a lot, yet crabs and beer and vodka aren't cheap."

"I'm not that altruistic," he says. "I make money on this."

"How so?"

"Tubbs and I each put in some money for the keg, punch, burgers, hot dogs, and crabs— two bushels from our buddy Tom, who has a jon boat with crab traps. He gives us a good deal, we ask friends to bring sides, and we charge money to get in, depending on if you're a guard or a guest. We make a nice profit, and everyone has fun. It's win-win."

"So, you're entrepreneurial. I like that. I should have paid admission, too."

"Not as my guest."

"Canoodling with the host has its advantages." I say.

"Oh, we're canoodling, are we?" He leans into me.

Someone throws a napkin at us and yells for us to get a room.

For the next few hours, he works the crowd with his arm around me. Girls flirt with him, but he politely moves them on. I meet the guy he shares a bedroom with, Troy Tuckett—they call him Tucky— and Tucky's girlfriend Rhonda. Tucky is short and muscular, with dark hair. He doesn't say much. Rhonda has blonde, curly hair; she's sweet and chatty. Kurt and Ingrid are star attractions; they arrive late and, when he sees me, gives me a big hug.

When I leave Sam to go to the bathroom, a few girls eye me with cool curiosity. The guys are friendly; some are too friendly. When I come out through the kitchen to go back outside, one of the guards nicknamed Vegas blocks me when I try to pass and puts his hands on my hips. He's kind of short, so we're almost eye to eye.

"Hey, there," he says. His breath is thick with the smell of beer. "Want a good time?"

I step back. He advances.

"Back off," I say. "I'm here with Shayne. I'm already having a good time."

"He doesn't have to know anything," he says. He sneers as he leans in to try to kiss me.

I shove him hard, and he stumbles back. "You're his friend. This isn't cool, and I'm definitely not interested." He's still trying to balance when I walk past him.

When I tell Sam, he checks that I'm okay. Then he chuckles. "Vegas is such a dog."

"You're not mad your friend made a move on me?"

His jaw tightens. "Oh, I'm mad, just not surprised. I'm sorry he did that to you. I have to work with him, though, so I'll handle it in my own way."

I tell myself to chill out. I wasn't hurt, just irritated. Vegas comes out of the house and acts like nothing happened. Sam tenses. I squeeze his hand.

"Let's forget about it and have fun," I say. "Nothing bad happened. No big deal."

He relaxes a little and kisses my cheek. We mingle with his friends. Some of the guests have brought brownies, cookies, and cake. Small groups sing to the music. Others peel off to find places they believe are private enough for making out.

When the crowd thins, I let Sam know it's time for me to go home. He offers to drive, and I accept. He's got a Mercury Comet GT—light blue with a black stripe on it. He doesn't open the door for me like Jake always did, but I let it slide. There's an equality to the two of us together that I like, and treating each other right is most important.

"Don't mind the junk in the back," he says. "I keep my gear in here."

His car is well kept; a cute little hula girl figurine sits on the dash.

"I like your car," I say. "Nice lines. Someday I want to get a Mustang."

"Thanks. It's definitely not new, but it gets me where I want to go. Mustangs are great."

I like that he isn't one of those guys who gets a car he can't afford just to impress girls, and then makes the car annoyingly loud with noisy mufflers. I can't stand that.

As we head north, I direct him to my place. He pulls up to the curb, he lets out a low whistle. "Looks like I got an uptown girl," he says. "This is a nice area."

"Don't get your hopes up," I say. "I wear Kmart jeans and pack peanut butter sandwiches for work. My mom helped us get in here, and I split the rent with three other roommates."

He laughs. "Well, don't get your hopes up, either. As you know, guarding doesn't pay well, but we throw great parties, and I can get you a good deal on sunglasses."

"We're not into each other for the money, I guess."

"I'll walk you up to your place," he says.

"No, thanks. I'm not ready for my roommates to pounce on you yet. Thanks for tonight."

"Thanks for coming. And just to let you know, if it's all right with you, I'm going to give you a proper kiss after our first date. This is just a warm-up."

He leans over and kisses me gently. This kiss lasts a little longer than the one in his kitchen; it makes me dizzy and warm inside. I want more, but he stops and leans back.

"That was a mighty fine warm-up," I say. "So, this first date you speak of... when will that be? I may need time to prepare for a proper kiss."

"I'm working on it."

"Patience is not one of my better virtues."

"Nor mine. I don't want to wait too long, believe me."

I want to ask him when I can see him again. I want to stay here with him all night, but I force myself to get out without another word, wave at him, and go up to the condo.

As he pulls away, I feel so thankful for such a wonderful night, and for feeling this breathless excitement. Being with him seems so right; I feel at peace.

Annie's car is out front, so she's probably in the bedroom, already sleeping. I put my keys on the counter and see a note from her for me.

*K - Your mom called. She said to tell you 'Jake knows.' What does he know??*
*~ Annie*

*There's something between us; a sort of pull.*
*Something you always do to me, and I to you.*

~ F. Scott Fitzgerald, *Presumption*

# Chapter 8

## FIRST RATE FIRST DATE

"So. What does Jake know?" Annie asks. I'm still waking up. She plops on the bed as she brushes her teeth.

"I don't know," I say. "Give me a minute to call Mom."

"Call her now. He better not be back in your life."

"I think you mean, 'how was your night with Sam,' right?"

Annie rushes into the bathroom to spit, then returns. "That's what I said. Jake better not be back in your life, and how was your night with Sam?"

"It was wonderful." I'm in a daze just thinking of him. "He's honestly too good to be true. I've never felt a connection like this with anyone before. He—"

"Blah, blah, blah. Call your mom."

I throw a pillow at her and go into the dining room, where the phone is.

"Jake knows that you work at the Carousel Hotel," Mom says.

"How?" I'm irritated that anyone in my hometown is talking about me.

"I don't know. Word gets around. I didn't say anything."

"How do you know that he knows?"

"Because he called here and asked me to let you know that he's coming to Ocean City to see you in July, when he has a break between his summer sessions. Says he's going to stop by the Carousel. He tried to get your condo number again, but I didn't give it to him."

"That would be a nightmare. What's he going to do, drive five hours here on a weekend and back again for a chance of seeing me? He can't just drop by my work."

"Don't put it past him," Mom says, "He wants you back."

"I don't care. He's had enough chances. I'll call him and tell him to stay away."

"Good luck," Mom says. "Sue says that you're seeing someone. A beach lifeguard?"

I give Annie the death stare. She isn't supposed to blab anything about my life to her mom or anyone else. "Nothing I want to talk about yet."

"It's good to see you move on from Jake. By the way, Sue and I are coming to visit over the July fourth weekend. I can meet him then."

"You're what?"

"I know, that's just two weeks away. The fourth is a Friday. I'll take part of Thursday off. We'll come back home early Sunday morning to dodge the worst traffic. Sarah might come. Dad and Uncle Al have to work, so it'll be a girls' weekend. Can you work out sleeping arrangements so we can stay at the condo with you? That would save us a lot of money."

"Umm, sure. I'll talk with Annie about it."

"I know you girls probably have to work, but we can keep ourselves busy."

When I get off the phone, I tell Annie what Jake knows, and admonish her for telling her mom about Sam. "Whatever your mom knows, my mom knows at the speed of lightning."

"Sorry, it just slipped out the last time she called," Annie says. "What can I say? I'm glad to see you happy, and it oozes out of me."

"Well, stop oozing other people's business. Also, Mom says they're coming to visit Fourth of July weekend. They usually avoid holiday weekends at the beach like the plague."

"Mom didn't say anything about visiting," Annie says. "Give me the phone."

Annie calls her mom, who confirms the upcoming visit. We don't like that they're springing this on us, but we'll have to deal with it. Bianca and Marion are fine with it; they both have plans most of that weekend. Bianca says she'll stay with a friend so Sarah can use her bed. Annie and I can sleep on the sofa bed so the moms can have our room.

In the meantime, I hope Sam calls. I already miss the sound of his voice and the feel of his hand on the small of my back. I've never felt this deeply connected to anyone before, and I long to see him again. His promise of a real date soon can't come soon enough.

Sam calls me after he's done working and invites me to meet him and his friends at Big Kahuna that night. I ask him for a raincheck on that because I've picked up a shift at the Carousel; I need the money. I ask him if he ever rests.

"How will I ever keep up with you?" I ask. "Do you guys go out every night? What's the party schedule of a beach guard?

"Let's see, Sundays we go to Bayside Pub, or Flipside, or Big Kahuna's with DJ Batman—keg yell-offs are the best. Monday nights to Bull Pen Lounge for dime time, then Fager's or Harpoon Hannah's. Maybe Salty Dog or Angler on Tuesdays. Wednesdays we usually do BJs deck party for live blues and cheap beer."

"I've been there a couple of times," I say. "Pretty good music and food."

"Their steamed shrimp is good," he says. "We sometimes go to MR Ducks after that. Thursday, maybe The Turtle on condo row. Friday it's OCBP night at Trader Lee's. We usually party at home

Friday and Saturday to avoid tourists. When there's a good band at the Electric Circus or Back of the Rack, we'll go there. I'll take you to see the Sharks sometime. I don't make every night out though, especially when I work at Tio's, but most nights I do."

I laugh. "I absolutely won't be able to keep up with you. You have to tell me what a keg yell-off is and, yes, DJ Batman is so fun."

"Everyone loves him," Sam says. "We've coined him 'the nighttime mayor of Ocean City.' He's the best DJ around, and a big friend of the guards. A keg yell-off is when he gives a keg away to the loudest group at the bar. You won't be surprised that we usually win."

"No surprise at all."

"He sometimes plays the theme to *Hawaii Five-O,* and we all throw ourselves down on the ground and fake-paddle the Hokule'a."

"I have to see that. So, seriously, when do you actually rest?"

"Sometimes Tuesdays and Thursdays if I'm not working at Tio's. Even now, though, when we're training for comps, we go out. Work hard, play hard."

"Comps?" I ask.

"Competitions with the other crews, and with lifeguards from up and down the east coast. The Mid-Atlantic comp is on the Carousel beach, which is handy since it's where you work, so I hope you'll be there. The Lifeguard Olympics are at the end of the month at Rehoboth Beach."

"I don't know how you fit it all in," I say. "Do you even have days off guarding?"

"Of course. A day and a half off each week. I usually take Tuesdays and Wednesdays off unless I'm switching with someone, or they need a lunch rover. We all have to show up for Monday morning meetings each week, even if we have the day off."

"How will you ever squeeze in a first real date with me?" I tease.

"For you, I'll make time," he says. "I'd say next Saturday, but that seems so far away."

"Saturday is good," I say. "But I hope we can see each other before then."

"Absolutely. Then the following Saturday is our epic Fourth of July party at the ranch. I hope you can come with me to that, too."

"The ranch? Is that a new nightclub?"

"It's a nickname for an old farmhouse in the middle of a cornfield in West Fenwick. We have a big keg party, and the barbeque grill going, and a band. We want to get Brad and the Bombers for the end of summer party, if we can. Hundreds of people show up. We have it on the Saturday of the weekends of Memorial Day, July Fourth, and Labor Day. I co-host and take a turn on the grill. If you come, I'll be with you when I can. These parties are legendary."

Why did Mom decide to come visit the one weekend when Sam asks me to go with him to the biggest party of the summer?

"It sounds amazing, but I can't make it. Sorry. My dance card is full."

He's silent for a moment. "It's the hottest ticket in town. I think you'd really like it. Do you have another date?"

"Yes, with my mom."

He laughs. "I'm relieved. I'd invite her, but I think she'd feel out of place."

"I doubt that," I say. "It's last minute; she just told me that she and Annie's mom are coming to town that Thursday," I explain. "They're staying through the weekend. Maybe my sister, too. I'm sorry. I can't even explain how upset I am about the bad timing."

"No problem," he says. "I'll see you before and after the party. But about our official first date next Saturday. I'll shower and change after work, and pick you up around seven?"

"That sounds good. I work tomorrow at the café if you want to come by on your break."

"I'll do that," he says. "It can't come soon enough."

"And I don't want you to think I'm getting all weird even before our first real date, but Annie told her mom that I'd met you, and now my mom is curious. Do you mind if we stop by your stand when they're here so she can meet you? Maybe Friday the fourth? Just to say hi."

"I'd love to meet her. I can't talk on duty, especially since the beach will be so crowded, but I get a half hour for lunch."

Later, when I get back to the condo, Bianca and I catch up in the living room in some rare time together. She has a fit when I tell her about the party, and that I'm not able to go.

"You're kidding me! I've heard all about these parties, and I'd give anything to get an invite. Can you get me in?"

"Can't you just show up?" I ask.

"It's out in the middle of nowhere, and your name has to be on a list. You have to be invited by a guard or a scoper. They have security, and you have to show your ID."

"What's a scoper?"

"Geez, Kristin, you're dating one of the hosts and you don't know any of this?"

"He just said it's a big party. I guess he did use the word epic."

"It's huge. Scopers are the guys or girls who go around taking pictures on the beach, and you get the pics in those little viewer keychains that you look through. The guards give them free entry and free beer if they invite hot girls, since they're on the beach every day meeting them."

"Genius. So, there's a cover charge to go?"

"Worth every penny. Please ask your guy to get me in. That would be totally awesome."

I call Sam while Bianca hangs off me. He says that she can come with four friends. I give him their names, and assure him that they're cute and fun, but not troublemakers. He also confirms that the beach guards partner with the scopers to invite pretty girls.

"That's quite a racket you've got going on," I say with a smile.

"It's a win-win. Unfortunately, the prettiest girl in town won't be there. Good thing I'm taking her out the following weekend."

In one way, I'm disappointed I can't go to the big party, but in another way I'm glad that I'm not going. Sam wouldn't be able to be with me most of the time, anyway, and it really isn't my scene. I tell myself I'm not missing much so that I won't be bitter about not being able to go because of Mom and Aunt Sue's visit. Annie and I are going to make the best of it.

As promised, Sam stops by the café during his lunch break, and I greet him on the deck with a diet cola and a smile. He can only stay a short time, but I'll take what I can get. Each time I see him, I like him even more. We have an easy connection. Every time he comes up to me, his vibrant blue eyes shine with a want of me that is more than sexual. I want more of him, too. He leaves me breathless.

"Kristin," he says before he leaves to run back on the sand to his stand, "I don't want to wait until Saturday to take you on that date. Are you free tomorrow night, or do you work?"

"I don't want to wait, either. I can ask Ashley to switch shifts."

His smile matches mine as he finishes his drink. "I'll pick you up at seven. Dress for a nice dinner but nothing too fancy."

"I'll bring my appetite," I say. I'm getting better at this flirting thing. He makes it easy.

"Good. I already have mine," he says. He kisses me on the cheek and then runs off into the hazy, hot day.

Our first official date the next night is a double date with Kurt and Ingrid. He tells me on the phone beforehand that it isn't Fager's, but that it is by the bay and has great seafood. Kurt and Ingrid are driving separately. I'm bursting with happiness; I'm so excited for this night.

I like that he's keeping the destination a mystery. I like that he's courteous and wants me to be comfortable. I also like that it's a double date, so there isn't so much pressure on either of us. It wouldn't matter to me if our first date is at McDonald's. I just want to spend focused time on him somewhere that isn't a party, and I want that kiss. I want it badly.

I'm so nervous, in a good way, that I can't eat anything all day. Annie makes fun of me, but also loves that I'm happy and excited. She likes Sam, but she's still cautious about him.

When he comes to pick me up and I open the door to him, we both just stare at each other. He's in faded jeans and a simple white button-down shirt that accentuates his tan. I swear, no man can fail with jeans and a white button-down, but he takes the cake. I feel warm inside.

His eyes caress me from my head to my toes. I'm wearing a tight, black, sleeveless top with a white jean skirt and black kitten heels—simple but classy. I borrowed black earrings from Annie and a simple bracelet to set it off.

"Drag him in here, Kristin. I want to say hi." Bianca makes her demand. She and Annie are waiting to see him; Marion is working a big event at the convention center.

We go into the living room and sit down. Bianca flirts with Sam, and Annie assesses him like a mother hen. After about ten minutes, we head out as Bianca gives a thumbs-up; Annie offers a warm smile of approval.

The conversation between Sam and me flows easily on the drive; sometimes we bask in comfortable silence. We go north to Delaware, which surprises me. Large condos give way to smaller motels and charming residential areas, and then we drive through stretches along Coastal Highway where there are just dunes to our right and the bay to our left. It doesn't really matter what direction we are headed; I love being alone with him on any road to anywhere.

"Taking me across state lines? Good thing I'm old enough."

He laughs. "Taking you to a place that has the best crab cakes around. Plus, not as many people know us here. We'll have more privacy."

"Oh, so beach guards are like celebrities in Ocean City?" I tease.

"It's just that locals know us there," he says, "and often come up and chat. Restaurant owners are good to us; they come over and say hi, and sometimes offer us free drinks and discounted food. That's nice, but tonight I want to focus on you. I thought having Kurt and Ingrid with us would make you more comfortable; they're fun."

"I'm glad they're joining us for dinner," I say, "but I'm also comfortable with just you."

He reaches over and holds my hand. Then he asks if he can call me Kit. "Short for Kristin," he says. "Also, like Miss Kitty from the TV show *Gunsmoke*. I have good memories of watching that show with my dad."

"I like watching westerns with my dad, too," I say. "So yes, I'd like if you call me Kit." Nobody else calls me that, just like nobody else calls him Sam.

We talk about our families and where we grew up. He grew up outside Annapolis and is the oldest of three kids. His dad owns a flooring company that does work for big corporations, and his mom is a homemaker and part-time church secretary. He's been on his own since he was eighteen, went to Towson for college, and loves being an OCBP lifeguard.

"And you're turning twenty-five next month, right? What day?"

"July the twelfth. A Saturday. It's no big deal."

"It is to me. Do you have plans, or can I book you for that night?

"The guys are taking me out to a club. A good reason to drink, they say. Come with me?"

"Depends how tonight goes," I say. I smile to let him know I'm kidding.

"Well, I predict it will go very well. Tell me more about you."

I tell him about my unremarkable upbringing in my small town, my fondness for books and animals, and my tendency to put ketchup on way too many things.

"I'll forgive you for being from Pennsylvania," he says. "The ketchup? Not so sure."

"How kind of you," I say. "I'll have you know I'm a good driver."

"Then you must not really be from Pennsylvania," he teases.

"We have our good qualities, which you may soon discover."

The night is fun. The restaurant overlooks the bay just south of Bethany Beach. Strings of lights add an air of romance on the back deck by the water. It has a great seafood menu, and we all eat well as Kurt and Ingrid share fun stories of Sam. They have an easy chemistry from years of friendship; I feel included and welcomed. I discover that Ingrid is a beach lifeguard, too.

"Does that get weird if guards date each other and it doesn't work out?" I ask.

Ingrid nods. "There's an unspoken rule that guards shouldn't date each other, but Kurt and I don't follow rules. We just enforce them."

Sam and I laugh. He squeezes my hand.

I ask them about rescuing people, and what that's like; they have plenty of stories about that. Every guard they know has rescue stories.

"Ocean City has more than 130 guards covering ten and a half miles of beach," Kurt says. "We average 2500 rescues a summer."

"It's scary and exhilarating," Ingrid says. "And though we don't have many female guards, our numbers are growing, and we've shown we can kick ass, too."

"Cheers to that," Sam says. We raise our glasses.

"That must be a great feeling. To know people are alive because of you."

"It's definitely a rush to make a rescue," Kurt says. "Most of the time we do ordinance enforcement for rules like no alcohol on the beach, no surfing ten to five, stuff like that. Plus, we post water conditions, help lost kids, and handle medical emergencies. Our main job is scanning the ocean and helping anyone in trouble out there. For that, there's no better job in the world."

"We have about fifteen crews from the end of May until late-September, and we rarely lose anyone," Sam says. "Drownings mostly happen when we're off duty. Being outside all day and flirting with girls are good perks, but this job is about saving lives. At least for us."

"Nothing better," Kurt says. We toast to that, too.

I admire and respect them. As a pool guard, there are rare occasions where I help people who are struggling to swim, but the ocean is different. It can be so unpredictable, volatile, wild, and dangerous, especially with rip currents. Swimmers who struggle in a rip current can easily die, and do, unless a guard is there to help them.

After an evening of easy laughter and good conversation, Sam and I say our goodbyes to Kurt and Ingrid, and then head back to Ocean City. As we pass the dunes, I ask him if we can stop by the beach.

"I'll never say no to that," he says. "Besides, I want to show you something."

He drives a little further, and then pulls off into a condo parking lot. There's a sign: Association Parking Only, and another saying to stay out of the dunes.

"I don't think we're supposed to be here," I say.

"We're not," he says. He smiles as he gets out of the car. "You coming?"

He comes over to the passenger side.

"We don't have to if you're uncomfortable. We can go somewhere else."

He starts to go back to the driver's side again, so I open the door and get out.

"I'm okay. Let's do this."

I like that he makes me feel daring, and that he's spontaneous and takes chances. This gets me out of my play-by-the-rules comfort zone. My heart races with excitement and fear as I take off my shoes and hold them with one hand as he takes my other hand and leads me through the dunes like a beachy maze toward the ocean.

We stand on top of a dune overlooking the beach. It's beautiful, and looks wilder and more unspoiled than Ocean City beaches. The crescent moon is bright as it casts a romantic light on the ocean, and the waves of the ocean crash along the shore.

"Sometimes I come here on my days off," he says. "Less crowded."

It's the perfect place and time for that kiss as the breeze gently rustles our hair and the salty air sprinkles our skin and lips. As we turn to face each other, and as he leans down to kiss me, a flashlight bobs toward us in the distance.

"Who's there?" a booming male voice shouts. "You're trespassing!"

I pull back, wide-eyed with fear, but Sam smiles and grabs my hand.

"Trust me. Run with me," he says calmly but firmly.

I do, and we weave in and out of the dunes away from the figure carrying the flashlight. I feel like we're in a movie running from a bad guy. When I shoulder check, I see a man in a uniform. He's either a policeman or a security guard; either way, I don't want him to catch us.

By the time we reach the car, we're both sweating and laughing. My heart is racing. We quickly jump in and take off, just as the man who was chasing us reaches the parking lot.

"Wow, that was close!" I try to calm down by taking deep breaths.

"Are you okay?" he asks as he pulls out of the parking lot. He reaches his hand to mine. "Sorry about that. Their rent-a-cop was awake on duty for once, I guess."

I laugh. "It was scary but fun."

"Glad you think so," he says. "I see that wild side sneaking out of you. A nice mix."

"You're a nice mix, too," I say. "Decisive and a leader, but also thoughtful and gentle."

"I guarantee none of my friends would call me thoughtful and gentle," he says.

"Well, that's what I see in you."

"I like that," he says. He kisses my hand while he drives. "Do you want me to take you home, or do you want to come back to my place for a while?"

I'm not sure how to answer that. My inside voice says yes, yes, yes.

"Not for what most guys would be inviting you back for. I don't want you to think that. I'd just like to hang out with you more tonight, if you want to."

"I'd like that very much. But I do want that kiss."

"Believe me, so do I. And you will get it."

I'm reintroduced to Sam's roommates when we get to his townhouse, including Tubbs and Tucky. Some other guys and girls I haven't met are with them in the living room drinking beer and watching MTV.

Sam introduces a guy named Jesse. He's tall and lanky, with shaggy, dark blonde hair and a boyish smile. He raises his red cup to me. "So, you're the famous Kristin who has Holiday whipped? Nice! Care to join us?" He has a charming Southern drawl.

"No thanks, Ratman," Sam says. He leads me upstairs to the bedroom he shares with Tucky and closes the door.

"Don't mind Jesse. He blurts out whatever's on his mind."

"He said I had you whipped. Is that a fact?"

Sam laughs. "I plead the fifth."

"Why do you call him Ratman? And why do they call you Holiday? Fess up."

"They call me Holiday because once some girl at a party said she only drinks on holidays and I shouted, 'Every day is a holiday!' Then I took a shot. Or maybe a lot of shots. That was when I partied almost every night. The guys have never let me live it down."

"Well, every day with you feels like a holiday, so I'll redefine it for myself."

"I like that," he says. "As for Jesse, before he moved in with us, he lived in a real dump with a rat problem, thus Ratman. It got so bad that he asked us if he could rent the big closet under our stairs for a couple hundred bucks a month. He's a bean and good guy, so why not?"

"Under the stairs? That's sad. And what's a bean?"

"A rookie. A first-year guard. We call them 'green beans' because they wear lime green shirts. And don't feel bad for him," Sam says.

"The rest of us share bedrooms, so he gets privacy in his oversized closet under the stairs. He gets a helluva good deal."

He opens the sliding glass door in his room; we step onto the deck overlooking the bay.

I take in the expansive view. The Milky Way is beautiful in the sky, and the lights of the stars and the city in the distance cast a romantic glow on the dark bay.

"This view is breathtaking," I say.

He takes my hand and looks at me. "It sure is."

It's a perfect summer night, and the nearness of him causes a weird mix of desire and contentment to stir within me. The sound of the water lapping against the wood is soothing.

"Do you know you have a dimple on just one side of your face?" He gently touches my left cheek. "Just this side."

His touch is electric on my skin.

"I had no idea. Do you like it?"

"Very much." He kisses it.

I touch the top of his lip and trace over it with my finger. "Do you know your top lip is the exact shape of the top of a heart? It's rather perfect."

"I had no idea. Do you like it?"

"Very much. I wonder, though, how it tastes."

"Do you?"

"I'm waiting for that proper kiss you promised."

"Is that what you want?"

"Very much."

He cups my face with his hand and leans into me. "I can't say no to you."

He kisses me slowly, gently, tenderly, in that magical setting for what feels like the most perfect moment in my life.

He stops, then, and looks at me with such desire in his eyes that it makes my heart hurt. His eyes seem to ask permission to continue. I put my hand on his face and draw him back to me. His kiss deepens, hungry, and is passionate to match my response. A low moan escapes me. We're in perfect synch, body and soul, and we can't get deep enough into each other to satisfy.

I feel him harden against me, and I feel my own longing for him deep inside. He touches my breasts as I slowly unbutton his shirt. I run my hands over his chest, as I've daydreamed countless times, and trace over his muscles and his light mat of golden hair. He feels even better than I have imagined. I want to touch every part of him and feel him inside of me; it's a primal hunger that reaches beyond the physical deep down into my soul.

He lets out a low moan as I start to unbutton his jeans, and he stops me with his hands as he pulls slowly out of our heated kiss.

"What's wrong?" I ask. I'm drunk on him.

His eyes look as hazy as mine. "I can't believe I'm saying this but, not yet."

"What? Don't you want me?"

"More than anything," he says. "But it's too soon. I want this to last. I want more than your body. I want all of you, on all levels. And besides, you said no sex on the first date."

"But it's more like our third date, and what if I believe you and let's get on with it?"

He laughs. "When we make love, hopefully for the first of many times, I want it to be the right time and place. I don't want Tucky barging in on us, or for you to wake up in the morning and wonder if it was too soon. I don't want you to have any regrets."

"I won't regret it. I won't."

"I won't take that chance. I love that you're both classy and sexy. I want more than anything to be with you like that right now but, for once, it's not about me. Can I take you out again Saturday, and again, and again? Get to know you better. We'll both know when it's the right time, and it'll be worth the wait, I promise you that."

I take his hand and put it on my breast.

"I can't believe you're turning this down. What kind of fool are you?"

He gently pulls his hand away and rests it on my hip. "The kind who respects you. Who wants you to be sure. Who gave you a proper kiss when the time was right and will give you much more when the time is right."

In that instant, I know he's right. I would've wondered if it was too soon. And that means, yes, it's too soon. He wants me. He's saying no in my best interest. Is he for real?

"Do you trust me?" he asks.

I nod. I reluctantly, slowly button his shirt.

He grabs my hand. "Okay, well if you keep doing that, I won't trust myself. You know how to get to me in every way."

"Ditto," I say as I adjust my shirt. "I think we're going to have quite the fabulous time when you stop playing hard to get and let me have my way with you."

"I'm counting on that," he says. "I think I'll have to take the next day off to recover."

"Definitely count on that," I say. I playfully punch him in the arm, and then grab my purse. "Now take me home before I change your mind."

I love flirting with him. Our banter is so easy and natural, and we can say so many things to each other through our eyes without saying a word. I feel a communion of spirit with him. It is powerful. Magical. Intoxicating. I crave more.

We plan another date for that Saturday, but don't wait until then to see each other. Sam stops by the café the next morning during my break, fresh from a three-mile run on the beach and a three-mile swim in the ocean. It's part of his regular training routine.

"It's not much of a day off if you still train so hard," I say as I hand him a diet cola.

"This isn't my hard training," he says, "it's a walk in the park."

"Showoff," I tease.

He reaches over to hold my hand. "I really liked last night," he says.

"Me, too," I say. "I can't stop thinking about it. About you."

"I have a proposition for you," he says.

I raise my eyebrow. "I'm intrigued."

"It's my day off. I'm hoping that you don't have a shift at the Carousel today, or that you can play hooky and come away with me. Is it my lucky day?"

I laugh. "As a matter of fact, in our switching days negotiations, Ashley asked me to trade today for Friday. So, when I get off my shift here, I'm free. What do you have in mind?"

"Just what I wanted to hear. We're gonna go tourist today."

"What do you mean?" I ask.

"You'll see," he says. "I'll pick you up at four at your place. Dress casual."

Later, after he picks me up, we drive to the boardwalk—the second oldest in the United States. He parks at the inlet and we move among the growing crowd, where I feel like I'm at a never-ending carnival, one far surpassing the mom-and-pop fairs in my hometown.

"So, this is 'going tourist'?" I ask him.

"You'd be amazed at how many locals never even come here, and it's one of the biggest attractions in town. Once in a while I like to just come here and feel like a kid again."

We spend the afternoon wandering—I don't even keep track of time. He holds my hand through the not-so-scary Trimper's Haunted House, where I nervously laugh the whole way through, and he triumphantly wins a blue bear for me at the balloon pop game. The carnival rides, shops, fair food, and arcade games stir my senses in a summer daze kind of way.

We play Skee-Ball, take photos at the old-timey photo place where I dress up like a saloon girl and he's a cowboy, and I beat him at air hockey at the arcade. Hunger sets in, so we get burgers from the Alaska Stand—it's been there since 1933. We then wait in the long line for some famous Thrasher's Fries. Sam points out the No Ketchup sign. I shake my head no.

"Don't you dare," he says. The only permissible toppings are vinegar and salt.

The Ferris wheel looms above, and we ride it to take in the sunset from a bird's-eye view.

Later, we top off our tourist day with ice cream from Dumser's Dairyland and carry our treats to a bench, where we sit and watch people while fending off seagulls.

The infamous Elvis, aka Norman, cruises the boards in his cowboy hat and polyester shirt and pants. He carries an 8-track cassette recorder that plays Elvis songs, and hums along with a kazoo. This is one of the more ordinary sights that we see.

After we walk around some more, he takes me to Shenanigans, a lively Irish pub on 4th Street, for drinks. "I want to splurge," he says. He orders a Black and Tan for himself and is surprised when I ask for an Amaretto Sour, one of the few alcoholic drinks I like.

"Is it okay if I order a special kind of amaretto liqueur for you?"

"Sure," I say. "I didn't know there's a difference."

"Only the best for you," he says. "Make it a Disaronno Sour," he says to the bartender.

We take our drinks onto the deck and look up at the sky. I love the taste of the drink, the magic in the air, and the light in his eyes. It's another simple but perfect evening.

The evening ends with a long kiss outside my condo. I'm in heaven.

After that, we see each other every day. We're magnets and have an easy camaraderie that is both loving and lustful. I've never felt more like myself with anyone, makeup or no makeup, dressed up or casual. I feel friendship and attraction with him in equal measure.

Our schedules are crazy, between my two jobs, his two jobs, and his training for the competitions. He swims in the ocean before he starts his guard shift, and runs on the beach before work, during his lunch, and after work. His body just keeps getting better and better, as does our connection, so my resolve to hold off sleeping with him gets weaker and weaker.

When I work at the café, he runs on the sand to see me during his lunch break. I'm in awe that this beautiful man makes such an effort for me. We chat for a few minutes, and then he runs back to his stand. When I work the day shift at the Carousel, he visits me when he gets off work; I spend time with him on my breaks when we can.

He leaves notes for me with sweet messages and poetry quotes. I keep each one in a shoebox. One of my favorites is tucked in my wallet at all times.

*Dear Kit,*
*You consume my heart and mind. I don't want it any other way.*
*~ Sam*

*p.s. You are always new. The last of your kisses was ever the sweetest; the last smile the brightest; the last movement the gracefullest. ~ John Keats*

When we're not working, we go to the beach, or swim in the pool at my place, or hang out on his deck and talk and make out. I sometimes go out with him and his friends to the bars and to see bands; other times, he goes out with the guys, and I spend time with Annie. It's a nice mix, and flows easily, effortlessly. Whatever great things I dreamed about this summer are no match for how much better this reality is now.

*Be thou the rainbow in the storms of life.*
*The evening beam that smiles the clouds away,*
*and tints tomorrow with prophetic ray.*

~ Lord Byron, *Bride of Abydos*

# Chapter 9

## WHEN THE MOMS COME TO TOWN

### JULY 1986

Every day is bliss with Sam, but by Thursday afternoon, Annie and I are nervous wrecks in anticipation of the visit of the moms, and maybe Sarah, which may be triple trouble. We have a good vibe going at the condo and with our lives, and the moms have a way of rocking the boat and stirring up tension. We want to make it through the visit in one piece, without any fights. We've both juggled shifts to be there when they arrive.

They arrive with little fanfare. Sarah is with them; they're all a little grumpy after the long drive. After the initial hellos and hugs, Mom critically eyeballs the living room and kitchen.

"You could've cleaned up for us," she says.

I shoot a 'here we go' look to Annie.

"We did," I say. She has no idea how hard we scrubbed the kitchen, and how many of Bianca's condom pouches we had to hide away.

Aunt Sue tries to lighten the mood by saying she'll put her magic touch on it later.

Sarah's straight brown hair is tied back into a tight ponytail as severe as her expression. "Nice place," she says. "Mom would've never let me live at the beach."

"I didn't 'let' her, Sarah. I told her not to," Mom says.

"She's always been stubborn," Sarah says as if I'm not here.

I'm not sure why Sarah is here. We aren't close. There's always been a chip on her shoulder with me. I'm not sure why.

"I had to see this to believe it." Sarah answered my unasked question. "Mom's been talking about this place and your new boyfriend. About time you dumped Jake."

"He's not my boyfriend, at least not yet. I'm just getting to know him." My defenses are already up.

"I'm getting to know him, too," Annie says. "He seems great."

I smile at Annie in camaraderie.

"What's his name?" Sarah says as she plops on the couch.

"Shayne. But I call him Sam."

"That's weird," Sarah says. "Why don't you just call him by his name?"

"It's a nickname. We can stop by his stand tomorrow so you can meet him."

"His stand?" Sarah asks.

"Kristin has herself a beach lifeguard," Mom says.

Sarah scrunches her nose in disapproval. "Must be nice to get paid to sit by the ocean and get a tan all day. How old is he?"

"He does a lot more than that. Like saving lives. He's twenty-four."

"Oh, older. What does he do the rest of the year?" she asks.

"I don't know. Like I said, I'm just getting to know him."

"I had a job, a kid, and a mortgage by that age," Mom says.

"Gary is twenty-five, and he's already a CPA. Good benefits. Good salary," Sarah says. "You have to think of the future. Looks aren't everything, you know."

I dare myself to ask her if by that she means Gary isn't good looking—which he isn't.

"We're just having a fun summer," Annie says. "Nobody's getting married."

"I hope not too much fun," Mom says. "Remember you have to earn money."

"We are. We're each working two jobs," I say. "And paying our bills."

Annie steers the conversation to restaurants she recommends for dinner. They're all affordable places to meet with the moms' approval. After they unpack, we head out the door for a bite to eat, and then we play a game of mini golf before returning to the condo for card games. We go to bed early. So far so good.

The next day, the Fourth of July, we wade through the throngs of people on the beach to Sam's stand in front of the Golden Sands. It's five condos south of our favorite childhood vacation spot, the Sea Watch. One thing Sarah and I always agree on is our love for the Sea Watch and Ocean City. Vacationing there each summer growing up was the one time that we had Mom and Dad to ourselves without the distractions of their busy work schedules. Whether Annie and her parents came with us or not, the focus was on us kids.

Dad and Sarah would body surf in the ocean while Mom and I relaxed under a beach umbrella and read books. We'd then take long walks together on the beach, play mini golf, go to the boardwalk, play games in the arcade, and swim in the Sea Watch's indoor and outdoor pools. Mom sometimes swam with us, but she didn't want to get her hair wet. She mostly lounged in the sun in her brown and white bikini and got appreciative looks from men.

Today, despite Sarah's cattiness, Mom's criticism, and my frustration at having to miss the big party with Sam, it's nice to be here with family. We've planned to spend a few hours on the beach by Sam's stand, and then go to the Sea Watch to eat lunch at our favorite sub shop in its courtyard.

We wade through umbrellas, families, screaming kids, obnoxious teenagers, girls soaking up the sun in barely-there bikinis, and guys staring at them but pretending not to. Sam looks gorgeous with his short red swim shorts and nothing else but his sunglasses. Golden hair covers his tan chest and highlights his muscles, which are even more defined now with all the training he's been doing. He smiles and waves when he sees us.

"Well, if he isn't a tall glass of water on a hot day," Aunt Sue says.

I totally agree with her.

"He's okay, I guess," Sarah says.

"You know he's more than okay," I snap at her.

"If looks are all that matters, sure, but you see where that got you with Jake."

"Don't let her get to you," Annie whispers. "Sarah couldn't get a guy like that if she had hundred-dollar bills coming out of her nun-inspired bathing suit."

"Sarah, I wouldn't be interested in him if he didn't treat me well, too," I say.

"Says the girl who keeps going back to Jake." Sarah is full of spice today.

"Please give him a chance, and don't embarrass me," I plead.

"Hey, I'm in your corner," Aunt Sue says. "I'll give him as many chances as he'd like."

"Sue!" Mom hits Aunt Sue's arm playfully with a book.

When the lunch rover guard arrives, Sam puts on a shirt and joins us on our big blanket for his break. I just want to abandon this crowd and be alone with him. I hope none of my family will embarrass me. This whole scenario is already awkward.

He's charming, as usual, and soon has enchanted them. He teaches them about riptides and how to swim out of them. He is himself, unpretentious and friendly, and finds ways to complement each of them. They drink it all in.

"I see where Kristin and Sarah get their good looks." He smiles at Mom. She lowers her eyes like a shy teenager; Sarah sits taller and grins.

Sarah isn't used to compliments about her looks, but Mom is.

"You and Annie both have the same pretty smile," he says to Aunt Sue. Aunt Sue was also a looker back in the day, and still maintains her engaging grin and trim figure, like Mom.

He doesn't lay it on too thick. He gives them tips on getting good deals at local restaurants and tells them about a shortcut back to Pennsylvania that will save them at least a half hour. He answers their questions about rescues and helping lost kids on the beach.

Aunt Sue asks him what all that 'flag waving' is with lifeguards on their stands.

"It's called semaphore," Sam says. "It's kind of like sign language with a flag in each hand, so we can communicate with each other from a distance. We move our arms in various positions to represent different letters, numbers, and special signs so we don't need electronics or technology to say what's going on—especially in emergencies, or when we're in the water."

"So, you don't flag 'hot girl coming your way in a blue bikini'?" Mom asks.

Sam laughs. "Once in a while, but we're not supposed to. Most of the time, it's about lost or found kids, or warnings, like if there's a rip current forming or a storm coming."

"So, what do you do when the summer is over?" Sarah asks.

He doesn't seem to mind her intrusive question and is quick to answer. "It depends. I was in Key West last winter with my friend, Stu, but usually I work as a bartender in Annapolis."

"Bartending?" Sarah does a disapproving nose scrunch.

"Bartenders make good money," Annie says. "Bianca makes more money at bartending than the rest of us combined."

"It's not really a lifelong career, though," Mom says.

I want to die. They are so damn snooty. What he does or doesn't do is none of their business, though this is all news to me.

"It is for some people," I say defensively. "Nothing wrong with that."

"Nobody is deciding a lifelong career today," Annie says.

Aunt Sue lightens things up. "What kind of sweet drink would you recommend for me?"

"Have you ever tried Sex on the Beach?" Sam asks Aunt Sue with a straight face.

Mom gasps. Sarah's mouth drops open. Aunt Sue, Annie, and I laugh out loud.

"If you're offering, I'll try it." Aunt Sue gets a case of the giggles.

"It's a fruity cocktail with a fun name," he says. "As for bartending, I make good money and I like it, so for now it's a good off-season job. Not forever."

When it's time for him to go back to his stand, he assures them that next time they visit, he'll get a good table for us for dinner at Fager's, so we have the best seat to watch the sunset over the bay. He has connections everywhere, so they're excited about that.

Aunt Sue fans her face with Mom's book when he leaves. "If it doesn't work out between you two, let me know so I can have him as a snack on the side. Don't tell Al."

"Mom!" Annie admonishes.

We all laugh; Aunt Sue is the saucy one. When we pack up to go, we say goodbye to Sam and head to the Sea Watch. We eat ham and cheese subs, play pinball and air hockey in the arcade, and have one of the best times we've had together in a long time.

Annie and I make spaghetti, salad, and garlic bread for dinner at the condo, and then decide we'll treat Mom, Aunt Sue, and Sarah to ice cream at Dumser's Dairyland. Going there is a family tradition.

We eat inside at a table, and when the check arrives, Annie announces that we're going to pay for everyone's ice cream.

"You've done so much for us, it's the least we can do," she says.

"Thanks for everything," I say as I pull out my wallet. "This isn't much, but we wanted to treat you."

"Well, thank you." Aunt Sue puts her purse away.

Mom purses her lips. "You're just doing this because Annie is."

Her words drop like a lead balloon. The goodness of the day suddenly slips away.

"What? No." I trip over my words. "Annie and I agreed. I know it's not much."

"Actually, Aunt Jeannie, it was Kristin's idea." Annie's voice is raised.

"I doubt that," Mom says. "You lead, she follows, like always. First college. Now the beach. Besides, I'm paying for that condo, and I'm supposed to be impressed you're buying some ice cream?"

Everyone is in shock, especially me. I'm humiliated and hurt. Tears spring to my eyes.

Awkward silence. Sarah doesn't even have anything to say.

Annie straightens her shoulders. I can tell she's mad.

"Aunt Jeannie, you helped us with the security deposit, and we're thankful, but Kristin and I and our roommates pay the rent for that condo, not you. And nobody makes her do anything she doesn't want to. Not anymore, anyway."

Mom gives Annie the death stare. Aunt Sue notices and doesn't like it.

"Jeannie, it's a nice thing for the girls to do. Let it go," Aunt Sue says.

Mom chuckles snidely in the way I know she's not finished. "Nice? You know what would've been nice? Not coming here this summer when I told her not to. Not wasting time or money. She's not going to have a cent left for college, and I'll be the one who has to pay for things she can't. And she wouldn't be here this summer if Annie wasn't here."

"And I wouldn't be here if she wasn't here," Annie says.

I watch the light go on in Sarah's eyes. The water is safe enough for her to go in.

"It's because she's spoiled," she says. "You've always spoiled her."

I'm blindsided. Where is this all coming from? I want to run and find Sam and bury myself in his arms until Mom and Sarah are gone. I've come too far and done too well here to just swallow all of this or slink away, though.

"Coming here this summer was my idea," I say. "Annie supports me and helps me to be brave and do things I want to do. You should try it sometime."

"That's rich," Mom says. "How dare you insinuate that I don't support you? That's all I do. Who pays for your college? Your car? Your rent at college? Who paid the fat security deposit on your condo? You didn't have enough for any place decent. You bleed me dry."

"Jeannie, that's enough. Watch yourself," Aunt Sue says.

I gulp. Tears escape and flow freely down my face.

"I've been working since I was fifteen," I say. "I'm not lazy or spoiled. It was your choice to help with the security deposit, Mom. You offered; we never asked you for that. We would've been fine living at a dump by the boardwalk."

"So that's the thanks I get?" She shakes her head.

I slam my fist on the table. "Thank you. Thank you. Thank you. How many times do I need to say it? You chose to get involved and tell us where to live and pay the deposit, and now you throw it in my face. I work hard and pay my bills. Can't you be proud of me?"

"Maybe I would be if you had listened to me in the first place."

"That doesn't even make sense," I say. "That would make you proud of your control, not of my independence."

Annie takes my hand to comfort me; I jerk it away.

I throw a ten-dollar bill on the table and run out into the parking lot. Here I am trying to do something nice, and she criticizes and humiliates me? Never as smart as Sarah. Always a disappointment. A follower.

Years of pent-up hurt spill out of me in the form of tears and sobs.

Someone puts their hand on my shoulder and asks, "Are you okay?"

This isn't Annie's voice. I turn around, and there is our waitress, a stranger, comforting me when my own mom or sister won't. She has black hair with severe bangs and bright red lipstick; her expression is soft and empathetic.

I shake my head no and sob more. She hugs me and pats my back.

"Whatever happened in there, I'm sorry."

Her kindness touches my heart. I'm about to ask her name, when Annie comes out in a huff and grabs my hand.

"Come on. We're taking the bus home. They can drive back and talk smack about us. Never in my life have I ever wanted to punch your mom more than right now."

The waitress hands me a tissue. "Thank you," I say. "Not just for the tissue."

She hugs me again and then turns to return to work.

"Who's that?" Annie asks.

"A guardian angel," I say.

"Sorry I didn't come out right away," Annie says. "I was busy telling your mom off."

"You did?"

"No, I'm too scared of her. But I thought about it."

My little burst of laughter at that eases my pain a little.

Annie gives me a big hug. "I did tell her that you didn't deserve any of that, and that she owes you an apology."

"I won't hold my breath," I say. I clean up my snot with the tissue.

The rest of the night is uncomfortable at best. When Mom, Sue, and Sarah get back to the condo, Mom doesn't say a word. Aunt Sue says, "Sorry, sweetheart" to me, but that's it.

Sarah looks at me disapprovingly. "Such drama," she says.

"Quite a show, right?" I say. "Congratulations. You got what you came for: a front row seat to family drama."

"Boo-hoo," she says. Her own drama continues with a slam of the bathroom door.

I can't believe I gave up the big party tomorrow night for this. I stay silent as I get ready for bed. Annie stays close to me, and we fall asleep on the sofa bed together.

Annie and I get up and go to work before the moms wake up. It's the Saturday of a big holiday weekend; nobody has it off. Mom, Aunt Sue, and Sarah stop by the Carousel later in the day to see where we work. It's awkward. Aunt Sue tells me they'll leave early the next morning as planned, which is fine by me. I wish they'd leave today so I can go to the ranch party.

I want to call Sam, but I know he's at the ranch getting things ready for the big event. If Mom hadn't come to visit, I'd go there right after work to be with him. I still want to; she won't care if I come back to the condo or not, but she'll use it against me in the future. *Remember that time you were so rude and went off to the party when we were your guests?* I can hear it now. I don't want to give her ammunition to use against me for future surprise attacks.

We all pretend the awful scene at Dumser's never happened. It's what our family does when there's conflict. We brush things under the rug and ignore it.

We go to a cheap buffet for dinner, as planned, and make small talk. Annie mostly talks about her work with the kids and a cute guy named Dean; he's her new supervisor. News to me; I remind myself to ask her more. Annie is doing the best she can to keep the evening flowing without another disaster flaring up. Bedtime is a silent affair again.

The next morning, Sunday, the moms and Sarah leave after breakfast and stiff hugs. I find a check for a hundred dollars on the kitchen table from Mom. I rip it up and throw it away.

Bianca calls from a friend's place to say the ranch party was a-maaaa-zing, and that she has a hangover but will be back later to tell me all about it. She says she thanked Shayne at the party, and that he was the perfect host, but that she didn't see him much because of all the people there. I don't really want to hear about it, but I'm glad she had fun. Marion is probably at Dave's, but who knows; she doesn't tell us a thing.

I work both jobs; it's the Sunday of a holiday weekend, so it's crazy crowded, and thick with people, heat, and bad traffic. I'm glad I'm busy; it keeps my mind off of how awful the visit was with Mom. On the way to the Carousel from my shift at the café, I stop by Sam's guard stand. I really need to see him, even if for a few minutes. I slug across the hot sand and wonder how Sam runs so effortlessly on it. Boom boxes are blaring, kids are running and screaming, tourists are getting sunburns, and scopers are taking pictures.

A tall, dark-haired guy is at Sam's stand; he must be a lunch rover. Sam is probably tired and hungover from the party, but he'd never miss work. He loves it too much and he's dedicated. I know I shouldn't talk to a guard on duty, but I'm desperate to see Sam, so I call out to him.

"Sorry to bother you. Is Shayne working here today?"

"Mac? Yeah. He just took a late lunch. Should be back in about fifteen."

I don't have fifteen minutes. Can't do anything about it. I thank him, and then hustle to the Carousel. When I get there, I'm hot and sweaty from walking on the beach. I'm not looking forward to sitting in the hot indoor pool area for the next six hours.

When I get to the pool area, I say hi to Kelly, the lifeguard with the shift before me. She has curly, short dark hair, and is really nice. We're becoming friends.

"Hey," I say. "Lucky you, you get to leave."

She laughs and shakes her head. "No, lucky you, to have Shayne MacCabe come in here looking for you. Lots of girls talk about him, but he's a hard one to catch."

I almost correct her to say that his name is Sam, but stop. That's only my name for him.

"He stopped by for me?" My spirits lift.

"Yeah, he ran here on his lunch break hoping to catch you. You missed him by ten minutes. He said to tell you he'd stop by here after he gets off work, and to give you this."

She hands me a card. My name is written in his neat, rounded handwriting.

I'm so happy he made that effort when I need it the most.

I take the card and thank her.

"I'll stay a few extra minutes so you have time to read it," Kelly says.

I give her a quick hug, and then go to an alcove in the atrium to read the card.

The card is illustrated with a smiling sunshine and the words, Here Comes the Sun. The inside typeset is: Thinking of You. Sam has included a handwritten note.

*Dear Kit,*
*The ranch party last night was fun, but I wish you had*
*been there. I can't wait to see you again. Can you still be my*
*birthday date next Saturday? It's the only wish I'm making.*
*Hoping for a yes.*
*Sam*

*p.s. I miss your sunny smile.*
*p.s.s. It was only a sunny smile, and little it cost in the giving,*
*but like morning light, it scattered the night and made the day*
*worth living. ~ Only, by Author Unknown*

I read it five times, and then put it in my pocket and start my shift. He wants to see me sooner. He quoted a poem for me. He's stopping by after five-thirty. I'll take my break then.

"Kristin, you're late." Russ intercepts me at the door.

I jerk out of my daydream. "No, I was here. Kelly asked me to—"

"And you DO know our phone policy, right? No personal calls here."

"I know. I never—"

"The only exception is an emergency. Not your boyfriend trying to get a hold of you."

"I don't have a boyfriend."

Could Sam have called the Carousel, and they assumed he's my boyfriend? I hope he will be, but he isn't yet. He's professional, though, and knows not to call me at the hotel.

"Well, someone thinks he is. Says he is. He called the front desk for you. Here's the message. Consider this a formal warning. Don't let it happen again. Our phone lines are only for guests. And start your shift on time."

He shoves a paper at me and huffs away. I look at the message. Everything becomes clear. Now I'm mad.

Message for:  *Kristin / pool lifeguard*
From:  *Jake (boyfriend)*
Message*:*  *Call Jake. It's important.*

*I write only to bid you farewell. The spell is removed;*
*I see you as you are.*

~ Jane Austen, *Lady Susan*

# Chapter 10

## THE VEX OF THE EX

I'm furious that Jake called me at the Carousel. I'm still not sure how he found out where I work. Who's talking about me in my hometown, and who would care? I'm not that interesting of a person. I can't wait to get back to the condo to call him and tell him off. He's doing all this so I'll get mad and call him so he can talk to me. His scheme clearly worked, but will come at a price. The only ray of sunshine is that Sam will be here for my break at five forty-five.

I feel a weird mix of emotions. I'm both angry with Jake and excited to see Sam. During my first break, I check to see if Annie has a moment; she's in her small office by the indoor skating rink; she flips when I tell her what happened with Jake.

"Oh no," she says. "Nope. He's not ruining anything for you this summer. Give me his number. I'll call him when I get home and give him a piece of my mind."

"I have to deal with him. He won't stop until I talk with him."

"See how he manipulates you? He's been doing that for years."

"Yeah, I see that more clearly now," I admit. "I'll call him later and tell him to back off. But for now, tell me about this Dean guy you like."

She points him out to me as he makes balloon animals for the Kids Club children by the skating rink. He's Filipino, with black hair, dark brown eyes, and a warm smile. The kids seem to love him; they laugh at everything he says.

"He's cute," I say. "I can't believe you didn't tell me about him before you brought him up in front of the moms."

"Not much to tell; he hasn't asked me out yet, but we flirt a lot, so hopefully he will."

"Not if he's your supervisor. Against policy," I say.

"Well, they can put that where the sun don't shine," she says. "You know it isn't every day that you really click with someone, so it'll work out if it's meant to."

I hope he asks her out. Annie deserves to feel the way I feel about Sam, and to have someone look at her the way he looks at me. I think she's ready after the Jeff heartbreak.

It's an uneventful day at work until Sam shows up. Then, all is well with the world and my stress melts away. While another guard covers for me, Sam and I go to the deck behind the hotel that faces the ocean. We sit down at a table, and he reaches for my hand to hold while we talk. It's just what I need.

"What's wrong?" he asks. "You aren't your usual sunny self."

"Thanks for the quote in your note about that," I say. "It's one of my favorites. It's often attributed to F. Scott Fitzgerald, but was actually published before he was born. See, this is my nerdy history side coming out. Few people care or get it right. But you did."

"Don't be too impressed. I got a book of romantic poems from the library. They got it right. Either way, it reminds me of you."

"Except I'm not so sunny now. My visit with Mom started out well, and then it turned awful. We had a big fight. And then I got in trouble at work because my ex called the hotel and left a message for me, and we aren't allowed personal calls at work, blah, blah. I can talk about it later, not now. I don't want to ruin our time together."

He stands as he keeps hold of my hand, inviting me out of my seat.

"Come here." He pulls me into a gentle, long hug. I don't want to cry, but I do a little. He tightens his arms around me and buries his head in my hair.

"I won't ask you about it, so you won't feel pressure to talk about it, but I'm interested in all of it. Let me know if and when you want to talk about it, okay?"

I nod and sniffle.

"You're cute when you cry, but I don't like to see you sad."

"I don't like to cry, but if I have to, you make things better."

He wipes a strand of hair out of my face. "One thing, though," he says. "Do I need to be concerned about this ex? Are there still ties there? I don't want to be a rebound. Those usually don't last, and I want this to last."

I shake my head. "It's over. Been over. No ties on my end. He's still trying, though. And there's no bounce left—nothing left to rebound from. Do you have any exes lurking around?"

"No. My last serious girlfriend was more than three years ago, before I started guarding. I've dated casually since then. I don't feel casual about you, though."

"No casual here, either," I say.

"Want to go for a short walk on the beach? Everything seems better by the ocean. I have to go back to the ranch to do some clean-up, but I have time for a short walk."

"My break is almost over, but yes, I can walk a little," I say. It's always yes with him. It's just what I need. He's just what I need.

⁓

After our walk, Sam leaves and I finish my shift. Derrick stops by as I'm leaving.

"Kristin? Can I talk to you for a minute?" he asks.

I realize there's a good chance he's going to ask me out—there's a swagger about him. I quick-think how I might turn him down nicely if he asks me out. Sam is my focus.

"I was working by the front desk today when my friend Vicki took the phone call from your boyfriend."

"He's not my boyfriend. He's my ex." I say.

"Oh. He said he was." His 'oh' sounds rather hopeful. I hope I'm wrong.

"He's trying to get back with me. He shouldn't have called here."

"I asked Vicki if I could give you the message privately; I didn't want you to get in trouble, but Russ saw her write it down. He grabbed the note. Sorry."

"That's nice of you. Russ gave me a warning. Thanks, though."

I'm mid-turn to go when he speaks again. "One more thing. Do you, um, want to go out for a bite to eat sometime? Or maybe the boardwalk for some Thrasher's?"

I know it's taken a lot for him to ask that, and I feel badly he's not going to get a yes.

"That's nice of you to ask," I say. "Until a couple of weeks ago, I was hoping you'd ask me out, and I would've said yes. But I've started dating someone, so I can't."

He looks bummed. "You just started to see him, though, right? So, you're not, like, in a committed relationship yet? Maybe you can keep your options open."

I could, but I don't want to. I only want Sam, even though it's still early for us.

"Not officially committed yet, I guess," I say. "So, I'll say that I won't instead of that I can't. He's already special to me, and I'd like to see where it goes. I wouldn't feel right going out with someone else. I'm a one guy kind of girl, even if we're just starting out."

He resurrects a smile. "Figures I waited too long. Let me know if anything changes?"

"I will. But I hope it won't."

He's a nice guy. I'm a nice girl. I've been honest. That's all I can do.

I call Jake the second I get home. He doesn't care that I'm mad, or that he almost got me fired. He won't say how he found out where I work.

"You got what you wanted," I say. "I'm talking to you. Congratulations. But now I'm really mad. Plus, you look like a stalker. Big win." He knows I'm truly mad when I get snarky.

"I'm sorry. I want to show you that I'm trying for you. I know I didn't do that enough before. I want to come to the beach to talk with you face to face. After all our years together, can't you give me that? I've made mistakes, but we've had good times."

"The only thing you deserve after this stunt of calling me at work is to never see me again. Just leave me alone."

"I'm going to take a weekend to come and see you. I'm asking for one conversation."

"No. There's nothing more to say. Besides, I'm seeing someone else."

"What? Already?" he asks.

"Already? We've been broken up for a while. I've moved on. You need to do the same."

"I'll let you know when I'm coming," he says. "It'll be soon."

"You'll be coming for nothing." I slam down the phone.

I'm so frustrated.  He'd better not come here. This is my world, not his.

Annie is furious when I tell her about the conversation, Jake's call to work, and his promise to come see me. She wants to call him.

"No. You're not my bodyguard," I say. "Just drop it. Sam's birthday is next Saturday, and I want to focus on that. I don't want Jake and his bullshit to ruin that in any way. I want to think about Sam, you, work, and fun. That's it."

When Bianca gets back to the condo, she talks about the ranch party, but I'm not interested. Marion comes in and goes straight to her room. She's so hard to read. Is she happy? Is she sad? Is she still dating Dave? She keeps a closed book on her life and doesn't ask the rest of us about our lives at all. Still, she's pleasant enough, so nobody pushes her about it.

I can't get over the irony of things. As soon as I finally let go of Jake, he wants me. As soon as I stop looking for real love, it lands on my lap. It's too soon to know if I love Sam, I guess, but I've never felt this level of harmony, attraction, connection, trust, and safety with anyone else, and I can't wait to see where it goes.

*Raise me a dais of silk and down;*
*Hang it with vair and purple dyes;*
*Carve it in doves and pomegranates,*
*And peacocks with a hundred eyes;*
*Work it in gold and silver grapes,*
*In leaves and silver fleurs-de-lys;*
*Because the birthday of my life*
*Is come, my love is come to me.*

~ Christina Rosetti, *A Birthday*

# *Chapter 11*

## THE GIFT

The week before Sam's birthday is busy and fun. On Monday, I pull out my emergency cash from inside a pocket in my suitcase and purchase something special for him at the Carousel's gift shop. I've been looking at it ever since I met him, and it's perfect. I can't wait to give it to him on Saturday; I hope he likes it. I spend Monday and Tuesday evenings with Sam, and it's hard not to say anything about it.

I take the day off on Wednesday to match his day off, and he takes me to Assateague Island to see the wild horses and spend a beach day away from everyone we know so we can focus on each other. It has a remote, wild feel about it, and is less crowded than the main Ocean City beaches. He brings a picnic lunch; we eat, soak in the sun, take a long walk, and talk.

We get back around five o'clock and go our separate ways because it's his bar golf night with his guard friends. They do this on a weeknight since bars are less crowded with tourists.

They meet at six o'clock at The Green Turtle—dubbed "the clubhouse" for this golf-themed event—by condo row, and then they all bicycle south along Coastal Highway to the inlet to start the event.

The goal is to play eighteen holes of bar golf in one night. Each hole is a bar. They must have one drink at each of the eighteen "holes" and ride north with a stop at each bar until they return to the clubhouse. They have to get each bar's specialty drink—at M.R. Ducks it's the Duck Call, at Tio Gringos it's a Corona or a Tequila shot; Brass Balls features the Rum Runner. Everyone wears a Hawaiian shirt and socks with sandals, or a similar "tourist look."

"That's a lot of drinks," I say before we part ways. "How many guards do this? How many usually last to the end?"

"More than fifty start; less than ten make it to the end. There's a pickup truck that follows us as we bike from one bar to the next that we call the golf cart. If you're too wasted to safely continue, you and your bike go in the golf cart. See, even with this, we think of safety."

"Do you usually make it to the end?" I ask.

"Every time," he says. "I told you I can handle my liquor. I only do this twice a summer."

"The whole thing sounds too crazy to be true," I say.

"I have evidence. We take a group picture at each stop. Then we make them into a slide show—chronological order, of course—and meet at Ingrid's a week or two after for a watch party. Each picture shows our gradual descent into madness. We have great stories."

"Well, have fun and be careful. I'd love to come to the watch party."

"You can come anywhere you like with me," he says. "Thanks for not getting all weird about this. We don't do it often, but when we do, it's a hell of a lot of fun."

"I like when you go out with your friends," I say. "It makes you happy."

"I appreciate that more than you know," he says. "Most of my friends with girlfriends get their balls busted about going out with the guys. Some with good reason, I guess."

"I trust you," I say. "You'd be crazy to mess up what we've got going on."

He kisses me. "That's for damn sure."

I share a much-needed evening with Annie; we grab a bite to eat, play mini golf, and then hang out by the pool at the condo. I wonder how Sam is doing. I know he's having fun and can handle the drinking, but I don't like the thought of him getting so drunk. I'll feel better when I know he's safe at home after such a wild night.

I have to laugh on Thursday when I stop by Sam's stand between my shift at the café and the Carousel. He looks rough when he takes his sunglasses off.

"I'll sleep it off when I get off work," he says. I end up napping with him later.

On Friday, I get off the bus a few blocks before my shift at the Carousel to order a dozen yellow roses from the flower shop to be delivered to his townhouse the next day. The color reminds me of the summer sun and his hair. On the card to accompany the roses, I write: *Happy Birthday, Sam. Here's to our endless summer.*

After work on Saturday, I race home to change, then head to Scandals on 66th Street where Sam's friends arrive with him for the birthday bash. The inside of the club looks like the inside of a barn; it's loud and crowded, but the music is great, and his friends buy us drinks.

After a few hours of eating, drinking, and dancing enough to work up a sweat, a slow song finally comes on. Sam holds me close, and then he takes my hand and leads me outside for some fresh air. We find a quiet corner away from the entrance.

"Thanks again for the flowers. The guys roasted me, but I loved them. A great surprise."

"Well, there's more." I reach in my purse and pull out a small present for him.

He smiles and tilts his head in surprise.

"Happy birthday, Sam." I hand the wrapped box to him.

"You didn't have to get me anything," he says. "Being with you is enough."

"You don't turn twenty-five every day. I know we haven't been dating long, but this seemed to have your name on it. I had to get it for you."

He unwraps the small box and opens it. Inside is a small, round, gold pendant with the outline of a swimmer inside of it, attached to a thin gold chain. It looks classy and golden, like him. I can't afford it, but he's worth it. I paid for it with my emergency money, anyway, so I just won't have any emergencies.

He runs his fingers over it.

"You don't have to wear it," I say. "I haven't seen you wear jewelry–"

"It's perfect," he says. He opens the clasp and puts it on. The pendant fits perfectly in the hollow of his neck, below his Adam's apple.

"Kit. I love it," he says. "Nobody's ever gotten me anything like this before. Thank you. For the necklace. And for you. You are the gift."

He gently caresses my cheek and kisses me softly.

"Take me to your place," I say. I feel heady from the nearness of him.

We leave soon after that and drive back to his townhouse. He holds my hand like he's afraid I'll disappear if he lets go. There is a heat between us even deeper than before, like a cleaving to one another that is a force of nature. Neither of us says much.

We go up to his bedroom in silence. Tucky is staying over at Rhonda's again, so we have the bedroom to ourselves. Sam pulls the mattress out onto the back deck and invites me to lie down with him under the stars. It's intimate and romantic, and he holds me in easy silence as we look up at the stars.

I get up on my elbow and look down at him. He returns my gaze and plays with my hair. We don't say a word; we just bask in each other's presence. After a while I lean closer to him.

"I don't believe you've made a birthday wish yet," I say.

"I already have it," he whispers. He kisses me. Warmth spreads through me like a wave.

I slowly undress him, and then undress myself. The balmy breeze caresses our skin and the soft light of the moon bathes us in its glow.

I caress his chest with my hands and my eyes, and then move lower until I've touched every inch of him. He returns the favor.

"Are you done playing hard to get yet?" I ask. I slowly move on top of him. His body is ready for me, and I am ready for him.

"Completely over that," he says, "But, are you sure?" he asks.

"I've been sure."

I guide him into me and start slowly moving up and down to the rhythm of the water lapping against the shore beneath us.

"Kit, you're stunning," he gasps. He grabs my waist, and we move perfectly together, as if made for each other. He then gently lifts me off him.

He gulps. "I don't want this to go too fast," he says.

He positions himself beside me as we just kiss for a while, which is as pleasurable as everything else. Now this is a proper kiss. I let out a low moan. I've never felt this level of communion and passion with anyone before. He then gets on top of me and enters me slowly; we move with each other with increased urgency.

He's tender, passionate, and giving. Being with him this way is even better than I had imagined, and we both release with a level of intensity that is more amazing than anything I've ever experienced. It's a level of intimacy that is way beyond lust; I feel cherished and loved.

After, he chuckles.

"What's funny?" I ask.

"I think I'm in trouble. I'm never going to want to do anything else with you now."

"So, this trumps, say, watching TV? Or a crab feast? Or taco night? Or happy hour?"

"All of the above. Anything. Everything."

"Same. We'll need a break once in a while, though."

"Maybe, but not anytime soon."

I kiss him in agreement. We melt together again and fall asleep in each other's arms under the Milky Way.

*Love swells like the Solway, but ebbs like its tide,*
*And now am I come, with this lost love of mine,*
*To lead but one measure, drink one cup of wine.*

~ Sir Walter Scott, *Lochinvar*

# Chapter 12

## THE SHOWDOWN

We wake with the sunrise and make love again.

"Best birthday ever. You're all my wishes come true," he says. We tangle our legs and bodies together like pretzels.

"Not a bad way to start a Sunday," I say. "I feel like I'm in an incredible dream with you, and I don't ever want to wake up."

"Me, neither, but reality calls. I have to be at work before ten."

We reluctantly get dressed and drag the mattress back inside to the bed.

After Sam makes breakfast for me, he drives me home and then heads to work. Fortunately, I don't have a shift at the cafe, and I don't have to be at the Carousel until three o'clock, so I look forward to a leisurely day reading and relaxing until then.

I walk in the door and see a note by the phone for me. It's from Marion, stating that Jake called and said to tell me that he's coming to visit on Saturday, so he needs a place and a time.

I go from cloud nine to a punch in the gut in a moment. I call Jake and tell him not to come; I tell him that we can just talk on the phone.

He says that he needs to see me in person. I don't want to see him, but I knew he'll probably show up at the Carousel if I don't agree, so I suggest that we meet Saturday at the Sea Watch courtyard at four o'clock after I get off work. It's within walking distance for me from work. I want the conversation to be public, quick, and done.

"I'm driving five hours to see you, Kristin," he says. "At least have dinner with me."

"I don't want you to come at all. It's your choice to drive all this way for nothing. We'll talk once, and then you'll leave me alone. Deal? And I hope you have something else to do for the weekend, because you won't be with me. I have other plans."

"With your new boyfriend?" he asks. "The beach guard?"

"How do you know he's a guard? Who told you that?"

"Not giving up my sources. But he can spare you for a weekend."

"You get one hour on Saturday. That's it. Or nothing."

"We'll see about that. I look forward to seeing you. I miss you."

I almost break the phone as I hang up.

Sam is going to be working and training most of the weekend since comps are coming up soon, so we haven't made any plans yet. Besides, we don't really make plans anymore. We just know we're going to see each other most days and have a casual approach to our time together. I hope Jake is bluffing, but in case he does come to see me, I have to tell Sam and Annie.

Or do I? Why do they need to know? Annie will have a fit. I don't blame her, but I don't want to hear it. As for Sam, I don't want to hurt him or have him think I'm even tempted by Jake. I'm not, so why bring it up? I debate with myself, but the answer is clear.

I will tell them. Because that's the right thing to do. Because there is nothing going on between Jake and me, and there won't be.

Because even though Sam and I haven't talked about commitment and monogamy, we live it. Plus, we've told each other we're not casual, and we certainly aren't.

I've known Sam a little over a month, but it feels like forever. I don't want to be with anyone else. He doesn't seem to want to, either. I never fret if he's with other girls when he goes out with his friends, and he never seems to mind when I go out with mine. It just feels natural and easy. I don't want to risk messing up what we have, and I don't think he does, either.

Yes, I will tell him. I'll tell Annie. I respect them both; I don't want to hide anything from them. And I don't have anything to hide. It's no big deal.

I see Annie at the Carousel and ask her if we can take our breaks together. We go out on the back deck overlooking the ocean.

"How's everything going with the kids and with Dean?" I ask. We chat about little things, and then she gives me 'the look' she gets when she knows something is up.

"What do you want to tell me?" she asks. "Good or bad?"

"Something you won't like," I say. "I don't like it either."

"Cough it up."

I never want to disappoint Annie or make her mad. I know this will do both.

"Jake is driving to Ocean City this coming Saturday to see me," I say. "He insists on talking in person. If I don't agree, he could come to the Carousel, make a scene, and get me fired. I'm already on thin ice with Russ. We made a deal that if I meet with him at the Sea Watch for just an hour, he'll leave me alone."

"No. His promises mean nothing. You know that."

"Well, I told him not to come several times, and it doesn't matter."

"Of course not," she says. "What you want has never mattered to Jake. Only what he wants. Geez, Kristin, grow some balls. You have a hot man here who adores you and treats you right. Why would you blow that? Why give into Jake's extortion? Tell me why?"

"I told you—to not get fired. Russ already warned me about personal stuff at work. I like this job and don't want to risk it."

"But you'll risk what you have with Sam?" Annie asks.

"No. I'll tell Sam. Explain it to him. He'll understand."

"Don't do this. Jake puts you under some voodoo spell when you're with him, and you lose every crumb of common sense. I've seen it. He knows how to play you and sway you.  You're better without him, happier, more yourself, more fun. Even before you met Sam, I saw a change in you. I love seeing you like this. And I like how well Sam treats you. Don't ruin it."

"I know I'm better without Jake. I did love him, but after a while I think I was just in the habit of him. He doesn't have a hold over me anymore. And I won't betray Sam."

She runs her hands through her short hair and shakes her head.

"I could put you in a room alone with Rob Lowe or any hot guy on the planet, and I know you wouldn't be tempted to do anything to risk what you have with Sam. But Jake is your biggest weakness. You wouldn't want to give into him, but you could. Don't see him."

"He'll see me one way or the other. I'm doing damage control here. Why is it when I'm a bitch to him, he can't live without me? So, let him come here, and then go for good."

She sighs. "You're so stubborn. I hope that you're right."

I know I'm right. I believe in Sam and me, and I believe in myself now. Jake doesn't have power over me anymore. I'm no longer interested in his poor imitation of love. Sam shows me what it's like to be truly wanted and respected. With him, I feel peace and passion, not pain.

Let Jake come and see, and then let him ride off into the sunset into my past for good.

I finish my shift, and then go home and change. Sam picks me up and we meet friends at the Sheraton, where we get ten tacos for a dollar and Bud drafts for a dollar fifty. When we're not holding hands, our arms are around each other. Always touching.

When we get back to his place, we watch a World War II documentary and then go upstairs and out onto his deck. I love how peaceful the bay is, such a contrast to the wild and moody ocean. I love both, and I love them even more when shared with Sam. The lights of the city and the moon reflecting on the water are idyllic.

He talks about training for the upcoming weekend comps and suggests we just chill at his place Saturday after work so he can take it easy. I agree. Jake will be gone by then.

As I'm about to tell him about Jake's planned visit, he grabs my hand and tells me I'm beautiful, smart, and funny, and that he's never felt like this about anyone before. The way he looks at me with such warmth and longing makes me melt.

I can't get the words out that I was going to say. It's not the right time. I pivot.

"I feel the same way," I say. "You're a brave, gentle soul with an edge. Nice on the eyes, too. A rare combination. I feel so centered with you. It's like I've known you a long time."

"What have you done to me, Kit?" he asks. "I can't stop smiling when I'm with you. Even when I'm not with you. The guys say I'm whipped. They're right. Happily."

"Annie says I'm glowing, I guess we're in the same boat."

He kisses me. I almost get carried away. I push back gently. I can't make excuses or wait any longer to let him know about Jake's visit, so I dive right in.

It hurts me to tell him that Jake is coming to see me, and that I've agreed to see him, but I do. I explain why. He says nothing. He walks over to the edge of the deck and hangs his head.

I go over and put my arms around him. "Sam. Please look at me."

He does. Those eyes! I can't bear the hurt I see in them.

"It's just an hour in a public place," I say. "Otherwise, he'll probably come to where I work and make a scene. I'm sorry. I don't know how else to get him off my back."

His jaw hardens and he shakes his head.

"He's trying to get back into your life, and it's working."

"No, it isn't," I assure him. "I can't control that he's coming here, but I can let him see that one conversation is all he's getting. I can come over here right after I see him."

"No. Take all the time you need. Let's meet up Sunday."

He walks from the deck back into his bedroom, sits down on his bed, and puts his head in his hands. I sit down beside him.

"I'm asking you to trust me," I say. "This is no big deal."

"It's a big deal to me. I wish you wouldn't see him, but do what you need to do."

I rub my hand along his back. "Sam, do you know that you don't have to tell me that I'm important to you? Every action you take tells me that. Every time you look at me, every time you touch me, the time you share with me, the effort you make every day to see me and to make me smile. I feel it, and see it, and I'm sure of it without a word. Don't you feel that from me?"

He pauses, and then nods.

"I'm asking you to trust that. Do you?"

"Yes. But I don't have to like it."

"I don't like it, either. I'm sorry. Jake's determined to see me one way or another, so at least this way it's on my terms. This is about his ego. Not me. You and I may be new together, but we're already stronger than he and I ever were. We're connected on a whole different level."

The mood shifts a little. He's quiet and sullen, but he holds my hand and puts his arm around me as we go back outside to look out over the bay.

"This isn't the evening I had in mind for us," he says. "Especially after last night."

"Me, either," I say. "This all just came about this morning."

"I was hoping you could stay over, but I need a little time to myself to digest this. Plus, I'm training hard tomorrow, so I should try to get some good sleep."

I don't like this shift in plans or his mood, but I understand it. I'm sure I would be taking this kind of news harder than he is if the situation was reversed.

He takes me home, walks me to my door, and quickly kisses me goodnight.

I touch his cheek and look deeply into his beautiful eyes.

"Please don't let this affect us," I say. "Please trust me."

He doesn't say anything as he leaves.

Part of me wishes I hadn't told him at all. He would've never known, and Jake would've come and gone without anything changing between Sam and I. Sam wouldn't be hurt, and I wouldn't be kicking myself for causing him pain that he doesn't need to have.

Later, I toss and turn before falling asleep. In sleep, I don't have to think about how I hurt Sam, and how mad I am at Jake and myself for getting into this situation to begin with.

Sam and I spend time together the rest of the week between work shifts and Sam's training. He's aloof and distant, but I can tell he's trying not to be.

By Saturday, we're both in bad moods, on edge about Jake's impending visit. Jake is probably already in town. Sam is going to have a busy day at work; July and August crowd numbers are staggering. About a quarter of a million tourists visit each week in the summer, and the ocean is full of people who can't swim, or who can swim but don't heed rip current warnings from the lifeguards. His focus must remain sharp.

The indoor pool at the Carousel is busy, but not as much as the beaches outside. People come inside to get a break from the hot sun and swim, and I have to be especially watchful of little kids who aren't being properly watched by their parents.

When I get to work, there's a medium-sized, wrapped package on the guard chair to the right of the pool room entrance. Ashley is already there, checking the chemicals in the pool. "Some tall, hot guy in cutoff jean shorts dropped it off," she says.

My heart falls. It has to be Jake. He's too stingy to buy real swim trunks. Why is he here? I'm already mad, and this makes it worse. I open the package, and there's a Walkman that has a cassette tape in it. A 'play me' note is taped to the Walkman.

It's not quite ten o'clock, so I have a little time before my shift starts. I tell Ashley that I'll be right back. I take the Walkman, find a quiet place near the broom closet, and press the play button.

Jake's voice says, "Kristin, I know I didn't tell you enough or show you enough, but I do love you. It was never just about the physical part. I'm sorry that I didn't tell you that more. Please give me another chance. I'll do whatever it takes. Let me show you."

After his voice message stops, the music begins. It's a mixtape of love songs, including an instrumental song from the *Somewhere in Time* film soundtrack, which Jake knows is my favorite. I listen to four of the songs—all filled with love and longing—and then stop the tape.

I slip into the broom closet and let my tears flow freely. I try to process the mix of my emotions, ranging from anger to sadness. Jake is doing and expressing everything I've always wanted from him. My stubborn heart had held out hope for so long; now it's too late.

Even if his efforts are sincere this time, I've tasted from Sam what it's like to be cherished, and to be treated with dignity and devotion from the start. I can't go back to less. I now know what it feels like to be enough without having to convince someone of it. Sam gives that freely and generously to me; I don't need to leave for him to show I'm important to him.

I wipe my tears and go back to the pool. Ashley asks if I'm okay and I nod, although that's not remotely true. The stress is overwhelming; Jake is here. This whole situation has hurt Sam, and that's my fault. I'm mad, sad, and nostalgic at the same time. My stomach is in a knot. I take a deep breath. I just want to get back into Sam's arms as soon as possible.

A little after noon, Sam walks in and sits beside me on one of the pool deck chairs, like he usually does during his lunch break. We talk as we both scan the pool; Russ doesn't mind; he's a fan of the guards, and of Sam. He knows our guests are even safer when he's here.

I feel more relaxed with Sam beside me. It's all going to be okay. I do a visual sweep of the pool, and my eyes stop at the opening door to check a new arrival. But it's not a hotel guest. My mouth drops open in shock as Jake walks through the door and toward me with a smug smile. He stares at Sam like a challenge and sits on the other side of me.

I'm in the middle between Sam and Jake. I'm horrified. Jake and I had a plan. We made a deal. He disrespected it all. The Walkman, and now this. I'm probably going to lose my job. I might lose Sam. I'm for sure going to lose my mind.

Sam remains seated by me but leans forward and stares at Jake.

What is this, a showdown at the O.K. Corral? This is ridiculous. This is the lowest thing Jake has ever done. I'm so angry I can barely speak, but I find my voice.

"Jake, what are you doing here?" The tension in the words speaks volumes.

He stares straight ahead. "It's my day with you. He gets you all the other days."

"This isn't a child custody case. You don't get a day. You get an hour with me at four o'clock at the Sea Watch—not here, not now."

"I'll go," Sam says. I know he's trying to dial down the situation to help me.

"No, please don't," I say. I turn to Jake. "Jake, this is Shayne, my boyfriend. He belongs here with me. You don't. I'm at work. Please leave."

"It's a free country," Jake says.

We all stare straight ahead. I have to keep it together. I'm still on duty, checking the pool.

Jake must've been lurking out on the beach in front of the Carousel. He's never met Sam, but I'm sure when he saw a beach guard come into the hotel, he put two and two together, so he came in to mark his territory. This is so wrong.

I have no idea what to do. I should've never agreed to see Jake; I suddenly realize it's all part of our pattern, and I helped to create that. Years of being wishy-washy with him, taking him back when he cheated, and not being firm perpetuated an ongoing cycle of me being a doormat and him not believing my 'no.' I had taught him that my 'no' means that if he gives me a minute to be mad, then it'll become a 'yes.' I blew it. I have to stop the cycle. I feel horrible for Sam.

"You're jeopardizing my job and stressing me out," I say to Jake. "Please go."

"I'm not doing anything," Jake says defiantly. "I wasn't going to come in here. Then I saw him come in. I figure that if he can be here, so can I." He crosses his arms.

"But *he* is my boyfriend and was invited here. You aren't. And you aren't a guest of the hotel, so please leave or I'll call security."

Jake looks at me in surprise. "You've got to be kidding me."

Sam stands up in front of me protectively. "She asked you to leave."

Jake stands and faces Sam. "You leave," Jake says.

People are looking at us. They see two alpha males ready to rumble. I see a shit show.

I stand between them. "You think a fight is going to make things better for me?"

"No," Sam says. "Sorry. I'll go. Will you be all right?"

Sam's anger is controlled. His jaw is set firmly, and his eyes are like steel. He's used to diffusing situations, and he chooses me over besting Jake.

Jake sits back down. "Good decision," he says.

I grab Sam's hand. "I'll be okay. I can handle this. I'll see you later."

Sam nods and leaves. I can tell he's upset, and I hate that.

"I can't believe you," I say to Jake. "You're showing me you don't care about me at all."

Tears form in his aquamarine eyes.

"But I do. I asked you for a chance to talk, that's all. I drove all this way, and he has to see you on this day? I didn't realize what a cold bitch you can be."

"Me? I was trying to be nice. You bullied me into a conversation. That's all I agreed to after you wouldn't take my 'no' for an answer. I realize I didn't always mean 'no' in the past, but this time I do. We've been done, and I'm not changing my mind this time. Please go."

I see the hurt in his eyes, but I can't let that soften me. He needs to know I mean it.

"I don't want to come across like that," he says. "I wanted to show you that I'm willing to fight for you. I did take you for granted. Now I don't. Did you get my mix tape?" he asks.

I sit down beside him again. My head hurts. Why am I feeling bad for him in this moment? I have too much history with him.

"Yes," I say. "Thank you for that. I realize you meant it sincerely. That kind of effort and expression was everything I used to want from you. It's just too late. Please go."

I scan the water. Do my job. Hope no one has reported me.

He stares ahead silently, sulking. "Okay. I'm sorry. This is all gutting me. I just want some time with you. I'll see you at the Sea Watch courtyard at four?"

"My God, Jake. What else do we possibly have to say?"

"Please, let's just meet like we agreed. I'll go now."

If it gets rid of him now, then so be it. That's what I tell myself. I made a deal, and I'll stick to it, and then it'll be done.

I nod, and he leaves without another word.

I feel numb and tight inside. I remember all the times in the past that Jake made any kind of effort, but only when he thought he lost me. Never when he had me. I think about the movies I've seen that mirror that kind of relationship. I'm embarrassed. How blind have I been?

I want to run to Sam and tell him how sorry I am about all of this. I'm fuming, at Jake but mostly at myself, for hurting the only man who has ever made me feel this special. My heart is racing. My breathing is shallow, and I feel dizzy. All the anger and stress builds and builds.

A teenager who keeps running around, despite my warnings, runs by me again, laughing. I stand up and yell, "Walk! Walk or get out! Get out!" Tears start running down my face.

A hush comes over the crowded area. Everyone is looking at me, and all I want to do is disappear. Be invisible again. I didn't realize the upside to that before.

"I'm sorry," I say under my breath. I don't know if it's to myself or the guests. I call Russ from the pool phone. This is it; I've really blown it. Time to face the music.

"Russ, it's Kristin. Can you come to the pool and relieve me for a few minutes, please?"

He comes over right away from the hotel's administrative offices with Dana, a girl my age who is sort of a rover; she helps as needed for coverage at the front desk, the ice-skating rink, and the pool, since she's also certified as a guard.

A look of concern washes over him as soon as he sees me.

"You don't look well, Kristin," he says. "Let's go out in the lobby and sit down. I figured we needed to talk, so I brought Dana to guard the pool."

Dana nods sympathetically while Russ and I go out the pool doors. The cool air conditioning is an instant relief. Russ leads me to some chairs on a quieter side of the lobby area and we both sit down. He hands his bottled water to me and tells me to drink. I comply.

I confess that I yelled at a guest.

"I'm sorry," I say. I'm still shaking. "My ex, the one who called here the other week, stopped by here uninvited. I told him to leave; it took him a while to do it. I just got so stressed."

Russ sighs and shakes his head. His usual tough demeanor is gone.

"Kristin, take some deep breaths. There you go. It's okay. Deep breaths. In and out."

"I understand if you have to fire me," I say. Fresh tears fall.

"Not at all," Russ says. "You're a good guard. Everyone likes you. We're all allowed a bad day once in a while. And I know exes can be problematic. I have one like that."

I sniffle. "Really?"

"She's done even worse. Anyway, do you want to take a break and come back, or take the day off? Dana can cover your shift."

I'm so relieved that I want to hug him, but that would be weird, so I don't. I want to go, but I also want to show him that I'm stronger than this and can be counted on at work.

"If I can have fifteen minutes to pull myself together, that would be great," I say.

"That's fine. She'll watch the pool until you get back. Are you sure you're okay?"

"Yes, thank you," I say. I really appreciate Russ at that moment. I walk out.

I don't want to see anybody, not even Sam or Annie. I feel

overwhelmed with a mix of emotions, and I can't handle them all together. My brain hurts, like it's short circuiting. I go to the broom closet, close the door, sit in the dark corner, and take deep breaths.

After about fifteen minutes, I pull myself together and finish my shift. This is already a difficult day. I want to get my last conversation with Jake done and over with.

❧

The interior, open air courtyard at the Sea Watch is in the same triangular shape as the building, with the parking garage at the wide base, two towers of condos on either side, and a narrow row of condos towering toward the sky as the "tip" of the triangle. Guests access the condos from the interior side, so that the exterior balconies have spectacular views of the ocean. The courtyard is decorated with plants, benches, and a small flowing fountain to enhance the ambiance. Offices and my favorite sub shop line the walkways.

People are still checking in when I get there; road-weary tourists are getting their keys, carting their luggage around, and finding their way to the lobby elevators. That's fine with me, because I don't want to be in a private, quiet area with Jake.

He's standing by a bench and cleaned up since I saw him earlier. Gone are the cutoffs. He wears a crisp, light blue shirt tucked into white shorts. His hair is wavy from the humidity. He looks a little lost. I can't believe I feel a bit sorry for him. Annie is right, there's a part of me still vulnerable to him. But my heart is now with someone else.

I think of Sam, then, and the beauty of him, who he is, and how he treats me. But this isn't really about him or Jake. Annie says it's about me respecting myself with better choices, and being with people who value me, flaws and all. Jake is my past; I have a different future.

Jake turns on his magnetic smile for me, but it doesn't move me anymore.

"Thanks for seeing me," he says. "Can we go somewhere private?"

"No," I say. "But over there may be a little quieter."

We walk over to a more secluded bench and sit.

"I've gone about this all wrong," he says, "I messed up. What I'm trying to say through all this is that I'm ready to commit to you. It's long overdue, I know. I'm sorry about everything. I love you. Let me make it up to you and prove it to you. Please."

He's been sincere and sorry before, and I suppose he means what he says and feels at the time. Once he gets what he wants, though, he goes back to his old ways. Six months ago, I would've swooned at this earnest and loving Jake. Now, not at all. Now, my 'no' is real.

"I won't keep talking about this," I say. "There are a lot of great things about you, or I wouldn't have loved you or stayed with you for so long. But you only want me when you can't have me. I deserve better. So do you. Please, let this all go. Let me go."

"I can't," he says.

"You can," I say. "You will. Believe me when I say that when you meet the right person, you don't want anyone else. Go find your girl, Jake. It's not me."

I stand up to leave. He stands up, too.

"You're leaving already?" he says. It's like he hasn't followed the conversation at all.

"Yes. There isn't anything else to say. And please don't call or stop by my work again. But if you do, I don't care. I won't let you hold that over me anymore."

"I won't. But wait, I don't have a place to stay tonight. Can I stay with you? I'll sleep on the couch. Maybe we can take a walk on the beach? I'll leave in the morning."

He sounds as desperate as I must've sounded a million times before when I tried to convince him to love me more, or stay with me, or be faithful to me. I can see how foolish and ineffective it is to beg someone to be with you.

"I know you're used to changing my mind," I say. "And you want more time to try. But it won't work. I'm not mad—I'm just done. You can find a cheap motel by the boardwalk."

"How can you be so cold about this?"

"Don't think this doesn't hurt me, it does. But you brought us to this point, not me. You'll always be in my heart, Jake, but you can't stay in my life."

"Kristin—"

"Goodbye, Jake. I wish you only the best."

I stretch up to kiss him on the cheek, and he turns his head to catch his lips on mine. I lean back immediately to avoid it, and he gets nothing. I only want Sam's kiss.

I turn and walk away.

I look at my watch as I walk out of the Sea Watch and onto the sidewalk that runs along Coastal Highway. It's five-fifteen. Sam gets off work at five-thirty, and I want to see him before he leaves since I don't know where he'll go after work. I feel a liberating sense of freedom, and I want to share that with him. I run on the sidewalk from the Sea Watch to the Golden Sands.

The humidity is suffocating, but I don't have time to wait for the bus. I have six big blocks to run. I gasp for breath from the start. It doesn't deter me.

By the time I get to the Golden Sands, run through the lobby, and go out back to the beach, I'm drenched in sweat and tears. Why did I do this to Sam? Why did I do this to myself? I was so blind. I let fear of losing my job influence me, and a sense of obligation to "be nice" to someone I've loved for so long, even though he didn't listen to me or respect my wishes. No more. Even though Sam and I have no formal commitment, I don't want to hurt him or risk what we have, which I did by agreeing to see Jake. It was boneheaded of me.

By the time I get to the beach, it's after five-thirty, and his guard stand is empty. My heart sinks. But I *feel* him here. He has to be here.

"Sam?" I call. I look around, searching for his blonde head among the crowd.

"Kit?" He steps out from behind four girls.

His shirt is on, and his gear is in his hands, so he's ready to leave. I'm suddenly glad that he's usually accosted by girls wanting to talk with him when he gets off his stand for the day, because otherwise he would be gone by now.

He's always professional at work, so we aren't affectionate while he's on duty. At that moment, though, he runs to me, takes me in his arms, and buries his head in my shoulder.

I hug him tightly as tears run down my face. I'm so relieved that my bad decision to see Jake didn't cost me Sam.

"Hey, hey, it's okay," he says. "Babe, are you all right?"

"I am now. I wanted to get you before you left."

He breaks our embrace, looks in my eyes, and wipes the tears running down my face.

"You got me," he says. "You've always got me." He pauses. "You met with him?"

He sounds hurt even as he says it, and that breaks my heart.

"It was a short meeting," I say. "Goodbye doesn't take long when you mean it. And I don't care what he does; he can't manipulate me anymore. I won't see him again. It's a freeing feeling. I couldn't wait to get back to you. I know you have to train for comps, but – "

"I'd rather be with you," he says. "Let's grab some dinner and hang out on the deck. I was worried you'd go back with him. Seems like a guy used to getting his way."

"Used to is right. Not anymore. I'm sorry I agreed to see him," I say. "That was wrong. I only want to be with you."

"You do what you want," he says. "I don't own you. I'm just glad you came back to me."

"So, we're okay?"

"More than okay," he says.

I melt into him in relief. I don't want to give up this good man and what we have together. I never want to hurt anyone, but I usually end up hurting everyone when it comes to Jake. At least I used to. My former attachment to him has caused hurt to other guys who tried to date me along the way. This time, I've hurt Sam, and I don't ever want to do it again.

We spend the night together cleaving to each other, keenly aware that this situation could've torn us apart. We make love, and then we do it again Sunday night following work, dinner, ice cream on the boardwalk, and slow dancing to no music on the deck.

The next morning, he wakes me up with kisses and breakfast in bed: Frosted Flakes and a chocolate bar. We sit in the bed sharing the feast.

"Too much of this and I won't fit in my bikini."

"You know we'll work it off, and then some. This is a great way to start the week," he says. Suddenly, his eyes widen, and he looks over at the clock by his bed. "Oh no."

It's ten minutes after nine. "What? You still have time to shower and get to work."

He chuckles and shakes his head. "I completely forgot; our annual group guard picture is this morning. At nine o'clock, before work starts. Guess I'm missing it this year."

I grab his hand. "I'm sorry. I didn't know. I'm sure it's important to you."

"It's on me, not you. The guys will razz me, but I don't care. You know why?"

"Because sex with me is better than being in a picture with a bunch of sweaty guards?"

He laughs. "That. And because every time I'll look at that picture, I'll remember why I wasn't there; I'll know I was with you, instead. There's no place I'd rather be."

He kisses me and I playfully push him away. "Careful. You can't miss work, too."

"No," he says. "But you can help me get ready." He pulls me out of bed.

"I think you need a cold shower. Is that what you have in mind?"

"Hot, cold, doesn't matter as long as it's with you," he says.

The shower takes a little longer than normal, but he still makes it to work on time, as always.

*I love her, and that's the beginning and end of everything.*
~ F. Scott Fitzgerald, *Dear Scott, Dearest Zelda:*
*The Love Letters of F. Scott and Zelda Fitzgerald*

# Chapter 13

## COMPS AND THE PARTY PULL

"Why is there a hamster in our living room?"

He's a small, white, beady-eyed cutie in a cage with an exercise wheel and toys.

"Bianca got him yesterday," Marion says. She is on the couch watching TV and eating cereal. I do a double take since our paths haven't crossed lately. "She named him Hairy Harry, in case you want to add him to the lease."

"Cute, but she knows we aren't allowed to have pets," I say.

"She does what she wants. She left a note that she won't be home until later. And if you're looking for Annie, she's filling in for someone at work today."

"When Bianca gets home, I'll tell her the hamster has to go."

"While you're at it, tell her to stop sleeping with guys on this couch," she says. "It's gross. I have to keep cleaning it, because she never does."

Marion keeps eating. She's edgy. Something's up. I ask about her work and Dave.

"Work is work, and Dave is history," she says.

"Oh, no. What happened?" I ask.

She doesn't answer, so I tell her about yesterday's Jake and Sam situation.

"So what if your ex stopped by? Did you and Sam agree to be exclusive?

"Not exactly. We didn't have a conversation about it, but we don't need to. I don't want anyone else. I'm pretty sure he doesn't, either." I sit down beside her.

"Can't be too sure. Maybe you're just the flavor of the month," she says.

"Why so cynical?" I ask.

"Why so naïve?" she asks.

I'm stunned. She's being so prickly with me.

"Was Dave seeing someone else? Is that what this is about? Not all guys are jerks. If Dave is one, I'm sorry. Don't take it out on me."

Marion delivers a steely gaze that rivals Mom's, without the obligatory unconditional love. "What's the worst thing that's ever happened to you, Kristin? A broken nail?"

"Hey, what's your problem? Jake cheated on me repeatedly, so I know about betrayals. Doesn't mean Sam will do that."

"Doesn't mean he won't," she says.

"What are you so mad about?"

"You're lucky if the worst thing that's happened to you is a cheater. Not everyone has constant sunshine up their ass like you." She gets up and heads to her room, slams the door.

The friendly Marion who was with me on the beach when I met Sam has been replaced by hurtful and crude Marion. That girl has issues. I shrug it off.

I see that Bianca has left a message on the table from my mom. I call Mom back before I start my work shift. Our phone conversations since the awful holiday weekend have been shallow and short; we never bring up what happened at Dumser's. She's deep-freezing me; it's her way to pretend bad things didn't happen. When she's mad at Dad, she's as cold as ice. She won't speak to him for weeks, and then one day resumes talking to him like nothing ever happened. I know she won't talk with me about our fight, so I don't talk about it, either.

Mom tells me that she, Dad, Aunt Sue, and Uncle Al are coming to Ocean City to visit us August tenth through the thirteenth. They're visiting from Sunday to Wednesday to avoid busy weekend beach traffic. They'll get a hotel. Sarah isn't coming. In related news, Sarah and Gary have set April as the month they'll marry. I yawn. Too far away to think about, and I don't care.

I'm relieved they'll get a hotel when they visit, but the word August reminds me this amazing summer will be over at the end of next month. I love my life in Ocean City; I don't want it to end. Mom asks when I have to be back at college, and I don't want to talk about it. She won't drop it, so I remind her that I have to be back the Friday of Labor Day weekend for band camp—a week ahead of when most students return for classes. I already don't want to go.

Annie and I are on the pom squad; it's a dance team that does pom-pom routines for the corps-style marching band that takes the field at home football games, some away games, and exhibitions and competitions throughout Pennsylvania and Maryland. There are about twenty-five of us, along with the band, majorettes, and color guards who do all the flag waving. We prance around with our colorful pom-poms during the shows, and then drop them for a feature dance in the front of the band, ending in Rockette-style line kicks. It's Annie's third year on the squad and my second. Band camp is where we all learn our routines for the fall season.

"It'll be here before you know it," Mom says. As if I need to be reminded that band camp and the end of summer will be here soon. Too soon.

As I hang up the phone, Bianca barrels through the door with her unending energy. I talk to her about getting rid of the hamster and ask her not to have sex on the couch. She just waves her hand dismissively.

When I see Annie at work later that day, she tells me about her night out at Scandals with Tina, and I tell her about what happened with Jake. She's relieved he's gone. So am I.

Sam and I see each other every day. He invites me to both lifeguard competitions, and I'm excited to see him compete. He had told me that comps are a good way to raise awareness of the beach patrol to the public, to hone their rescue skills, and to keep in shape for the summer. "We have to be in shape to make rescues," he says. "Sometimes victims are twice our size."

Both comps are on weekdays in July and draw big crowds. The USLA Mid-Atlantic Regional Championships are held in front of the Carousel on Wednesday, July 23, so I work an early shift, and then come out to watch the run, swim, and rescue competitions. More than three hundred guards from New York to Virginia compete in teams and individually. I don't understand a lot of the competitions, but I enjoy rooting for Sam and taking pictures.

Sam's athleticism is impressive—he has such focus, talent, and passion for competing. I love watching him, and I love it when I catch a glint of the gold necklace I gave him for his birthday. He places in the top five of several events, which means he'll go on to the national competition in Galveston, Texas in early August. A handful of other OCBP guards win events that day, including Ingrid; they'll advance to nationals, too.

The Lifeguard Olympics are later the next week, in Rehoboth Beach, Delaware. I arrange my schedule to be sure I can attend. Sam will need to keep training, but for now, given the accomplishments at the regionals, everyone agrees it's a great reason to party at BJ's deck party.

I'm more comfortable with Sam's friends now and have a lot of fun. He always makes sure I'm included in conversations, and he knows when I've had enough of the crowds and want some quiet time together. We're a good balance for each other.

We're opposite in so many ways; he's an extroverted athlete and I'm an introverted artistic type, yet we complement each other, learn from each other, and have a deep and easy chemistry that keeps growing deeper. Every day with him is magic.

⁓

Sam needs some rest, and wants a relaxing, off-duty beach day. I love these days with him, when we walk hand in hand by the ocean, relax on beach chairs, and engage in easy conversation and flirtatious banter.

He takes me to the 130<sup>th</sup> Street beach, which is near my condo in North Ocean City, and where things are more chill. There are no quiet beaches in Ocean City in the thick of July, but this one is less crowded than most, away from the high-rise condos and popular attractions further south. The weather is hot and humid, so the cool ocean water is a draw for everyone.

We walk near the guard stand, and Sam waves at the tall, beefy guard on duty with short, dark brown hair and big muscles. I recognize him as one of the best athletes at comps. He nods to Sam, and then resumes his intense focus on the ocean.

"That's John. We call him The Hulk. You can see why," Sam says. "Most muscle guys like that are strong, but can't run worth shit, but John can do it all. A great athlete and guard."

We place our beach towels and chairs on the sand by the shoreline. Sam scans the ocean.

"Easy," I say. "You're not on duty today."

"Look at that thirteen-foot surf," he says. "Great for body surfing if you're a strong swimmer, but most people aren't. John's gonna have his hands full. Even though there are red flags to alert everyone to dangerous conditions, people ignore them."

Sam keeps his eyes on the water and clenches his jaw. He tries to relax when we come to the beach on his days off, but he's a guard at heart, not just on the clock. The beach is crowded with tourists, and the surf is rough, so he's on high alert.

We soak in the sun while we talk, laugh, and make loose plans for the weekend. "I was hoping we could go for a swim today, but not in this surf," he says. "Bad rip currents, too."

"I don't usually swim in the ocean, anyway," I say, "even when the water isn't so rough. I love the ocean, but usually do my swimming in the pool. Calm water. No sharks."

"We can come back another day and go beyond the breakers where it's calm. That's where I do all my swimming."

"What are the breakers?" I ask.

"It's where the waves curve, and then break into the white foam you see."

I hesitate. "Maybe someday."

He takes off his sunglasses to look at me. His blue eyes match the deep blue of the summer sky. "What's wrong?" he asks.

I'm ashamed to tell him of my fear. "You know I love the ocean," I say, "but I almost drowned in it when I was six years old. A lifeguard saved me just in time. I guess I'm still afraid of it. I love swimming, but in calm water like pools or lakes."

"Sorry that happened to you," he says. "The ocean has kicked my ass a lot of times. Let's just take a walk today. If you ever want to swim with me out there, though, let me know. It's amazing, and I won't let anything bad happen to you. But only when you're ready. Okay?"

I nod. I appreciate that he doesn't tease me about that, or pressure me to swim. I trust him, and I want to overcome my fear. He can help me with that someday, but not yet.

Suddenly, three sharp whistles sound in quick succession. Sam leaps up and looks over to John, and then out to the ocean.

I follow his lead. There's about ten people scattered beyond the big waves. They're young, maybe between the ages nine to fifteen. Some are going under. Those who aren't are being pulled out to sea. I gasp. "They're all in trouble out there," I say.

I've learned from Sam that three whistles from a guard indicates a life-threatening situation; immediate help is needed. Guards from stands on either side of John will respond, but that's not enough to help all those kids.

Sam turns to me. "John probably radioed this in, but have someone call 9-1-1 now." He runs into the ocean.

I race through the crowd toward the condos and hotels to find a phone. People start to gather at the shoreline to see what's going on. I reach a condo building where people are coming out on their balconies to see what all the commotion is about. Crowds are thick by the ocean now, with people yelling and watching four guards, including Sam, attempt to rescue all those kids in the rough ocean. I yell up to some people that I see on a second-floor balcony.

"Please call 9-1-1! Those kids are drowning out there!"

The woman waves. "Doing that now," she says.

She goes inside, and people from other balconies call down to me, "I'll call, too."

I run back down to the shoreline. It's hard to see what's going on. I'm worried about Sam. The ocean is so rough, and he went out without his rescue can.

It's hard to see what's going on, and everyone is asking about what's happening. I can see Sam's blonde head bobbing and swimming toward the kids.

"Where are the parents?" someone nearby asks.

"So many kids out there." "Can they get to them all?" "Not enough guards. Should we go in to help?" The comments come from various people gathering on the beach.

"The guards said not to," another says. "Surf and rip currents are too rough."

I feel helpless. John returns to shore with a girl in his arms. He hands her to a group of people with blankets, and then runs back into the surf. Another guard brings in a teenage boy. A female guard has joined them and has just reached one of the kids pretty far out. Just then I see Sam, a kid in each arm. He fights the current, waves crash over them, and they all tumble under.

I close my eyes, remembering the horrible feeling of nearly drowning when I was a kid. I was trying to get to Dad and Sarah, who were body surfing pretty far out. Mom was reading a book; she didn't see me walk into the water, didn't see a big wave sweep me off my feet, and didn't see me get pulled under. The ocean tumbled me like a washing machine. I remember murky water, a strong force holding me down and rolling me, gasping for air, and swallowing salty water. Darkness surrounded me, and then I felt a strange sense of peace. Then, a strong arm pulled me up into the light. I don't know his name or remember his face, but he saved my life.

Now, Sam and the other guards are doing the same for these kids. I pray they'll be all right; I know there is only so much you can do against the force of the ocean. They seem to be under too long, and then suddenly they emerge from the breaking waves, like they're being spit out of the mouth of a whale. Sam rises, his arms still protectively around a boy and a girl, laser-focused on bringing them to shore. People run out to help; Sam returns to the water.

Each time John, Sam, and the other guards bring kids to the shoreline, people on the beach and the balconies burst into applause. The guards don't seem to notice. Exhausted, each immediately turn back and dives into the base of the waves to help more kids.

The ambulance finally arrives, and the medics assess the kids. By then, the parents of the kids—apparently part of a big family reunion—have emerged from their rented condos to see what's going on. They quickly discover that their children are the ones in danger.

"We were playing gin rummy while the kids went down to swim," one says.

"My baby, my baby!" A mom has to be held back by two bystanders as she realizes her daughter is not in the group of those who've been rescued yet.

"I don't understand, they're all good swimmers." Another member of the family chimes in with panic, confusion, and a hint of defensiveness.

Sam makes three more trips into the water before all the kids are accounted for; he and the other guards bring them all to the shore. He collapses on the sand, and I run to him, but the medics get to him first. They give him, John, and the other guards oxygen, but they're soon up talking to the police and the OCBP sergeants and lieutenants who showed up.

After Sam talks to the medical professionals, parents, and the other guards, he makes his way back to me as people pat him on the back and thank him for rescuing the kids.

He practically falls into my arms. I shake with relief as I hold him.

"I'm okay," he says. "So lucky we got them all."

"Lucky my ass," I say. "You guys saved those kids. You're fearless. They have a future because of you. Quite a feat for your day off."

His face is covered in droplets of water; his hair is matted to his head. His necklace clings to his neck; he hasn't taken it off since I gave it to him. I hand him a towel.

"We're never off duty at the beach," he says. "I didn't expect this. Usually, it's one or two people at a time for a rescue. This was a lot. We call mass rescues like that a party pull, and this was one hell of one. I've never been part of anything like that. So glad we got them all."

"I think you need a hot shower and a cold beer," I say as I help to dry him off.

"And maybe some food, and sleep, and you," he says as he leans in to kiss me.

⌒℮↻

We go back to my condo. We have it all to ourselves. He showers while I make him a meatball sub and a salad. We eat and watch TV on the couch; he falls asleep in my arms and doesn't wake up until the sun is setting in hues of pink and purple. When he stirs, I lead him back to my bedroom and into my bed.

"Get some more sleep," I say.

He pulls me into bed with him and starts to kiss me. "I have something else in mind."

I laugh. "You're kidding. You must be exhausted."

"I'm getting a second wind."

We forge ourselves to each other and fall asleep in each other's arms.

⌒℮↻

I wake at midnight, intertwined with Sam. My eyes fly open wide, though, when I think of how Annie must've come home and seen us in bed. I don't want to put her out of her own bedroom. I thought Sam and I would wake up and leave long before this.

I look down at Sam, and I know that I love him. The moonlight kisses his hair and face, and so do I. His long, golden lashes look like they're sprinkled with fairy dust. His perfect lips are slightly parted; he looks like a Greek sculpture upon my bed. My heart hurts with joy.

I get up to go to the bathroom and notice a note by the foot of the door. I open it to see Annie's cursive handwriting and her signature smiley face.

> *Hey Kristin, saw Sam's flip flops by the door, I won't come in.*
> *Looks like you got lucky tonight. Or – I should say – he did.*
> 
> *I'll sleep on the couch.*
> *Love ya – Annie*

I return to the bed and look at Sam. I'm completely, ridiculously in love with him. Should I tell him? No. Not yet. I want to keep this perfect night with him going forever; I don't want to complicate anything. What if it spooks him? I don't want to risk it.

I curl back into his arms and, in his sleep, he tightens them around me. I nestle my head on his chest and wrap my legs around his. I place my hand on his heart and whisper, "Be mine." Rousing slowly from a deep sleep, he kisses my forehead, then my cheek, then my lips, and then we unite again in perfect harmony under the light of the moon.

∽

I wake to gentle kisses on my cheek. "Good morning, Kit. I love waking up to you."

We spend a few hours in bed laughing and talking. That feels even more intimate than the sex. It's his day off, but he has to train for the Lifeguard Olympics coming up on Thursday, so I make a quick breakfast for him of scrambled eggs and toast as he showers.

On my way to the kitchen, I spot Annie on the balcony reading a book; I wave at her and let her know Sam is leaving soon and I'll be out to join her then. The other girls must still be in bed or gone for the day, because nobody else is up and around.

Sam and I eat breakfast in bed and then I walk him to the door.

"Kit, just so you know," he says, "I'm hopelessly in love with you." He kisses me on the cheek and leaves.

He loves me? He loves me! He said it so casually and matter of fact, that it takes me a minute to process it—and by then he's gone. I'll savor those words all day, all my life.

I don't have a shift at the café, and I don't need to be at the Carousel until much later, so I go out to the balcony and sit beside Annie. She's not working until later, either. I'm glad we have this time to catch up.

"Well, well, you're glowing. Must've been some night."

I tell her about the big rescue at the beach, and how the day and night unfolded, though I don't give details. I apologize that we took the bedroom all night.

"I'll find another spot any time to see you this happy," she says.

"Annie, I've never felt like this before. It's not frenetic, obsessive, or crazed. It sounds corny, but it's like that song, a peaceful, easy feeling. Calm. In sync."

"I know. I can see it. I love to see you this happy."

"Are you happy, Annie?"

She nods. "This is a great summer. I'm glad you and I are still close, and that we have other friends and interests. I like the beach and my work. The best decision we ever made."

"It's going by too fast," I say.

"Then let's enjoy every moment," she says. I wholeheartedly agree.

After work, and after Sam completed his training exercises, we have a fun evening with Kurt, Ingrid, and some other friends at Big Kahuna. We say goodbye to them, go to his place, and pull the mattress out onto his back deck overlooking the bay. It's become a habit. We share some wine, and he tells me about his hopes to climb the ranks in the beach patrol to someday be captain. I tell him that, someday, I want to be a published writer, though it's probably unrealistic.

"You can do anything," he says. "I'll support you a hundred percent."

I've never shared that with anyone before. It seems silly, so I've stopped thinking it's possible. But here, now, with Sam, I believe it can happen.

I lean over and kiss him gently, then passionately. I pull back before I lose myself.

"Sam, I need to tell you something," I say.

"Tell me."

I can't seem to get any words out. I'm caught up in how he looks at me, how the stars form a blanket above us, how his hands run seductively through my hair, and how my body craves him. Before I get lost in him, I tell him how I feel.

"Sam, you've put a spell on me. I love you, everything about you. And I love the way you love me. Thank you. You're the greatest gift I've ever been given."

"I love you," he whispers. "I've never been more sure about anything in my life."

He kisses me again, and again, and then he pulls me down to him on the mattress. We make love under the hazy sky to the sounds of the water lapping against the deck, Madonna's "Crazy for You" on a distant radio, and our beating hearts.

*I love thee, I love but thee*
*With a love that shall not die,*
*Till the sun grows cold*
*And the stars grow old…*
~ Bayard Taylor, *Bedouin Song*

# Chapter 14

SAPPY TRUTH INTERLUDE

AUGUST 1986

I love him.

First, the shallow things. I love the way he looks in his short, red guard swim trunks. I love the curve of his calves, and his high cheekbones, and the blonde hair that clings to his legs, arms, and chest—I love that he doesn't shave that like most swimmers do. I love how masculine he is, and his muscles, and the line of hair that runs from his stomach to his groin. I love the way his blonde eyelashes are long and sparkle in the moonlight. I love the sound of his voice, the brilliance of his smile, and the set of his jaw, square and determined. I love the way he stands leaning back a little, with his hands on his hip bones, relaxed and at ease. I love the shape of his lips, and how tenderly and passionately they kiss me. I love the way his body intertwines with mine, and that his arms automatically tighten protectively around me, even in sleep, when I stir. I love running my hand over his chest as I fall asleep. I want to feast on him every time I see him, and even when I don't see him. He is fit and sculpted, and I don't care if every girl on the beach looks at him. He is gloriously mine, with his dark skin, pale hair, and intense blue eyes.

What I love the most, though, is who he is. I love his soul, his intellect, his courage, and his passion. I love how he is both confident and humble. I love that he likes to help people, that he gives a hundred percent to everything he does, and that he loves me so fully, authentically, and respectfully. I love that he is so dedicated to his job—and how good he is at it. I love the way he follows through on what he says he'll do, and that he's bold in expressing his opinion, even if it's unpopular. I love the way he looks at me with unmasked love. I love his gusto and grit, and the way he holds my hand like he doesn't ever want to let me go. I love that he adores me in front of his friends, and that he's respectful with my friends, even the ones he doesn't like. I love his athleticism, and the way I feel safe with him. And his eyes. Beyond the color, I love the way they light up when they see me, look into my soul, and make me feel seen. Really seen.

I love, love, love him. Even his faults; we all have them. I get pouty when I don't get my way, and snarky when I get mad. He gets quiet when he gets mad and can be opinionated and moody. I care what other people think; he doesn't.

Once, back at the Lifeguard Olympics, a guy who is part of Sam's crew was really critical of Sam, and I got more upset than Sam did about it.

"What's a nice girl like you doing with a guy like Sam?" he had asked me. His name is Tim. He's arrogant, tall and muscular, with moss-green eyes.

"Excuse me?" I'd asked. I was surprised, because Tim had never talked to me before.

"Yeah, he's a jerk. Thinks he knows it all. Loves a power trip."

For a moment, I hadn't known what to say. He had some nerve saying that to me.

"Well, aren't you a charmer?" I'd said. "He can be a little sharp with people sometimes when they're out of line, but they usually deserve it. He isn't like that with me."

Tim had laughed. "Of course he's not. But he is with everyone else."

"I see him a lot with his friends and other guards. He's not a jerk," I said.

"Well, he's like that with me. He's my crew chief. I was late once. Once. He ripped me a new one and wrote me up. I do a good job, and he does that? Not cool."

When he had said that, I wondered if it was true. Yes, Sam is opinionated. And, as someone's boss, he's going to expect them to do their job. He won't hesitate to tell them if they aren't. Some people can see that as harsh, I guess. I care about how he treats others, but what I see about him—even when he doesn't know I'm watching—is kind, but not a pushover.

I figured that Tim wasn't telling me this out of the blue for no reason.

"And who do you think is good enough for a nice girl like me?" I asked, fishing.

"That would be me. A true Southern gentleman."

"Ahhh, who is the real jerk?" I had asked him. "A gentleman doesn't throw his brother under the bus. Aren't you guards a family? A brotherhood? Here you are, talking smack about him to his girl, and hitting on her."

"I'm just saying, if anything happens, I'd love to take you out. Show you the difference."

With that, he had sauntered away.

Later that night, I'd told Sam about it, and he'd laughed. "Tim will steal the shirt off your back. He'll especially steal your girl if he can. And he often does. He's a good guard, though."

"It's weird that you don't mind when your friends hit on me," I'd said.

"You're a beautiful girl. I don't blame them. And with these guys, nothing surprises me. Besides, we have a code. You can flirt with another guard's girl, but don't sleep with her."

"Weird code. But is it true? About you being hard on him when he was late one day?"

"What I learned from our captain, I carry through to my crew. If you're early, you're on time. If you're on time, you're late. If you're late, you're fired. I didn't fire him."

"A write-up is pretty strict, though. Can't you give just a warning the first time?"

"Not with this job. If you're late and someone drowns in that time, that's obviously a big deal. That won't happen on my watch, or with my crew. He'll get over it."

"I see what you mean. But could you change it this once with just a warning?"

He nudged me playfully. "Did ol' green eyes get under your skin?"

I nudged him back harder. "I just want people to like you like I do."

He nuzzled his nose into my neck. "I don't care about being liked. I care about doing my job well and saving lives. But you like me, huh? Even though I'm bossy and mean?"

I nodded and kissed him. "I wish they could see you the way that I do."

He pulled me close. "The ones who matter, do. If someone on my crew doesn't like me, I know that at least they respect me. They know I'd give my life for them, and that I expect their best. I may break rules in life, but not here on the beach. It could cost someone their life. If I have to be the bad guy to enforce rules, so be it."

I kissed his shoulder. "Good girls are supposed to like bad boys. It's a thing."

"Is that so? Then yes, I'm bad. Very, very bad."
"Show me."
And he did.

*I'm yours for ever – for ever and ever.*
*Here I stand; I'm as firm as a rock.*
*If you'll only trust me, how little you'll be disappointed.*
*Be mine as I am yours.*

~ Henry James, *The Portrait of a Lady*

# Chapter 15

## TRIALS, TRUST, AND TEMPTATIONS

### AUGUST 1986

A week before my parents visit, I get crabs—not the kind you pick and eat.

It's a terrible way to start the month. The weekend before he leaves for nationals, Sam tells me to go to the doctor to get checked for them. He's just found out he has them; he gets a prescription cream to treat them. He says I'll probably need a prescription for the cream, too. When he tells me exactly what these kinds of crabs are, I'm horrified, mad, and suspicious.

"This is sexually transmitted, Sam. Have you been with someone else?"

"No," he says. "I swear."

"Then how did you get them?"

"No idea. You can get them from towels or bed sheets of someone who has them," he says. "It probably came from my place. Jesse said he had critters, so we all got checked, and we all have crabs. He sprayed his junk with Raid, thinking that would get rid of them—can you believe that?" Sam laughs at his story. Laughs at crabs.

"This isn't funny, Sam. You expect me to believe that's how you got it?"

"I hate to say it, but we all use whatever towels are in the bathroom, and they could've spread that way. Or it could've been your couch, since Bianca sleeps there with different guys, and you and I have slept there a couple of times. It isn't funny. Jesse is funny, though."

I don't like that this makes me doubt Sam's faithfulness. I'm so used to Jake and his stories to cover cheating, that my automatic thought is to assume he's lying. Plus, sex is the most common way to spread crabs. Is he spinning a story? I want to believe him, but I'm skeptical.

I make a doctor's appointment and, sure enough, I have them. I'm furious and grossed out. I get the cream, and it clears things up while Sam is in Texas at nationals, but my anger lingers. I have to tell Annie, since we share a bed; fortunately, she doesn't have them.

I never thought something like this would happen to me. I thought being monogamous would prevent getting anything like this. It doesn't work, though, if the person you're with isn't also faithful. Has he cheated on me? I'm sure he has temptations every day; what if he gives in to them? The cloud of doubt I always carried with Jake does not fit well with Sam.

I admit that I'm sometimes tempted, too. I'm human. Nothing is as tempting as what I have with Sam, though. I get asked out, but I say no every time. I wasn't even swayed by Jake's swan song to get me back. I even walk away from a close call with Derrick one day when Sam is at nationals; I don't see that one coming, though I should have.

Wednesday the sixth, when Sam leaves for nationals for three days, Derrick and I run into each other during a work break at the Carousel. I mention Robert Frost's "Fire and Ice" poem as we watch people skate on the indoor ice-skating rink. He says he has a collection of first edition poetry books at his place, including one from Frost; many are inscribed and signed. It's rare to find one first edition book, let alone a small collection.

"No way," I say. "How many? I don't see you as a big poetry guy."

"I'm not," he admits. "My dad teaches Lit at Towson. He keeps most of his collection at our house in Timonium; the others he keeps here at the condo that he and Mom own. That's where I live for the summer with a few friends. They pay a little rent, but not much."

"Nice," I say. "You probably don't even need to work."

"Not really, but I want to. I like to fix things and be productive. Hey, would you like to see the books Dad has here? They don't interest me but might interest you."

"Yes, please. Can you bring some to work tomorrow?"

He shakes his head. "They might get damaged. Dad would kill me. Why don't you stop by my place to see them? I live off Old Wharf Road by the bay."

That isn't too far south of where Sam lives. It would be weird, though.

"I don't think so. I have a boyfriend."

"You've made that clear," he says. "Why don't you stop by after work? My roommates will be there; it's taco night. It won't take long. Bring your boyfriend if you want to."

I relax when he invites Sam, but I know that seeing a bunch of old books would bore him. Besides, he's away at nationals. I don't have any plans after work, anyway, since Sam is in Texas. I can take the bus there from work, see the books, and take the bus back to the condo.

"I'll stop by around five if that's okay, but I can't stay long."

"No problem," he says.

Later, when I get to Derrick's place, none of his roommates are there.

"They decided to go out to eat, instead," he says.

His parents' condo is even nicer than my rental, with real leather furniture and new carpet that isn't stained or worn. Most of my new friends who live in Ocean City for the summer live in run-down places; this is clearly the vacation home of people with money.

I feel uncomfortable that his roommates aren't there, but I don't say anything.

He offers a glass of water or wine, but I decline and tell him that I can't stay long. He says the book collection is in the master suite, so I follow him to the door of the bedroom. He walks to the other side of the room and points to two rows of books in a mahogany bookcase.

"Check them out," he says. He picks up a book. "He has a few from the 1800s."

Something doesn't feel right. It's the slow creep of fear, and the realization that I don't know Derrick well enough to be alone with him. For all the talk of equality, men are generally stronger than women. I put myself in a vulnerable situation, and I wonder if I'm safe with him. I can't help but think of that frat party where I wasn't safe, but thankfully I got away in time.

"I thought the books would be in, like, a common area like the living room, and that your roommates would be home," I say. "This feels weird."

"Sorry," he says. "I thought they'd be home, too. Let's do this another time, then. I don't want you to be uncomfortable. I'll walk you out."

I nod, but don't turn away. He doesn't move, either. I feel strangely tethered to the floor.

Seeing my hesitation, he locks eyes with mine and walks slowly toward me with the book in his hand. The air is suddenly thick with sexual chemistry. Like, whatever chemistry we have at work times ten. What have I gotten myself into? I tell myself to leave, but I'm frozen.

As he gets closer, my heart starts racing with desire. I'm aroused, and he isn't even touching me. This is pure lust. It has to be. It lacks the sweetness and deeper connection of my chemistry with Sam, but it's powerful. I now realize how people can have casual sex. If I wasn't with Sam, I would've let Derrick take me then and there, without love as part of the equation.

Derrick comes so close to me that our bodies almost touch. His amber eyes lock into mine, and he smiles seductively. He knows that he has me in a trance.

Why am I not moving away? This isn't an easy no. It can be a pleasurable yes. Am I committed to Sam or not? Do I trust that Sam is faithful to me, with all his temptations? Can I do this, and Sam would never know? Yes, but I would know. I don't want to risk it. Sam is worth denying a fleeting moment of gratification. Sam is pleasure on all levels, not just sex.

Derrick leans down to kiss me. I force myself to step back.

"I don't need to see the books, after all," I say. "I, I have a boyfriend."

He smiles. "You keep saying that. Yet here you are. Come on, you didn't come here just to see some old books. And having a boyfriend doesn't matter to anyone around here."

"It matters to me," I say. "And I actually did come here to see the books."

He steps back. "Oh, okay. I'm sorry. I totally misread things."

"I didn't mean to send mixed signals," I say. "I'm attracted to you, but I don't want to risk what I have with my boyfriend. I need to go now. I'll see you at work."

He sighs and steps back further. "Understood."

I practically run out the door. I run until I reach Coastal Highway, where I catch the bus and go back to the condo. I'm shaking. I almost did something stupid that would hurt Sam and myself. I've never experienced the strength of temptation like that. As much as Jake's cheating had hurt me, I can now see how it can happen, even if you're committed to someone. I also know that walking away from it is possible; I did it. I chose Sam. He's all I need.

When Sam gets back from nationals late on Friday, I run into his arms and hold him tightly. I am his and he is mine. I won't mess it up. I won't hurt him. I won't lose him.

He asks me what's wrong. I think about telling him about my visit with Derrick, but what good would that do? I didn't do anything with Derrick except be tempted.

"I just had a rotten few days without you," I say, "but everything is better now."

It is better. Sam always makes everything better. I decide that I'll avoid Derrick at work, and never be alone anywhere with him again. I also decide to trust Sam about what he told me about the crabs and move on. If I'm naïve and wrong, I hope I never find out.

I'm discovering how naïve I am about a lot of things. I guess I've lived a sheltered life and have lots of lessons to learn. Most involve guys and their motivations. The Saturday after Sam gets back from nationals and the day before my family comes to visit, a regular café customer surprises me. Not in a good way.

Frank is in his mid-fifties, distinguished and sophisticated. He and his wife, Dottie, own one of the condos in the building. They live somewhere in New Jersey, but travel to their condo a few times a month. They eat at the café often, and tip generously. Sometimes Frank comes with his buddies. He's handsome for an old guy, with salt and pepper hair; Dottie is an aging beauty dripping with diamonds and too much lip filler.

Frank doesn't give me creepy, lustful looks like most men of many ages. He's never flirty with me, even when Dottie isn't around, and doesn't undress me with his eyes like a lot of guys do. He isn't one of them. At least I didn't think so.

That day, he shows up to the café alone. After I serve him lunch with his usual Dirty Martini and he tips me twice the cost of his bill, I feel him watching me as I serve the other tables on the deck. He pulls out a cigar and smokes it as he watches me work, then calls me over.

"Do you want another drink?" I ask. "And where's Dottie?"

"She stayed home this weekend. A big bridge tournament. Just me this time."

"Well, please tell her I said hello. Would you like some dessert?"

He smiles slightly. "As a matter of fact, I would."

He takes off his Persol sunglasses and looks at me intently.

After a moment of awkward silence, I start listing our desserts; we don't have many.

"I don't mean that kind of dessert," he says. "I mean the kind I take up to my condo."

I stare at him blankly, trying to figure out his meaning. I don't equate him with anything remotely sexual, so my mind is not going in that direction.

He sighs and smiles. "I have a proposition for you, Kristin."

"Oh," I say, still not understanding. "Do you need a waitress for a private event?"

Sometimes condo owners have cocktail parties or dinners in their condo and hire café staff to serve meals and drinks. It's good under-the-table money, but I always decline because I want time with Sam in the evenings when I'm not working at the Carousel.

He stands up to talk to me and gets a little too close. His dark brown eyes scan my body. I can smell his expensive cologne and see the beads of sweat around his temples.

"You told me once that you're in college, right?" he asks.

I step back a bit, but don't want to be rude. "Yes, sir, in Pennsylvania."

"Not sir. Be a good girl, call me Frank, like you always do."

"Okay," I say. I feel uncomfortable now with this man who usually puts me at ease.

"What would you say if I offered to pay for your college this coming year?"

"Why would you do that?" I ask. My voice grows colder as this all comes together.

"Because you would keep me company when I come to town the rest of the summer, when Dottie isn't with me, of course. I would also pay your rent here for the rest of the summer. Gifts and jewelry as you wish, of course. A mutually beneficial arrangement. What do you say?"

I stare at him blankly, trying to process it all. I feel angry and disappointed that a man I respect, trust, and think of as a good man turns out to be just another guy who wants in my pants. I suppose his offer would appeal to some girls, but I'm not one of them.

"No, thank you. Excuse me. I have tables to serve."

"Think about it," he says as I walk away.

I finish my shift in a daze. He doesn't summon me over again, but he watches me for a little while longer before he goes back inside.

That night, wrapped in Sam's arms on the mattress on the back deck under the glow of a crescent moon, I tell Sam about Frank. He laughs about it.

"What's so funny?" I ask. I'm annoyed at his cavalier reaction. "Isn't that disgusting? You aren't mad that some old guy treated me like a prostitute?"

"I think he has good taste," he teases.

I hit him playfully in the arm. "He offered to pay for my college."

"He must know you're that good in bed."

"Stop it. Seriously, who does that?"

"Rich, horny men. Kit, this happens all the time. I'm just surprised it's the first time it's happened to you." He kisses my forehead.

"What do you mean it happens all the time? Like what people does it happen to?"

"Pretty, young girls. Ingrid and Fran and the other girl guards get propositioned all the time. Most of us guys do, too."

My eyes fly open in shock. "What do you mean?"

"Rich ladies offer to give us cash, or pay for our rent, or take us to nice dinners—you name it—in exchange for sex, or sometimes just for company. Sometimes men do, too."

I don't even know what to say to that. I really have been living under a rock.

"Did you ever take anyone up on their offer?" I ask.

He pulls me closer. "Nope. I may have slept around before I met you, but I've never taken money or gifts or anything for sex. Like you, I can't be bought."

"Someone must take them up on it," I say.

"Sure. Lots of people do. It's a quick way to make ends meet. And some girls only date guys with money. If that was you, you wouldn't be with me. Can't be my bank account or car, yet here you are. Must be love. Lucky me, because I can't afford to pay for your college."

"How can I ever face Frank again?"

"Pretend like he never said anything. Act nice like you always do. Or quit."

"Quit? I can't. I need the money. Besides, I won't let him scare me off."

"You always tell me you don't make much there, anyway. Maybe work somewhere else."

"I don't want to start over somewhere else at this point."

"I have a proposition for you. Not as sweet of a deal as Mr. Old Rich Guy, though."

I turn to him and raise my eyebrows. "I'm intrigued. Go on."

"The summer is flying by so fast. What if you quit the café and ask the Carousel for more hours, but only day shifts? I'll quit Tio's. We can have all our evenings together."

"I'd love more time with you, but I need the money from the café. I have rent, phone, electric, groceries, and I haven't saved anything for college."

He caresses my face. "I don't like to think about it, but you have to go back to college in three weeks. I'm selfish. I want all the time with you that I can. If we both get off by six and take the same days off, we'll have more time together, even if it's just for a week or two. I'll host another kegger party and crab feast to make some fast cash, pay bills, and help you with yours."

"I don't know," I say. "One of my goals this summer was to make it on my own with no help from my parents or anyone else. It feels good to be able to do that."

"And you've done that. I'm good with whatever you decide. If I had all the money in the world, I'd give it all to have more time with you. It's going by too fast."

I am so taken by this perfect moment in his arms. I see that he's offering me his heart in a new way. This isn't a dirty proposition, or an exchange of anything tawdry, or an attempt to control me. It's to spend more time with me, and that means a lot to me.

"Let's do it" I say. "More time with you is priceless to me."

I talk to Marty and Serena about leaving and offer a week's notice, but they tell me I can make this my last day if I want. They're not mad at me, it's the opposite. They're happy for me.  Serena says she can cover until they hire someone else. I take them up on that and thank them for giving me the opportunity to learn so much. I say nothing about Frank.

"The reason we bought this business was to be able to spend more time together, so we get it," Serena says. "Good luck to you. You've been a big help here."

She gives me a big hug. "Doing anything for love is the best reason," she says.

I couldn't agree more. My focus is Sam. We had a little bump in our relationship with the crabs thing, but we resolved it quickly. I choose to believe Sam when he says he didn't have sex with anyone else. I choose to not get stuck in a state of constant doubt and suspicion that had marked my trust issues with Jake. Sam is worth that risk. I don't want to overthink everything.

In the meantime, Annie has her own temptations. It turns out that Dean has a girlfriend back in West Chester, Pennsylvania, and that they won't see each other much over the summer. Dean tells Annie about her, so Annie keeps her distance from him. They kiss one evening after work on the beach; Annie feels guilty, so she starts scheduling her shifts so that she doesn't work with him.

"Figures the one guy I really like is taken," she says.

"He seems pretty taken with you if he kissed you," I say.

"I can't let my heart go where it can't stay," she says. "One kiss was tempting enough. It was fantastic. I have to meet someone else who is available and can match that."

"Someday you will. And he will be worth the wait. Just like Sam."

*All my heart is yours, sir; it belongs to you;*
*and with you it would remain,*
*were fate to exile the rest of me*
*from your presence forever.*
~ Charlotte Bronte, *Jane Eyre*

# Chapter 16

## MOVIE MOMENTS

Annie and I pool some cash to pay a friend of Marion's to clean the condo. The hamster is still here, but not in his cage. He has to go, but not the way he has. He's escaped, and I'm on Bianca's case because he needs to be found. I don't need him climbing up my mom's leg, freaking her out, and letting it be known that we have a pet when the lease forbids it.

"Hide the cage and your hamster food in your bedroom closet," I tell Bianca. She agrees and hides it all. We just hope Hairy Harry will remain lost.

The next day, the parents show up after they've checked into their hotel. It's the first time Dad and Uncle Al have seen the condo; they immediately toss humor into the mix when the moms get too uptight. The fact that they're staying at a hotel instead of with us at the condo helps everyone; it gives us all space and fewer opportunities to clash.

"You got yourself a nice place here, Krissy," Dad says.

"We may have to rent this on our vacation next year," Aunt Sue says.

"It does look nicer than last time," Mom says.

Annie shoots me a look of relief. I'm glad we decided to have it cleaned.

Thankfully, Hairy Harry remains elusive, and we have a nice visit without him. We spend the next few days hanging out at the beach near Sam's guard stand, playing mini golf, chowing down at the Paul Revere Smorgasbord buffet, which we've done for endless years in a row, and cooling off with ice cream from Dumser's. At night we play cards.

Sam reserves a nice table on the deck for us all at Fager's with beautiful bay views. Dad and Uncle Al insist on treating, so I just order soup. I can see why it's a first date place; it has stunning scenery, delicious food, and different areas to suit any mood. After dinner, we walk onto the pier to the white gazebo to watch the sun disappear from the multi-colored sky into the silky water. My heart is full to have the people I love together and getting along.

Everyone loves Sam, especially Dad and Uncle Al. They laugh and yuck it up like old friends. When Sam wins at cards, they let him know he's officially part of the family by calling him a cheater while patting him affectionately on the back.

When the parents stop by the condo on Wednesday around lunch on their way out of town, Mom asks about Annie and I scheduling the walk-through with Ron to get the security deposit back. She also asks about us returning to college at the end of the month.

"I don't want to talk about it yet," I say.

"Well, you have to. It's just a few weeks away."

"It's too soon," Annie says. "We want to enjoy the time we have left. We'll call in a week or so and work out the details. Okay?"

Mom opens her mouth to speak when, surprisingly, my dad beats her to it.

"Let the girls enjoy the rest of their summer. It'll work out," he says.

Aunt Sue interjects before Mom can respond. "Thank you for a great visit. Tell Sam thank you for everything, and we hope to see him soon," she says.

When everyone else heads outside to the car, Mom pulls me aside.

"Kristin, I want to talk with you for a minute."

I look at her expectantly. She smiles, and that puts me at ease a little bit.

"I'm proud of you for working hard and paying your bills here. And I'm glad you found Sam. He seems to treat you right."

I feel hot tears form in my eyes. Hearing her say all that means a lot to me.

"Thank you. Is there a 'but' somewhere?"

"Not really. Seeing you this happy makes me happy. I know it'll be hard for you to leave here. To leave Sam. Please promise me that you'll go back and finish college."

"That's the plan," I say. "I mean, I'll be sad to go back because I love it here, and I'll miss Sam. He'll visit a lot, though, and I'll visit here. It'll work out."

"Long distance relationships are hard. Tell me you won't quit college to be with Sam."

We stare at each other a moment, assessing the situation. She's being careful with me so I'll give her the promise she wants. I'm being careful with her so this visit ends on good terms.

"I said I would, so I will," I say. "College and Sam. I can have both."

"Sometimes love can distract us from important things we need to do for ourselves."

"Sam and college are both important," I say.

"I like Sam. I wish he was more ambitious, though," she says. "I think that could be an issue in the future. You may love him, but you'll want someone with a real, year-round job, stability, and good benefits when you graduate and want to settle down. You like nice things."

How did this go from her being proud of me to her wanting me to marry an accountant?

"He does have a real job," I say.

"You know what I mean."

"No, I don't. How many lives have you saved in your real job, ever?" I stare her down.

"Don't take this personally. You'll want more than this someday."

"More than love and sunshine and the ocean? I don't think so."

"You're idealistic. You'll want security, and a house, and—"

"Don't tell me what I'll want," I say. "I want a good man more than any material thing. Sam will get that kind of job when he wants to. I like that he does what makes him happy, instead of conforming to anyone else's expectations. Do you know he's been on his own since he was eighteen? Nobody pays his way. Nobody puts security deposits down for him. Nobody pays his rent. Nobody buys him a car. He earns it all himself. I respect that. "

"I respect that, too, I really do. And I am glad he treats you well. I'm trying to look out for you. I'm just saying, please stay in school. You're in a bubble right now."

"College is a bubble," I say. "Life in our small town is a bubble. Be glad I'm happy."

"I am," she says. "Just, keep your promise to stay in school."

She offers a stiff hug. I try to return it. I know she means well. I've heard that mothers and daughters become friends later in life. I hope so. Right now, it's hard.

Downstairs, Annie and I wave goodbye as they drive off. Annie, who knows me better than anyone, puts her arm around me.

"What's wrong?" she asks. "It was a good visit. I know you don't want to talk about leaving, but we have to do it sometime."

"I know," I say. Tears flow down my face. "But not yet. Not ever."

"You've been pretty emotional lately. Are you okay?"

"I will be. "I just don't want to think about leaving. I need to see Sam."

Although I just saw him last night when we were with my family, I miss him. I took off work today to be with him since it's his day off, but he was called into cover someone who called in sick. I want to catch the bus to go hang out beside his stand on the beach just to be near him. Feel the sun on my face. Be with him when he takes his breaks. I don't often do that, but today I will. Then we can grab some dinner and go ride the Ferris wheel, be closer to the stars.

Tomorrow night is the annual guard dinner, and although that will be fun, it'll be with a crowd of people. I want Sam all to myself this evening.

I sit down on the couch to eat a quick lunch, and then lean back and close my eyes, just for a little bit. The next thing I know, I've slept away most of the afternoon.

I startle awake. It's almost five o'clock. I'm bummed that I slept the day away. I run to the bus. I want to reach Sam before he gets off work; he isn't expecting me. I feel a sense of urgency to just be near him.

We don't have to be doing anything out of the ordinary, yet every minute with him feels extraordinary, no matter what we're doing. We also have so many memorable moments, like out of a movie, filled with fun, romance, and the undercurrent of sand sifting through an hourglass.

By the time I get to Sam's stand, it's almost five-thirty. Time for him to get off work. Time to be with me. Time to be us. The tourists are dispersing to tend to their sunburns, but a few people remain. Fishermen start to come out and drop their lines in the ocean. People from the Golden Sands condos lounge on their balconies overlooking the ocean to wind down.

I love the sounds, sights, and smells here. I love the feel of the sand beneath my feet. I love the sound of the seagulls and the crashing waves. I love the salty air and how people laugh a lot here. I love how blue the sky is on a perfect summer day and the moodiness of the ocean. I love Sam. I love it all. It all feels like home, and I can't bear the thought of leaving.

As I near Sam's stand, I stop to just watch him. He doesn't see me yet, and I feel like one of the girls who sunbathe by his stand to try to catch his attention and flirt with him. I don't want his attention yet, though. I just want to look at him—to drink him in—to imprint the image of him in my mind and heart forever. The thought of not being with him every day is too much to bear. I want every last ounce of him before I have to leave this picture-perfect summer behind.

He turns toward me, then, and sees me. He smiles in surprise and delight. His look wraps me like a warm blanket from the inside out. He checks his watch and motions me toward him.

I walk to his stand, and just as I get near it, he grins, stretches each arm out wide like wings, and jumps from the stand down to the sand in front of me. It's like slow motion. He has an unsteady landing, and the force of his motion causes him to tumble and take me down with him into the sand. I land on my back with him on top of me. We both laugh, and then we kiss deeply, with no care as to the sand getting in every crevice of our bodies or the people around us.

We are in our own world until the clapping begins. We look up to see and hear the people on the beach and on the condo balconies applauding us. Some are hooting and hollering. Sam blushes—it's the first time I've ever seen that. He stands up, offers his hand to me, and helps me up. Caught up in the moment, he takes me in his arms and twirls me around as everyone continues clapping. It's like a scene from a movie—unscripted perfection.

He kisses me again, and we wave at everyone as we gather his gear and walk off the beach.

"So much for your rule of not showing affection on the beach," I say.

"With you, I break my own rules. Seeing you made my whole day better. The second I was off duty, I wanted you in my arms. I couldn't wait."

"Well, let's go to your place and do some more of that, but without an audience or any clothes," I say.

"Roger that," he says. We run to his car like giddy teenagers.

We spend the evening up in his bedroom with the door locked. Tucky usually stays overnight at Rhonda's, but this night he's at the townhouse, and he's mad that he can't get in his own bedroom. We don't care. Sam tosses some clothes out to him when he bangs on the door saying he needs to get changed from work.

Later, we sneak out of the room for quick bite to eat, and then draw fake tattoos on each other for fun. We talk about the future and how we want to travel to beaches all over the world, foster dogs, and have our own place with a bay view like this one with sunset views every day.

We're up practically all night, sleeping and making love, and repeating the cycle in his bed, on the floor, in the shower, and on the deck under the winking stars.

At three in the morning, I go downstairs to get a drink of water. As I turn to go back upstairs, Jesse comes out of his closet bedroom; we both are startled.

"Jesse, oh! You scared me."

"Hot damn, girl," he says in a sleepy drawl as his gaze travels down my body.

The only light is from the moon, which casts a soft glow in the silence of the night. I see him quickly look away and mumble something as he rakes his hands through his hair.  I realize that I'm wearing my short, white babydoll nightgown, which nobody but Sam should see. Jesse grabs a throw blanket from the couch and tosses it to me. I cover myself with it.

"Sorry I woke you," I say.

"Not a problem." He looks away. "Most people forget I'm here."

As I start to climb the stairs, he calls my name. I turn around.

"I just wanna say I ain't never seen Shayne so happy," he says. "He's whipped for sure, and it gives me hope that I can find a gal who does that to me someday. He's a lucky guy."

"Thanks, Jesse. And I'm a lucky girl. Good night."

He goes back to his room under the stairs as I head back into Sam's bedroom and into his arms. I raise myself on my elbow and just look at him for a while, memorizing every line on his face so I can unwrap the memory of him over and over again in the weeks ahead when I can't be with him each night. It hurts to think of being without him near me.

Inspired, I get up and pull a pen and small notepad from my purse. I write a passage from one of my favorite poems, which now I can completely relate to. I put it on the nightstand beside his bed, where he'll see it first thing in the morning.

> *Sam, my love,*
> *…For the one I love most lay sleeping by me under the same*
> *    cover in the cool night,*
> *In the stillness in the autumn moonbeams his face was*
> *    inclined toward me,*
> *And his arm lay lightly around my breast — and that night I*
> *    was happy.*
> *~ Walt Whitman, When I Heard at the Close of the Day*

I slide back into his arms and look at him some more, in wonder that such a beautiful, brave, kind man can love me like he does. I could stare at him forever, but eventually I fall asleep in the only place I want to be. With him. Always with him.

*Happiness, not in another place but this place...*
*not for another hour, but this hour.*

~ Walt Whitman, "A Song for Occupations" from *Leaves of Grass*

# Chapter 17

## HARRY AND CHARLEY

Untangling from each other with the soft morning sun shining on us isn't an easy task. We shower together and he drops me off at my condo before he goes to work. I work from eleven to four at the Carousel so that I can get back to the condo and have some time to get dolled up for the guard dinner without being in a big hurry.

As I get a snack in the kitchen, Marion comes out from her bedroom, dressed for the beach in her bikini and coverup. Things have been tense between us since that awkward conversation about Dave and Sam. I offer a 'good morning,' but don't expect a response.

She stops at the door and turns to me.

"Kristin, I'm sorry about what I said before, and how I said it. I really am glad you're with Sam and that he's good to you."

I didn't expect this.

"Thanks," I say. "Whatever happened between you and Dave, I'm sorry."

"Me too," she says. "But it's not just that. I've had a lot happen in my life, and it just seeped out that day with you. Don't take it personally."

I go over to her and hug her. She returns it. "Thank you," I say.

She leaves, and as I get ready for work, I feel a weight lifted from me. I'm glad Marion and I are back on good terms, and the vibe in the condo seems brighter again.

∽

Sam may have missed one annual guard tradition—the group photo—but he isn't going to miss the annual guard dinner. I'm making sure of that. The dinner is held every year on a weekday in the middle of August. This year it's on a Wednesday, and it's the only official OCBP event where the guards get dressed up. They can each bring a guest and must behave because the captain is there. I'm excited to be Sam's date and be part of this tradition.

After work, I rush home to get ready; Sam is picking me up at six o'clock. Annie is working a long shift at work, but Bianca is there to help me piece together a decent outfit. I'm putting on some mascara when I hear a knock at the door. We aren't expecting anyone, and Sam wouldn't even be off work yet, so I know it's not him.

I open the door to our downstairs neighbor, an older woman with bottle-red hair who looks mad. She holds a covered Tupperware container.

"Yes?" I ask.

"Is this yours?" She opens the container. Inside is Hairy Harry. He pops his white head out, which causes the lady to shriek as she hurriedly puts the lid back on.

"Um, no, it's not mine," I say.

"I think it is. Your roommate has been asking around about it. It ran up onto my bed last night and almost gave me a heart attack. Made my teeth fall out when I screamed. Fortunately, I was able to get him in here with a broom and not have to touch him."

I try not to laugh at that image as I take the container from her.

"Well, it's hers, then. But not mine," I say.

"I know your landlord. You're not supposed to have pets," she says. "We owners don't like renters around here, especially you college kids. You cause too much trouble. Like this."

"I'm sorry. We try to be good neighbors. We don't have parties, and we aren't loud. We'll find the hamster a new home right away." Our landlord can't know about this.

"You bet you will. And I'm telling your landlord."

Just as I'm going into panic mode, Bianca comes out of her bedroom, all smiles and rainbows. "Mrs. Kinney!" she says. "Thank you for bringing Harry back. It's my sister's hamster; she brought him with her when she visited a few weeks ago, and he escaped. She wants him back desperately. There's even a reward. Be right back."

Mrs. Kinney is speechless. So am I. Bianca goes into her bedroom and quickly returns with a wad of cash. She hands it to the shocked woman, who tentatively takes it.

"I don't know if I need a reward for a hamster," Mrs. Kinney says.

"Oh, please take it. For your favorite charity. And please don't say anything about this. I feel terrible that he got out and bothered you. I'll return him to my sister right away."

Mrs. Kinney slips the money in her pocket. "If you insist. But no more pets."

"No more, promise." Bianca's sweet smile is powerful enough to close the door.

After the lady leaves, Bianca and I burst out laughing.

"You could sell air conditioners to an Eskimo," I say. "You're a scary good liar."

"I'm the daughter of a judge," she says. "I have to be able to get away with anything."

"You'll find Harry another home today?" I ask. "We need the security deposit back."

"Yes. I'll give him to a friend from work. She'll adore him."

☙

With Mrs. Kinney bought off and Harry returned, we can focus on the guard dinner.

"It's at the Garden Gourmet Restaurant," I say to Bianca.

"Not bad, not bad," she says. "I have just the perfect thing for you to wear."

She's goes into her room and comes out with what she calls her purple hottie outfit. It's a ribbed, purple, V-neck crop top with a matching straight skirt that goes down to my knees. With it, I wear low white pumps with white earrings and a chunky white bracelet.

"Perfecto!" she says. She also helps me fluff my hair to what she calls goddess goodness.

Sam picks me up on time; he looks amazing in a white Oxford shirt, gray tie, and charcoal pants with a black belt and dress shoes. He's slicked back his hair and looks like a movie star. I whistle.

"You sure clean up nice," I say.

"You're stunning," he says. "Can I take you home with me?"

"Anytime, Mister."

At the restaurant, I do a double take on everyone. The guards look so different all dressed up. Though they look great, most of them look uncomfortable. I'm sure they prefer their red trunks and bare feet to ties or dresses and tight shoes.

We sit at a table with Kurt and Ingrid, Tucky and Rhonda, and Jesse with Eva, his girl of the week. Kurt is the life of the party, as always, and everyone swaps stories of past and recent rescues, pranks, comps, ranch parties, crab feasts, and off-season plans.

I bring my camera and take pictures throughout the night as we eat, dance, and celebrate together. It's a tight-knit community. I'm glad to be a part of it for this special event.

The big talk of the night is the forecast of a hurricane for early the next week. I ask Sam if I should be worried, and he says, "Not with me." I know it's true, and that he and the other guards will be kept up to date on the latest information, be prepared to handle emergencies, and ensure we're all safe. I trust Sam completely.

After dinner, we go back to Sam's place with his roommates and other guard friends. They quickly discard their formal attire and are back in their usual state of half-naked undress playing drinking games and watching TV. I'm tired and have to work the next morning, so Sam takes me home around midnight and stays only a little while.

"Thank you for taking me. It was fun. Everyone seemed so happy."

"Yes, especially me, because of you," he says. "Let's do it again next year."

"It's a date."

Sam and I make plans for the upcoming weekend, including a trip to Assateague to see the horses, plus a romantic dinner in Berlin. The weather has other plans, though. Hamster Harry is gone, but Hurricane Charley is on his way. It's due to hit Ocean City on Monday, the eighteenth, and all the guards must be available to help the police and firefighters prepare. All frontline workers will be at the ready as the storm continues to work its way up the east coast.

Charley is apparently a force to be reckoned with. The guards have to pull all the beach guard stands and trash cans out to the street to be picked up and secured, help the beach rental operators get the umbrellas and beach chairs off the beach, rescue people stupid enough to go into the violent ocean, be on call with the Coast Guard, and go door to door to evacuate residents and tourists. If anyone refuses to leave, the guards have to get them to sign a waiver.

Sam is exhausted by the time he briefly stops by our condo on Sunday, when the weather is already scary. He wears his bright red windbreaker and has been working since Saturday morning. He'll barely have time to get decent sleep before starting over again in the morning.

"I'm on my way to the firehouse headquarters on 14th Street. They want me to answer the phones and talk to the local and national press," he says.

"That's great that they picked you to do that." I hand him a grilled cheese sandwich, potato salad, and a beer to gulp down.

"They know I love to talk," he says. "While I'm here, I need to tell you to evacuate or sign a waiver."

Marion has already left town to stay with a friend in Baltimore. Bianca is on the phone inviting people over to our place for a hurricane party. Annie and I are in the living room talking with Sam about whether to stay or go. The party sounds fun, but we don't want to be in danger.

"What should we do?" I ask Sam. "We trust whatever you recommend."

"Officially, I recommend that you evacuate; unofficially, I'd stay here and enjoy the party. You're not by the water and, from what I'm seeing, we won't get the worst of it. It's your decision, but I have to stay in town to work and be available to help anyone."

He stays for a half hour, and then has to leave. He calls later to say he'll be working around the clock, and that if people are coming over to our place for a party, to have them leave early or stay overnight through the next day when the hurricane hits.

I admit it's scary, but I trust Sam's knowledge and instincts. Bianca's friends come over in the evening; we eat pizza, drink beer and soda, dance to the radio, play cards, and compete in beer pong. Some leave by midnight; others stay over and sprawl out in the living room.

Monday morning, the wind gusts are up to thirty-five miles per hour, and we've had more than four inches of rain. Bianca's friends have left; she, Annie, and I are glued to the TV all day. Sam's voice comes through the air from many of the newscasts as he gives reporters updates from headquarters. The hurricane is not as bad as it could've been, but it's still rough.

Monday night he calls me. "Still here and will be for a while. Hope I can see you tomorrow when Charley is on his way out."

The next day, the weather is not as volatile, but it's still nasty, and the ocean is still a rough, savage beast. The guards post 'No Swimming' signs everywhere. At least Sam is back to his regular schedule, and I can see him.

When I go into work, I'm not surprised that the Carousel pool is crowded because of the bad weather. Hotel guests have to do something indoors. I'm surprised that the beach guards still have to go to work, though.

"Why?" I ask Sam when he visits me at the Carousel pool during his lunch break. "Surely nobody is swimming in the ocean today."

"They sure are. Lots of rescues on bad weather days. There are always people who ignore common sense and the no swimming signs, and then need to be rescued."

"They don't deserve to be saved if they're stupid enough to swim in water like that."

"It's our job. Besides, everyone deserves to be saved. Even stupid people."

"Of course, you're right. I'm just mad they risk your life like that."

We're together for dinner and overnight; I'm so glad to be with him again. He shares that he and other guards made several rescues since I saw him at lunch. It's the sort of thing that's not reported much in the news, but the guards do it every day—even in rough weather.

That night, Sam is rewarded with a back rub and a peaceful night together in bed listening to the sound of the steady rain. I like the bad weather days as well as the sunny days; any day with Sam is a great one.

I feel safe and at home when I'm with him. We live in the moment, grateful for each one we have together. There is nowhere I'd rather be, and no one I'd rather be with.

The summer clock is ticking, though, and we both know the day I have to leave to go back to college is coming soon. Desperate to stop time or prolong it, we cling to each other like vines, savoring every precious, fleeting moment.

August flies by in a dizzying blur of work, tourists, humidity, sunshine, happy hours, dancing, parties, and time with Sam. Quitting the café to spend more time with him has been a good decision. I've also been able to balance life a little better and spend more time with Annie. Tonight, a week before I have to leave, she and I are having a rare dinner out.

"Kristin, you look miserable. Am I such bad company?" Annie asks.

I try to smile. "I'm sorry. I just really miss Sam."

"One day without him and you melt into a puddle? What's going to happen when we go back to college?"

"I don't want to think about it. I'm sorry, Annie, give me a minute to snap out of it."

"Hey, I practically abandoned you when I was dating Jeff. You took it like champ when sometimes I wouldn't see you for weeks. I know our time is short here, and I'll have more of you when we're back at college. So, it's okay."

"Thanks for understanding. Let's order. I'll be fine." I pick up the menu.

She takes it from me and stands. "Come on, let's go. I'll take you to Sam. Where is he?"

"No. This is our night out."

"Our dinner is postponed. I'm taking you to Sam so you can moon over him in person, and I'm going to go home and finish the book I started. In a few weeks, I'll have all the dinners I want with you. Let's go."

This is my bestie. I love her.

She takes me to the bar where Sam said he'd be with his friends. The bouncer knows me from being there before with Sam; he lets us in. We see Sam sitting with a couple of the guys, drinking and laughing.

When he sees me, he smiles and extends his arm to me. I fold into him, and he kisses my hair. His friends say hi to me; they don't seem to mind me being there.

"All he does is talk about you, anyway," his friend, Vince, says.

"You okay?" he asks me. "I thought this was your night with Annie."

"I ruined it because I missed you too much."

He pulls me closer. "I missed you, too. Thanks for coming here."

Annie pats him on the back. "Tag, you're it. You take home the prize tonight."

"Thanks, Annie. I can't think of anything better. Please join us."

His friend Rocco, a cute guard with dark, curly hair, sees Annie and pipes up. "Yeah, stay. My name's Rocco. Let me buy you a drink."

I plead with Annie with my eyes to stay, and she does. Rocco flirts with her while Sam flirts with me, and we end up having one of the best nights of the summer so far.

*Everything is more beautiful because we are doomed.*
*You will never be lovelier than you are now.*
*We will never be here again.*

~ Homer, *the Iliad*

# Chapter 18

## THE SUMMER SUNSET

With a week left before I have to return to Pennsylvania, I pack a little bit each day. It's weird to think that soon I won't come home to Bianca and Marion anymore. Annie and I will still see each other, but we may or may not run into them at college. We say we'll get together, but who knows? We are here for a season, and I'm thankful for that.

Sam works the hot, crowded August days on the beach and plans for the ranch party set for the Saturday of Labor Day weekend, the same day I'll be starting band camp at college. I wish I could stay and go to the party with him, but wishing doesn't do me any good.

Sam has to work until the third Sunday following Labor Day Monday, but that means he can't visit me until late September. Many of the guards don't work through September, so the ones who are left are a skeleton crew; a weekend off is unheard of. Still, Sam makes some workday trade deals with other guards, and talks with the captain so that he can come to visit me the weekend of September 13—my birthday weekend.

With time running out, there's something I must do before I

leave Ocean City. One evening, as Sam and I watch another perfect sunset from the deck, I ask him to take me swimming in the ocean soon, beyond the breakers.

"Are you sure?" he asks. He looks for the truth in my eyes, where he always finds it.

"No," I say. "I'm still scared, but I trust you and I feel safe with you. I see the joy you have when you're swimming out there, and I want to experience that with you."

He kisses me. "I'm proud of you. Facing fears is a big deal."

"So is trust. I trust you and feel brave when I'm with you."

"Let's go this Saturday. Your last Saturday here this summer. A good milestone."

"It's a date."

Two days later, on that last Saturday of this sensational summer, I meet Sam after work by his stand, and we make our way to the water after his shift ends. Although he calls everyone else out of the water, as all the guards do when their shifts end each evening, a few people remain to swim. At least they know he is going off duty.

The crowd has thinned out by this time; many tourists have had their share of sun and have left the beach. The vibe is peaceful, and the sun's intensity has calmed.

Sam is already in his swim trunks. I remove my shirt and shorts to reveal the one-piece bathing suit he recommended so I won't have to wonder if a bikini top or bottom will go the wrong way with the waves. I look out to the ocean trepidatiously. The waves are rather tame today, but the thought of going through them still rattles me.

"We'll be back before it gets dark, right?" I ask.

"We're not swimming to Spain," he says.

"Smartass."

He reaches for my hand and holds it. "It's going to be great."

"Are there sharks out there?" I ask.

"Odds are you won't meet Jaws. If you do, I'll punch him."

"Jellyfish?"

"You don't want to see what's under the water. Kit, you love the ocean. Let it love you back. She's a moody bitch, but I've got a good handle on her. You'll love it. But if you don't want to, there's no pressure. I'm happy just to be with you, land or sea."

I look into his eyes, and I see love and safety there.

"Let's go," I say.

He leads me by the hand into the breakers, and tells me where and when to dive down, let the wave pass over me, come up, and keep paddling. He stays close to me the whole time, and we soon emerge on the other side of the waves where the sea is calm, welcoming, and gentle as a reward to those who dare to venture that far.

Our heads bob up from the final wave, and he smiles reassuringly at me. I look around, amazed. I've never seen the view from here; endless water on one side, and the shore, beach, hotels, and condos to the other side in the distance. It's a different, tranquil world.

Sam is watching me. "It's amazing, isn't it?"

"I love it. I see why you swim out here."

"At least twice a day. I feel free out here. Let's swim."

He slows his pace to match mine. I swim freestyle for a while, and then breaststroke, while he switches between freestyle and the butterfly, which is hard, but he makes it look easy.

I feel as if I'm part of the ocean, in a snow globe without the snow. The blue of the sky and the ocean meld, surround me, become part of me. I'm glad to experience this with Sam. When fear tries to sneak into my head, I look at him and am reassured that he'll never let anything bad happen to me. I relax and let myself have fun.

He knows when to bring me in, sensing when I've enough of the experience and exercise to be invigorated by it without being exhausted by it. Coming in is easier than going out, and when we reach the shore, he picks me up in his arms.

"You did it!" he says as he spins me around. The moment is romantic and intoxicating.

"That was amazing," I say. "Thank you. I would've never done it without you."

"My pleasure," he says. He kisses my hand. "Come here, I have something for you."

He reaches in his black duffle bag and pulls out a small blanket that he spreads on the sand. We dry off with the towels that I brought and sit on the blanket to watch the pastel colors in the sky. We sit in silence for a few minutes, his arm around my back, to enjoy the view and each other. He reaches back into his bag and pulls out a card and a small ring box. I gasp.

"Don't worry, it's not an engagement ring. At least not yet. Your mom and dad would kill me, and I'd like to live a lot longer to be with you."

I laugh. "We'd elope before she could kill you."

"It isn't much, but I wanted you to have something you can look at every day to remind you that you have my heart. My commitment. All of me. I love you, Kit."

I open the card, which features a watercolor painting of an ocean scene. On the inside is his handwriting:

*Dance with me, now and forever. I love you.*
*Always,*
*Sam*

Beneath that, words from Lord Byron:

There's a lump in my throat. I'm full of love and gratitude. I open the small box. In it is a ring, delicate and gold, with a small oval ruby complemented with a small round diamond.

I look up at him, tears in my eyes.

"It's beautiful, Sam. Perfect. I love it. I love you. Thank you."

I put it on the third finger of my left hand; it fits perfectly. I want to say it's too much, that he can't afford it, but I know what it must've taken for him to save money for it. I don't want to take that away from him. That he sacrificed for me is an honor.

I kiss him as the sun sets; it's another movie moment, perfect, magical, and so completely right in every way. I lean into him. We sit in contented silence as the day fades away and the sound of the waves became a lullaby.

The next night, my last Sunday at the beach, I sit in the condo living room with Sam and Annie eating hamburgers and fries.

"How are you getting back to college?" Annie asks. "You have to go back on Friday to be there for camp Saturday morning. Remember, I'm not driving back until Tuesday."

Until this moment, I'd forgotten that Annie won't go back to college the same day I do. She has her car; my car isn't here. How will I get there?

My face tells her everything she needs to know.

"This is why I don't let you plan things," she says. She's laughing, and yet there's an undertone of none of us wanting the summer to end with me stuck without a ride back.

"I'll take a bus back," I say. "I still can't believe Bernie is letting you come late."

Bernie is the band director at our college; a rare mix of loved, respected, and feared. He keeps more than a hundred and fifty students in line and prepares us for the upcoming season. Band camp starts the Saturday of Labor Day weekend and runs the week before classes start. It's a critical time when the band learns their music, and the rest of us learn routines and formations.

"He doesn't have a choice," she says. "He could've dropped me, but he didn't. I told him I signed a work contract through Labor Day weekend at the Carousel and can't get out of it."

"They didn't make you sign one?" Sam asks me.

"No," I say. "The Kids Club gets especially busy on holiday weekends, so they need to hang onto their staff. They don't have as much of a problem finding pool lifeguards."

"They're paying me double," Annie says. "I'll catch up on learning the pom-pom routines and, Kristin, I'll help you learn any routines that you may get stuck on."

Annie usually helps me learn the dance routines. Just like math is difficult for me, so is learning those routines. Once I have them memorized, I kill it on the field, but it takes me a long time to nail them. Last year, Annie spent extra time outside band camp helping me.

"I'll call the bus station tomorrow for schedules," I say.

"No. I'll take you," Sam says. "When do we need to go?"

"You can't take off Friday; it's a holiday weekend."

"We can leave Wednesday after I get off work. I'll take you back to college and stay over at your place until Thursday. You can show me around campus, and then I can head back to work Friday and the weekend."

"Are you sure?" I'm touched that he's made this offer.

"I'll see the campus and where you live, so I know where to go for future visits."

That sounds like a good plan. None of the other roommates at our college house will be there, so Sam and I will have the place to ourselves. I'll have Friday to myself to get settled in.

"You two will visit each other a lot, and the school year will go by fast," Annie says. "We'll be back here next summer before we know it. As for me, I'm going out with Tina tonight. Rocco may stop by the club."

"Go Rocco!" Sam says. We all laugh.

Annie and Rocco have gone out a few times since they met at the bar. She still likes Dean, but they're just friends since she's made it clear that she's nobody's side piece.

Sam and I look at each other. I don't want to go. I want to stay here with him. I start to tear up. He holds my hand. Living apart long distance will be hard. This is what Mom had warned me about. I'm already feeling the hard reality of that truth, and it's painful.

*Day by day and night by night we were together –*
*all else has long been forgotten by me.*
*(Often quoted as: We were together. I forget the rest.)*
~ Walt Whitman, "Once I Pass'd Through a Populous City"
from *Leaves of Grass*

# Chapter 19

## THE BREAKDOWN

Monday evening, Sam runs a few errands after work. I sit on the balcony alone, thinking about this beautiful summer. It was and is real and fabulous, bubble or not. I'm living what I didn't know I needed until I now have it—to feel fully alive. To be happy. To be authentically loved. To feel at home. To feel like my true self. I feel all of that here, now. It's an ideal alignment of the right time, place, and person.

I've done many things this summer, met many people, and experienced new things, yet the one overriding element is Sam. Sam, Sam, Sam. He *is* this summer. Spending each day and night without him in the future is inconceivable. We'll find a way to keep connected, somehow, some way, when we are apart after the sunset of this extraordinary summer.

Bianca had suggested that I switch to a Maryland college to be closer to him. I'd looked into it, but I would need to make up a lot of credits there, so it would take longer to graduate.

"Maybe he can move there," Bianca had said.

"The ocean is seared in his soul—he's summer personified. I don't think he'd be happy so far away from it."

"I don't think he'd be happy so far from you, either," she'd said.

Sam and I don't know how we will work it out, but we will. We aren't used to planning ahead and trying to figure out the future. We take things day by day. Looking ahead means looking to a time when we're apart, and we don't want to deal with that until we have to.

The next day, Tuesday, August 26, is my last day at the Carousel. Russ, Ashley, Annie, and Tina bring in lunch. We gather on the deck to talk about our summer and the stories we've collected along the way. We've had a great summer together; I'm going to miss them.

Sam throws a bon voyage party for me at his townhouse that night. His roommates are there, along with Kurt, Ingrid, and ten other guards and their girlfriends. Annie and Bianca come; Marion declines because she doesn't like parties or goodbyes. I wish I could find the Marion that emerged that day we went to see Dave, but she has disappeared.

Tomorrow, after Sam finishes his shift, he'll drive me to college. I'll manage without my car until I can ride home with Annie some weekend in September. For now, I don't want to think about that or any upcoming logistics. I want to enjoy the party.

Sam asks his buddies to man the bar and the grill so he can be with me, and I hold onto him like he'll slip away at any moment. I love my life here with Sam, and don't want to leave it.

"We'll make it work," Sam assures me. "And we'll come back here next summer. In the meantime, we'll visit each other a lot, and maybe I can find a winter job closer to you."

He'll stay in Ocean City to guard until the third Sunday following Labor Day, and then he'll move to Annapolis until it's time to return to Ocean City to guard next summer. He already has a bartending job set up at a nice restaurant there for the winter, and will rent a room in a house near there. Bartenders make the most tips on weekends, but he's going to work weekdays every other week so that he has some weekends free to visit me when I don't have away band events or competitions to attend.

"I'll do whatever it takes to see you," he promises.

The party is fun, and everyone wishes me well. I know I may never see some of them again, since some guards get full-time jobs elsewhere in the fall and won't return next summer. Nobody talks about that, though; we all want to be in the moment.

When the guests have gone home, and Annie and Bianca have left for the condo, Sam and I pull the mattress out on the deck for one last night under the stars for this fleeting summer; I vow we'll return to a similar deck and view sometime in the future. He probably won't be able to rent the same townhouse next summer, but we'll find another one like it. We spend the night glued to each other, not saying a word. Not needing to.

The next morning while Sam is at work, I finish packing what's left of my clothes, clean up around the condo as best as I can, and say goodbye to Bianca and Marion, who will be staying until Saturday. When Annie gets off work, she helps make sure that I don't leave anything behind except my heart. We wait for Sam to get off work to pick me up and leave.

Annie will be at the condo when Ron the realtor does the walk-through on Sunday to make sure everything is good, and that we'll get our security deposit back. She'll then stay at Tina's Sunday night, and head back to Pennsylvania Monday evening after her last day of work.

Annie and I sit out on the balcony before Sam arrives. I grab her hand.

"This summer was more wonderful than I ever dreamed it could be," I say to her. "Thank you for saying yes to coming here. You helped me to have the confidence to do it, and to experience the happiest days of my life."

She squeezes my hand. "Same here. I wouldn't have done it without you, either. I've loved every minute here, and seeing you blossom. You're different than when you came here. More confident, more relaxed, more you. Happy."

She hugs my tears away.

"Sam is such a part of me now. It hurts to think about being away from him."

"It'll be okay. This is only the beginning. You two will figure out how to see each other, and you and I will kick ass at college and have more adventures. We're in this together."

The door opens and Sam enters with smiles and positivity. I know this is hard on him, but he isn't showing it. He has to work and plan for the big ranch party while dealing with his own emotions of me leaving. I felt his hot tears as he held me on the deck the night before, but I didn't say anything; I just held him closer. He's being strong for me, and I'm grateful.

We pack up his car. Bianca and I have said our goodbyes; Marion left a note saying she'd see me around campus. I hug Annie, and then Sam and I take off across the Route 50 bridge to a whole new reality. I keep looking back, longing to turn around and never leave again.

"Don't look back," Sam says. "We have a great future ahead."

That's the attitude I need to have. I don't turn around again.

"I'm looking forward to showing you my world at college," I say, "because you're going to be a part of it. Plus, my bed has been sitting alone all summer. We'll break it in."

"Now that is something to look forward to," he says.

Ten miles outside of Ocean City, the car lurches and vibrates; it makes a loud sound and starts to lose power.

"Oh, shit," Sam says.

He shifts the car into neutral, puts on the emergency flashers, and pulls off to the side of the road. Steam rises from the engine. He puts his head down on the steering wheel in frustration.

"This isn't good, Kit. Unless we rent a car, I won't be able to get you back to college in time. I'm so sorry. This is a shitty time for my car to bail on me."

Neither of us has the money to rent a car, especially now that Sam will have to pay for his car to be fixed. Seeing him frustrated and down inspires me to be strong to help him.

"It's okay. Like you always say, we'll figure it out."

"We need to get to a phone," he says. He's in solution mode. "I'll call Kurt or one of the guys to come and pick us up. We'll get the car towed to an auto shop I trust midtown, and then look into the bus schedule for you. At least we have an extra day built in to get you back."

We walk about a half mile to a gas station. He uses the pay phone to call Kurt, who comes to get us. He takes us back to Sam's place, where I call Annie to update her. She offers to take me back to college and then return to finish her weekend at the Carousel, but that's too much on her. I wish I had brought my car so I didn't have to inconvenience anyone.

Next, I call Mom and explain the situation. "I'll take a bus."

"Hold on, your dad wants to say something."

Dad never gets on the phone with me. His voice is firm and soothing.

"Krissy, we'll come and get you. Take you to college. Don't you worry about it."

I hear Mom saying something in the background, and then Dad talks in hushed tones to her. "I'll take a sick day… Well, then don't go… You go to work, and I'll go get her myself."

"Dad," I say, "you don't have to take off work. The bus is fine."

"No, Krissy, You're not taking a bus. I'll get up early and be at your condo by eight or nine tomorrow morning. Don't you worry about it."

Mom gets back on the phone. "I'll take a sick day, too. I'm coming with him."

"Mom, you don't have to." She'll be in a mood, and I don't want to deal with that.

"It's fine. Your dad and I will worry too much if you take a bus."

I don't know what the big deal is about taking a bus, but I'm touched that Dad and Mom will drive five hours there, then back home in the same day. Mom suggests that I can take my car from there. They're doing that for me. That's a lot. I feel loved by them, and by Sam and Annie.

I try to look at the bright side: I get one more night with Sam on the deck by the bay. I'm disappointed, though, that he won't be taking me back—that I won't have one more day with him to transition to the new world we're about to encounter without our daily dose of each other.

Sam and I order pizza, talk about our crazy day, and go upstairs. As we hold each other on the mattress on the deck, we both cry. Earlier, we had a breakdown with the car. Now, we have an emotional breakdown. It's all too much to pretend it doesn't hurt to say good-bye to the life we've created together that was destined to change. We've known it all along; it still hurts.

"There is a line in the Jane Austen book, *Pride and Prejudice*," I say. "It's simple and romantic, and I've always dreamed of being so in love with someone that I'd be able to say it with complete sincerity. I can say it now, to you."

"What is it?" he says. He kisses the top of my head.

"My heart is and always will be yours."

"And mine yours," he says. "Always. Doesn't matter if we're together or apart."

"I never felt like I belonged anywhere," I confess to him. "I always felt like there was something missing, or something else I should be doing or looking for. Nothing ever felt quite right. Until you. Until this summer. You're home to me, wherever we are."

"I feel the same. I have good friends and good times, but being with you is a whole different level. I try to explain you and I can't.

You're adventure and passion and peace all in one to me. I'm glad we found each other."

The moon is full and hazy above us, mesmerizing like a sultry mistress. The laps of the water seemed to whisper, "goodbye, good-bye, goodbye." We have each other, and that is all we need. This final night in Ocean City for the summer of 1986 is ours, and all we can do is hold each other and merge our tears, souls, and bodies until the sands of this place and time slip away.

*I loved her – love will find its way*
*Through paths where wolves would fear to prey...*
~ Lord Byron, *The Giaour*

# Chapter 20

## THE BETRAYAL

### SEPTEMBER 1986

Sam takes me to the condo the next morning in Kurt's car. We put my luggage on the sidewalk, hold hands, and talk like our hearts aren't breaking. Mom and Dad show up around nine o'clock in their white Chevy Cavalier. They unfold their tired bodies onto the sidewalk. Dad puts on a smile, gives me a quick hug, and shakes Sam's hand.

"Thanks for taking care of our girl," he says.

"Always my pleasure, though she takes pretty good care of herself."

Mom gives Sam and I each a hug. "Sorry your car broke down," she says.

"How bad is it?" Dad asks.

"I'm waiting to hear. Sorry I couldn't get Kristin back to college. I tried."

"We know. We appreciate that," Mom says.

"We can pack my things into your car, then why don't you come up and rest a while," I say. "Annie still has some groceries in the fridge. I can make pancakes and eggs."

Sam says he'll come up too, but can't stay long. He has to get to work. "I'll need extra money to pay for the car, so the guy relieving me is okay if I take my shift back."

"We can't stay long," Mom says. "We have to get back. Dad works night shift tonight."

"Oh, no. Dad, that's too much. I'm sorry," I say.

"We can rest a bit, Jean," he says.

He did the driving, so he's the one who needs a break. "And it's no problem, Krissy," he says. "I'll get a cat nap before I go to work."

He must've switched daylight shift for night shift with someone instead of taking a sick day that he probably doesn't have. Working at the steel mill is hard labor, and he works swing shifts, switching every two weeks between day shift, evening shift, and night shift. His body never really gets used to any rhythm or flow. He never complains.

He works hard to provide for us. So does Mom. This trip here and back to their house, especially with heavy traffic the Thursday before a holiday weekend, is taxing for both of them, and a show of love. I need to remember this, even when I long to hear the words more often.

We pack up their car and go upstairs to have breakfast. Annie and the other girls are gone, so we have the place to ourselves.

While I make breakfast, Dad dozes off on the couch; Mom goes out on the balcony to have a cigarette. When nine-thirty rolls around, I walk Sam downstairs, and we stand by Kurt's car in a tight embrace. Tears roll down my face; I can't let go. Finally, he gently pulls away.

"I'll see you in a few weeks for your birthday weekend. You can show me around campus and point out all those cornfields you have there. Okay?"

I nod as he wipes my tears. "I'm staying over at Mom and Dad's tonight. I'll drive my car to college tomorrow. You have Mom and Dad's number, right?"

"Yes. I'll call you there tonight."

He looks into my eyes, and we speak a million words without saying a thing.

"You're the best thing that's ever happened to me," he says.

"And you to me," I say.

"We'll have decades of summers together, and all the seasons in between."

We kiss and cling to each other like we're drowning. When we pull apart, he puts his head in my neck and hugs me again before he pulls away and gets in Kurt's car. We wave as he drives away, forcing light smiles that betray our heavy hearts.

The ride back is quiet. Mom asks me about what classes I'll be taking, when my other college roommates will be back, and the weather forecast.

I curl up in a ball in the back seat. "Mom, thanks, but I'm not ready to talk yet."

Dad turns on the radio. I cry quietly.

The landscape gradually changes from flat to the familiar rolling green hills and valleys of my home state. It's pretty. When we pull up to the house mid- afternoon, Smidge is in the big bay window looking out at me. I've missed him. We take my suitcases into my bedroom, where I'll switch out some summer clothes for warmer fall sweaters, leggings, sweats, and pants from my closet. It strikes me that it's a childhood bedroom, still decorated with pink and white striped wallpaper. Why have we kept it this way for so long?

Smidge is Dad's buddy when I'm not here, but when I'm home, he's all mine. He rubs against my leg, purrs, and lets me cry into his fur as I sit on my bed. I'm emotionally exhausted, and not looking forward to driving to college the next day alone. Annie won't be back until Monday night, and our other two roommates won't be there until the following weekend. I'll have Friday to get settled, and then start band camp early Saturday morning.

Sarah and Gary stop by the house that evening. They drive an hour from Harrisburg to see me, which is weird but nice. Dad makes my favorite meal—haddock with homemade fries and peas—and then he naps before he has to go to work at eleven o'clock.

Gary helps Mom with the dishes while Sarah and I go out to the carport to sit and talk while the bug zapper loudly electrocutes the innocents. The tradition is for the whole family to sit out there while Mom and Dad smoke; we listen to the music or to the crickets. Our house overlooks a ridge, on a back road with few houses, so it's otherwise peaceful and quiet.

"I wanted to say I'm sorry for the way I acted when we visited you at the beach," Sarah says. It's a rare moment of sisterly friendliness. "I think I was jealous."

I give her the side-eye, unsure if there's an agenda.

"Of what? You're the one who has it all. The good job, the nice place, a good income, and a good guy you're going to marry. I'm always playing catch-up to you."

"Remember my friend, Wendy? She invited me to be a Girl Scout camp counselor with her in upstate New York one summer. I really wanted to go. I knew Mom would say no, so I didn't even ask. I wish I'd have been brave. Like you. Seems like you had a great summer."

"The best," I say. I can't say more, or I'll burst into tears.

"Sam seems really nice," she says as she reaches over and squeezes my hand. "Doesn't hurt that he's nice to look at, too."

I squeeze her hand back. This is an unexpected moment I didn't know I needed, but I did. Sarah is rarely affectionate, and I'm glad she's going easy on me now when I'm vulnerable.

"He's the best. I love him. I miss him already."

"Love doesn't go anywhere, even when the person you love does," she says.

I turn my head and smile at her. "See, this is why you're the smart one."

"Since we're on the topic of love, would you be my maid of honor at my wedding in April?" She is still holding my hand.

I beam with joy that she asked me. I care about her wedding, after all.

"I'd be honored."

"Good. Thank you. I promise I won't make you wear an ugly dress."

"I promise I won't wear an ugly dress."

She laughs. "Wanna go in and play a game of Hearts with Mom and Gary?"

I need the distraction. "Yes. And thanks, Sarah. Love you."

"I love you too, Sis."

⸎

The next morning, I load my car, which has been sitting in Mom and Dad's driveway all summer. When dad comes home that morning from his night shift, he slips his customary twenty dollars and a Hershey's candy bar into my hand before I leave.

"I wanted to tell you that I think it's my fault Jake knew where you worked," he says.

This catches me by surprise. "How so?" I'm curious, not mad.

"The guys at work were talking at lunch one day about what our kids were doing for the summer. I said what you were up to. Didn't think anything of it. Turns out, one guy is married to a gal who works with Jake's mom. Word spreads. Sorry about that. I was just real proud of you."

I smile and give him a hug. "That's okay. And I'm real proud of you, too, Dad."

An hour later, I pull onto a side street near my college and park in front of the older, two-story house I rented with Annie and two other girls since last year. They'll graduate in May. I still have another year to go after they're gone, and I don't know where I'll live my senior year. I can't think about that now, though.

I lug my suitcases and duffle bags upstairs to the largest bedroom, the one I share with Annie. It's light blue, and has two double beds, two dressers, two small desks, a big closet, and two windows with simple white curtains. The house feels stuffy, so I open the windows to let some air in, even though it's hot outside. I'll turn on the window air conditioners soon.

Two other small bedrooms are upstairs; I open those windows, too, to air out the rooms. Donna will be back next week, and so will Carly and her boyfriend, Steve, who may as well live here since he's stuck like glue to her, much like I have been stuck to Sam.

My old diary sits on my desk where I left it. My life is so different now from when I last wrote in it. I'm not even interested in reading it to remember.

Annie's boom box is still on her desk. I think about turning on the radio or playing one of her cassette tapes, but decide I want silence. Last night with family was nice. A reset, even. But I'm tired of noise and conversation. I'm thankful to have the day alone to come to grips with being without Sam and Ocean City.

Five minutes later, the silence in the house is deafening. I feel so discombobulated. I want the condo. I want the ocean. I want the sand, and bay, and annoying tourists, and laid-back locals, and the smell of salty air. I want Annie and Bianca and Marion. I especially want Sam. None of that is here. This is a world I vaguely remember, and don't want to return to.

After I unpack and clean the house from the dust that has built up, I go out to get a few groceries. Being alone isn't as good for me as I thought it would be. I have too much time to ache for Sam. I want to jump in my car and drive back to the beach, quit school, be back in his arms tonight and every night. Instead, I turn on the TV and most of the lights; I intend to keep them on all night. Stupid band camp. Why didn't I try to get out of it?

Sam calls and we talk for two hours. He's getting ready for the ranch party the next night, and I wish so badly that I could be there to go with him.

My mind is racing and feels cluttered. Should I transfer to a college in Maryland? Should I leave here for good? I want to. This place isn't my home anymore. Sam is home. I wish Annie could've come back with me. She is home to me, too.

Why am I being so emotional? Why am I so tired? My need for Sam is unbearable.

So much is going on inside my head that I have to get it out. I go upstairs and open my old diary. I need to pour out all of my thoughts on paper so they won't clutter my head. I write, like I used to, in streams of thought. I write about the summer, the love I found with Sam, the future I want with him, and the freedom to be myself that I discovered.

I'm so tired. I put the pen down and go to bed. I fall into a deep sleep so I don't have to think about all I'm missing, and about the empty space beside me that Sam used to fill.

I don't sleep well. I wake late. I scramble to get dressed and to the field in time for band camp. I drive onto campus, past the historic Old Main building, and behind the sprawling buildings, dorms, and classrooms to the big practice field behind the football stadium.

It's nice to see everyone again, especially the other pom girls and the percussion line that practices and marches behind us in most of our formations.

I find my friend Bear, a trombone player who looks like a football lineman, and is the sweetest soul. I jump into his arms. His real name is Ted, but he's such a big teddy bear that everyone calls him Bear. He's like a big brother to me, and just the emotional support I need. Annie and I met him my first week in band, and hung out with him and his buddies all last year.

Bear is gay, but he doesn't feel comfortable being real about that. I don't care who he's attracted to or loves. I care about him, and I love how warm, funny, and kind he is. I'm also glad to have a guy friend who isn't secretly wanting to have sex with me; it's refreshing.

We talk about our summers, and then separate into groups. The two pom captains teach us the routines. I'm overwhelmed; I wish Annie was here to help me learn them.

I keep thinking about Sam. I think about his smile, the feel of his skin, and the way he looks at me. I have to put that all out of my mind and concentrate on the routines I have to learn. I'm frustrated that I'm slow to remember them, and I'm still so tired. Sleep sounds so enticing.

Lunch break can't come soon enough. I'm hot and sticky when I get back to the house, and I stop in my tracks as I approach the porch. Jake is sitting on the swing. A big, stuffed trash bag sits by the door.

Instead of bursting into expletives, I burst into tears. All the stress and pent-up emotions pour out of me. I miss Sam and our life together. Band camp is challenging. I'm hungry. I'm overheated and tired. So, so tired. And now, Jake has resurrected from the land of final goodbyes. Why? It all comes to a head. It's too much, too much.

Jake stands and approaches me. "What's wrong?"

He tries to hug me, but I turn away.

"What are you doing here?" I ask. "How many times do I need to tell you we're over?

He steps back, and I can see the hurt in his eyes.

"I had some of your stuff still at my place. I thought you'd want it back. Your favorite fall coat—the black one with the big buttons. Your purple blanket. Some bracelets. I know I could've dropped them off at your parents' house, but I wanted to see you."

"Why? You should've called first."

"I knew you'd say no. I remembered that you'd be here for band camp, and I thought I'd take a chance. We didn't part on the best terms last time. I was hoping to change that. Hoping maybe your thing with that guard guy was just a summer fling."

"It's not. I love him. I told you all this in Ocean City. I don't want to hurt you, Jake, but whether or not I'm with anyone else, it wouldn't work between us again. Please stop this."

He hangs his head. The fight has gone out of him. And me. My heart softens. I don't see Jake, the ex I'm mad at; I see Jake, the guy who took me roller skating and to my first concert, to prom, and to ride horses at his family's farm. I see the guy who taught me the constellations in the sky, and who I had loved for so long. I don't want to hurt him, but I have to.

He forces a small smile. "I'll carry these things in the house, and then I'll leave. For good. I want you to be happy. If that's not with me, then okay. I know I blew it."

I unlock the door, and he hauls in my stuff. I tell him he has to go. I walk him to the door and give him a hug. His embrace has a finality about it that I didn't feel before. I'm glad and sad. I want to believe he really gets it this time.

He pulls back, and before I can say anything, he leans down to kiss me. I don't know why, but I let him. For a moment I'm seventeen again, and this is familiar and normal—and then it isn't. No, there is nothing normal about it anymore. It isn't Sam. My Sam. I only want Sam.

I pull away and step back. "Jake, no. You've caught me when I'm emotional and stressed. That was wrong. I love Sam. I'm not the one for you. Please go."

"I know," he says. "That was goodbye."

He grabs my hand for an instant, and then lets it go and is gone.

I collapse on the couch and put my head in my hands. I feel horrible about the kiss. That shouldn't have happened. Why did I let it happen? I need to get all the jumbled thoughts out of my head, so I go up to my room and write in my diary again.

*August 30, 1986. There was a time when I couldn't imagine not having Jake in my life. He consumed it so much, and now it seems a lifetime ago. He disrespected me so much, and I let him. I see it so clearly now, especially with having been properly loved this summer by Sam.*

*Jake stopped by today to return some of my things—and to see if Sam and I are still together. I assured him we are. I think he finally gets that I won't go back to him. Ever. Before he left, he kissed me. I let him. I shouldn't have. It was a final goodbye for us both. A parting gift?*

*One thing is for sure. Jake is my past. Sam is my present and future.*

I feel better now that my thoughts are down on paper. Time is running out for my lunch break. I grab a quick sandwich and head back to the field. Two more days and Annie will be with me, so I focus on that to get me through the challenges of the days ahead.

When Annie arrives Monday, I almost knock her over with my hug. She tells me all about her final few nights in Ocean City, complete with a rundown of her special night with Rocco, and a vow to never drink rum again.

I tell her about my emotional roller coaster, my good talk with Sarah, and what happened with Jake. She's so mad about the Jake kiss that she storms out without saying a word. She comes back an hour later practically steaming.

"Why do you try so hard to sabotage yourself and the great thing you have with Sam?" she asks. "Why are you so self-destructive? What's wrong with you?"

"Why do you say that? I didn't even know Jake was coming."

"One day you're crying that you'll miss Sam so much it hurts, and just a few days later you tell me Jake was here and you let him kiss you. How can you turn so quickly?"

"I didn't turn," I say. I'm madder at myself more than she ever could be. "I wasn't thinking straight. I'm feeling so out of sorts and off-kilter. I don't know, Annie. I love Sam."

"You have to tell him about this," she says.

"Why? Nothing happened. I don't want to hurt him."

"Something happened," she says. "You kissed Jake. That's a big deal."

"*He* kissed *me*. It didn't mean anything except goodbye," I say. "I felt nothing."

"That's beside the point! How would you feel if Sam kissed someone else?"

"Horrible," I say. "Betrayed. It was wrong. But I didn't plan it or want it."

Annie paces like a caged animal. "Your naivety isn't cute, you know that?"

"What do you mean?"

"You need to grow up and get your head out of your ass. You've spent years with Jake normalizing his bad behavior. You think shit like that is okay, just because you 'didn't mean it.'"

"I'm not so naïve," I say. "I know that Sam must be tempted by girls that flirt with him at the beach and at his parties. He must think about kissing them or having sex with them, but he doesn't act on it because he loves me. I do the same for him. I made one mistake. I didn't sleep with Jake, and I stopped the kiss. He's gone now for good."

"I've heard that before," she says. "Tell Sam. I love you and want you to stop doing stupid stuff so you don't lose the best thing that ever happened to you. I'll meet you at the field."

She storms out. I sit on the bed and hang my head in shame.

How can I mess things up so badly just a few days away from Sam? How can he love me when I'm so messed up? I can't bear the thought of hurting him over something so insignificant. That kiss was no big deal—it just confirmed how completely over it is with Jake, and has been. Sam doesn't deserve pain from my momentary stupidity. No, he doesn't need to know.

*Meet me at sunrise, or sunset, or the new moon—*
*the place is immaterial…*
*With host or alone, in sunshine or storm,*
*in heaven or earth, some how or no how –*
*I propose, sir, to see you."*

~ Emily Dickinson, a letter to George H. Gould, February 1850

# Chapter 21

## SPECIAL OCCASIONS

September is a strange and new transition; I don't like it. Sam and I wrestle time, schedules, and logistics to see each other as much as we can, but it's not the same as the daily flow we had with each other. I have a full load of five classes, plus I volunteer as a writing tutor, work part-time at the library, practice and perform with the band, and hang out with friends when I can. I'm busy and exhausted, yet am still consumed with missing Sam and the beach. I walk most places in bare feet with my shoes in my hand and Sam's ring on my finger.

Sam comes to visit, as promised, the weekend of September thirteenth. My birthday is on the fifteenth, so we celebrate early for this special occasion. He shows up on my doorstep with a dozen red roses, Hershey's chocolate bars, and a delicate gold bracelet with a heart charm dangling from it. I love them all, but the best gift is Sam himself. I pounce on him, and my soul sings with happiness to be in his arms again, to feel his soft kisses, and to look into his eyes.

Annie sleeps on the couch that weekend, and I have to force myself to get out of bed with Sam to show him around campus and introduce him to my friends. I want him all to myself, but I also want to show him off. It's weird to see him in jeans and a jacket instead of shorts and OCBP t-shirt. He attends a home football game to watch Annie and I dance with the pom squad. He tells me he especially likes the pom costume on me—knee-high white go-go boots, a short, white shiny skirt, and a white puff-sleeved blouse with a tight red vest over top of it. The outfit doesn't stay on long when we get back to my place.

It feels weird to be together away from the beach. It's like we're Barbie and Ken, taken from a dream house and plopped down in a new location to explore an entirely different world together that doesn't feel quite right. We both love the ocean, not being landlocked.

We could be dropped in Antarctica, though, as far as I'm concerned. Sam and I are fine as long as we're together. He'll soon move out of Ocean City to Annapolis to start work at the bartending job he lined up until next summer. We explore options to be together year-round so that I can stay in college and graduate next year, yet still be with him. Even if we can find a solution, that probably can't happen until next semester at the earliest.

"We'll make the best of it," he says. "I'll come to you, you'll come to me, we can meet somewhere in the middle and spend the whole weekend in bed at a cheap hotel. Make it fun."

"Doesn't matter to me as long as I'm with you," I say.

When he leaves Sunday early evening, a blanket of sadness covers me. Annie takes me out for dinner on Monday for my birthday, but I feel half of me is missing. I twirl my ring and keep looking at my bracelet; they are beautiful but poor substitutes for Sam's presence.

Two weeks later, the last Saturday in September, another special occasion brings us back together—his sister's wedding. I finally get to meet his family and hometown friends. The stars align to make our schedules work out for it. He's done guarding at the beach for the season, and the college football team has an away game that the band and poms don't need to attend.

We stay at his parent's house; they clear out the guest bedroom for us.

"Shayne's never brought a girl home from the beach," his brother, Brett, says.

"Don't be telling my secrets," Sam says.

"If you get him to settle down, I'll believe in miracles," his sister, Ava, says to me.

Sam's parents warmly welcome me. I immediately feel like part of the family. Sam looks a lot like his dad, who is friendly yet edgy; Sam has his build, intensity, and striking eyes. Sam's mom is tall and elegant, with a warm, wide smile and a gentleness that reminds me of Sam.

The wedding is at the local country club, with a delicious buffet and a live band. Sam is in the wedding party; he looks like a model in his light gray tux. He can rock any look. His hair is getting long, and I love how it falls down his neck and curls at the ends. I wear a shiny green dress with a plunging neckline; I feel like a million bucks beside him.

"The camera loves you two," the photographer says. He snaps several shots of us. "You're glowing. I wish the bride and groom looked as in love as you two."

"We're taking bets as to how long my sister's marriage will last," Sam whispers to me.

"It's nice to see Shayne this happy," his mom says to me. "I'm so glad he brought you home to meet us."

"He makes me happy, too," I say. "You've raised a good man."

She raises her glass of champagne, and we toast to that.

When we leave, his mom invites me back for the holidays. I accept and look forward to coming back to be with everyone again.

Returning to college from such a fun weekend with Sam and his family is difficult. Every moment with him is sacred, and every moment apart is painful. I don't want to ruin any of it by bringing up Jake and the kiss. It would hurt Sam unnecessarily and topple our delicate transition to this strange new chapter of our lives of being apart for weeks at a time. I just want to love him, do better by him, be better for him, and make him happy.

Every time he has to leave me, he leaves a note—usually as part of a cute or funny card, like the one he gave to me the first time he came to the Carousel looking for me. We write letters when we're apart. He continues his tradition of leaving a passage from a classic poem or book at the bottom of each letter. It touches me that he does that, despite not really liking that stuff, because I like it. I keep them all in a cigar box by my bed and read them often.

*I offer you my hand,*
*My heart, and a share*
*In all of my possessions.*
*I ask you to pass through*
*Life at my side –*
*To be my second self,*
*And best earthly companion.*
  *~ Jane Eyre, by Charlotte Bronte*

*You must allow me to tell you how ardently I admire and love you.*
  *~ Pride &* Prejudice, *by Jane Austen*

*I arise from dreams of thee*
*In the first sweet sleep of night,*
*When the winds are breathing low,*
*And the stars are shining bright.*
  *~ The Indian Serenade, by Percy Bysshe Shelley*

*Shall I compare thee to a summer's day?*
*Thou art more lovely and more temperate.*
  *~ Sonnet 18, by William Shakespeare*

Everything he does is an act of love, from the cards he writes, to the poetry or classic book passages he includes in them, to the long trips he makes for short weekends just to see me. He even calls bars in my small college town to see if they have openings for bartenders so he can move closer to me, even though he won't make nearly as much money as he can in Annapolis.

We have to figure something out. The chill in the air reminds me that autumn is here, and winter is coming. The transition away from our summer is difficult, but we're adjusting together, just as we will for all seasons. Nothing can stop us as we navigate these unfamiliar waters. I don't know what my future holds, but I know Sam will be with me in it, every step of the way.

*The thorns which I have reap'd are of the tree*
*I planted; they have torn me, and I bleed.*
*I should have known what fruit would*
*spring from such a seed.*
~ Lord Byron, *Childe Harold's Pilgrimage*

# Chapter 22

THE DISCOVERY

OCTOBER 1986

Sam visits me in mid-October.

He's tired after working and then immediately driving to see me. After attending the halftime show performance to see Annie and me dance, he leaves the football game to go back to the house for a nap. We plan to go out to eat and to see a movie when I return.

I rush home after the game and can't find him. His car is gone.

I call out to him in the house, outside the house—everywhere. When I go upstairs again, I catch my breath. My diary is on my desk, spread open to the pages where I had written about Jake's visit the Saturday of Labor Day weekend, and about him kissing me. The necklace I had gotten Sam, that he'd not taken off since I gifted it, sits on top of the diary.

My heart sinks. *No, no, no, no, no!*

Leaving his necklace on the diary tells me more than any note ever could.

I'm frozen in a flurry of mixed emotions. I'm furious that he read my diary—I feel violated and offended. It's my most private space. My deep offense is not as powerful, though, as the fear that I've lost him. I'm horrified and sad for how hurt he must be after reading that Jake was at my place, and that I had let him kiss me. It was a betrayal. I'm terrified that I may have lost him because of what I've done; I've never felt fear like this. I have to explain. I have to tell him how sorry I am and remind him how much I love him. I feel sick and scared.

I hope Sam read the rest of what I wrote, the part about loving only him and wanting my future to be with only him. Still, what I wrote about Jake must've cut him deeply.

I'm inconsolable. Annie tries to calm me, but I'm sure she's thinking I'm getting what I deserve. It's true. How could I have been so thoughtless and stupid?

Sam won't be at Annapolis for another hour, given when he must've left the house after reading my diary. I put on my coat and grab my car keys.

"Where are you going?" Annie asks.

"To find Sam. He hasn't gotten a new phone number yet, but I have his address. I've got to go see him, beg his forgiveness."

"You hate driving in the dark, especially in a strange city. I'll drive you."

I hug her. "Thanks, but no. I love how you love me, Annie, even when I do dumb things, but I have to do this myself."

"I do dumb things, too," she says. "Go get Sam."

I open the door to rush out to the car, and there is Sam, standing at the door, with hurt so deep in his eyes that I know it'll haunt me all my life.

Relief sweeps me like a current. I rush to hug him, but he backs away.

"Why, Kit, *why?*"

I take a deep breath to calm myself; I take his hand. "Sam. Sam, thank God. I was just coming to find you. I'm so sorry. Come in. Please. Let me explain."

He comes in and sits down. I hate myself for doing this to him. He says he was halfway to Annapolis, hurt and angry, but that the part I'd written about loving him and wanting to spend my life with him kept nagging at him. That part made him turn around and come back.

"It's not just that you kissed him; that's bad enough," he says. "But you didn't tell me. You let him near you. All of it. I don't know if I can get over this, but I love you enough to try."

"Thank you, thank you." I cry in relief.

That one thoughtless moment can wipe away everything I've built with Sam hits me like a brick. He means so much to me; I can't bear to lose him.

We talk most of the night. I try to tell him a million ways how much I love him, and I promise that nothing like that will ever happen again. He holds me until we fall asleep.

We see each other again at the end of October and go to a Halloween party in Annapolis with some of his friends, but things aren't quite the same. He's trying, but I've broken his trust. Everything about us has always been so honest and true, and I blew it over one moment of vulnerability. I didn't sleep with Jake, but kissing him and not telling Sam is bad enough.

There's a small but noticeable distance between us now; I hope it goes away. How could I have sabotaged my own perfect love story? I know I'll never betray him again. I've never been so scared as that moment when I knew he'd left and might not come back. I know it will take time to heal from this, but I also know our love is strong enough to survive anything.

*And sometimes I have kept my feelings to myself,*
*because I could find no language to describe them in.*
~ Jane Austen, *Sense and Sensibility*

# *Chapter 23*

THE SECRET

NOVEMBER 1986

I'm sitting in my bed, studying, the first week of November—I don't remember which day. Nobody is home. It's getting dark outside. I reach over to turn on a light, and a sharp pain cuts across my abdomen. I've had mild cramps all afternoon and have been spotting for a few days. Weird spotting. Not like my normal period. My lower back has been hurting and the dull pain has grown worse every hour.

Another sharp pain hits again. And again. And again, until it is one continuous stabbing. This isn't like my normal period cramping. It's much worse, like someone is wringing my insides like a wet towel.

When was my last period? I can't remember. I'm never regular. I never pay attention. That's what it has to be, but I've never experienced anything like this.

The cramps intensify; they tear into me and then subside every twenty minutes. Then every ten minutes. The bad, stabbing back cramps get worse. No position helps. Then the searing abdominal cramping comes—scary awful, like someone is stabbing me from the inside out and ripping me apart. Twisting, stabbing, twisting, stabbing. What is happening to me?

Something goops out of me and I run to the bathroom, doubled over. Then there's a weird brownish discharge, thicker and darker than anything I've experienced with my period, mixed with bright, big red clots.

I cry out to God, to Sam, to Annie, to Mom. *Help me!* Where is Annie? More big, bloody clots seep out of me. More unbearable pain. What the hell? I feel like I'm dying.

Doubled over in a fetal position on the cold bathroom tile. Doubled over on the toilet. Doubled over in bed. Repeat. Bloody underwear. Bloody floor. Bloody, clumpy clots and balls in the toilet water. Tears. Flush. Pain. *Help me!*

I feel lightheaded. I splash cold water on my face. I try to clean up. I double over again. I want to call Mom, but she's an hour away, and I don't want to worry her. I want to call Sam, but he's even further away, and would feel helpless. He can't help. *Where is Annie?*

I open the medicine cabinet, desperate for anything to relieve the pain. Midol? Yes, swallow. Back on the floor. Back on the toilet. More clots. More pain. Doubled over. Flush.

Something is seriously wrong. I'm afraid. The college health clinic is closed. I need a doctor. Am I dying? *Help me!*

I change my underwear, stuff it with three thick pads, grab my keys, and somehow make it out the door and to my car, doubled over. I drive fifteen minutes to the hospital and stumble into the ER; the cramping is intolerable. I collapse at the front desk.

They take me back right away.

Calm down. Take off your clothes. Spread your legs. Cold table. Faces and hands in my crotch, looking, probing, swabbing. Pain. A pill for the pain. It doesn't help. An IV. *Help me!*

"When did the spotting and cramping start?"

"I don't remember."

"When was your last period?"

"I don't remember."

"A month, two?"

"I said I don't remember!"

Ultrasound, outside and inside. "We're going to give you something to relax."

A cold, sterile hallway. People all around. Bright lights. Headache. Tears.

Sam. Annie. Mom. *Help me!* Please. Please. Sam, Sam, Sam …

Where am I? Sleepy, so sleepy.

I wake to bright lights and muffled sounds. My head hurts. Mild cramps.

"Miss Spaide, wake up. We gave you something to relax. It's wearing off now."

Big, bald doctor, creviced but kind face.

"What happened?" I ask. Groggy. "Where am I?"

"You're in the hospital. I'm sorry to say that you've had a miscarriage."

The pain is mild now. Still so sleepy. I didn't hear him right.

"Wait, what?" I ask.

"A miscarriage."

"No."

"Yes. I'm sorry. Looks like you were thirteen weeks along."

"I'm pregnant?" I'm seared with shock.

"You were." He sits on the rolling stool beside the bed. "It's okay. Happens all the time."

Okay? No, not okay. When was I pregnant? Thirteen weeks? That's more than three months. That long without a period and I didn't notice? I was never regular, but three months? I didn't have nausea or sore breasts or anything.

A miscarriage? Doesn't happen all the time to me.

"No rhyme or reason to miscarriages," the doctor says. "Hard to know why. Looks like you've had a complete miscarriage, so no need for a D and C, but if you get a fever or—blah, blah, blah—take this pill—blah, blah, blah. Here's a prescription, get rest and drink plenty of liquids—blah, blah, blah—you're young, back to your usual self in no time."

I'm so confused. I flashback to the summer, the glorious summer. Yes, I've been tired a lot since then, but I had a lot going on. These months back at school, unusually emotional, sure, but that's because I've been missing Sam so much.

A nearby nurse, tending to someone else but in earshot of us, turns to me as the doctor walks away. She takes my hand. "I'm so sorry, honey," she says. "They don't tell you to do this, but I strongly recommend seeing a counselor about this. I can give you a referral."

I shake my head no. I'm fine. I'm fine. I'll be fine.

But I am not fine. I thought I knew what dark spaces were, dark times, pain. I had no idea before this day. I can't talk about it. I can't think about it. It hurts too much.

After a few hours of observation and some more pain medication, they release me. I walk in slow motion to my car. I drive back to the house in a daze. Everyone is home now. They're watching late night shows in the living room.

"Kristin, where were you? What's wrong?" Annie asks.

"I'm exhausted," I say. "Bad cramps. I went out to get Midol. I'm going to bed."

Nobody questions a girl having bad cramps. And it is true, I do have bad cramps. Anything to get her and the others to stop asking questions.

I go upstairs. Annie follows me.

"There were bloody balls of toilet paper in the bathroom trash can," she says. Worry clouds her face. "And some blood on the floor. I had to clean up a little. What's really wrong?"

I manage a small smile. "Sorry. A really heavy, bad period. I'll be fine. Really."

I go into the bathroom. Lock the door. Change my pads. Go to bed. Stare at the ceiling.

I was pregnant. Was. Not anymore. A baby. Far enough along to have fingers and toes and a heartbeat. A perfect union of Sam and me. How did I not know?

What have I done? Why did I lose the baby? Did I not eat right? Was I dancing for the pom squad too much? Did I overdo it? Was I too stressed? So much stress.

How did I not know?

I would've taken better care of myself. Had doctor visits. Taken vitamins. I would've told Sam. He would've said it will be all right, that we will work it out somehow, take it one day at a time. We would've had the baby. He would've been an amazing dad.

How did I not know?

I flushed my baby down the toilet. Our beautiful baby—down a toilet. What have I done?

I'm sorry. I'm so, so sorry, baby. I didn't know.

My baby. Our baby.

I feel in my bones that the baby was a girl. We would've named her Summer. She would've had her dad's butter blonde hair and cobalt blue eyes with long golden lashes, and my dimple and stubborn streak. She would've been a swimmer and an artist and a brave beach guard like her dad. She would've been, she was, a beautiful blend of Sam and me. She existed.

I'm sorry. I'm so, so sorry, baby. I didn't know.

I sob into my pillow. The residual physical pain is nothing compared to the pain in my heart, my soul, and deep in my bones. The ache, a true heartache.

It hurts so much. Not physically anymore. Emotionally. Make it stop, make it stop.

When I wake, it's almost noon the next day. I cry some more. Luckily, Annie has gone to class. She doesn't need to know. She can't help me. Nobody can.

I failed my baby. I didn't give her a safe home in my body. I flushed her down the toilet. Like trash. How could I not have known that I was pregnant? Or suspect it? Sam and I never used protection—how could I not have thought that was a possibility? It's common sense.

I can't tell anyone. What's the use? Sam is already dealing with the hurt of the Jake thing. I don't want him to feel more pain. He can't do anything about it, anyway. He'd be devastated and would feel bad that he wasn't here to help me through it. It's one more big thing that I've messed up and done wrong. I don't want to hurt him anymore.

As for Annie, I don't want to feel her pity. She'd be desperate to alleviate my pain and would feel helpless that she can't. Why put her through that?

I can't tell Mom and Dad. I don't want to hear lectures about not using birth control, or consequences of bad choices, or how a miscarriage was probably for the best so I can graduate college and get a good job. That I shouldn't have had sex before marriage in the first place.

I especially don't want to hear anyone say, "It's for the best." It's not.

I want my baby. I want her back. I want her to be a part of me again, so I'll *know* and actively love and protect her. She was Sam's and mine. She was ours. We were a family. She was alive inside of me, and I lost her without even knowing she was there. The thoughts of the bathroom, the blood, the toilet, and the flushing won't stop. They consume me.

*I didn't know!*

There's only one solution: shut it out. Pretend it didn't happen. It's our family motto— ignore bad things. Don't talk about it. No big deal. No big deal. Shut it down. Shut it out. What choice do I have? I can't live with this pain or guilt. I'll go crazy.

It happens all the time. Isn't that what the doctor said? No big deal.

Just a bunch of cells, isn't that what they say? Not a baby. A fetus. Does that help? To use semantics so we won't call it what it is? A baby. Our baby. Was alive. Now dead.

No, it doesn't help. Yes, a baby. Fingers. Toes. A heartbeat. I'm sorry, baby.

I can't live like this. The logic of no big deal doesn't align with my heart and spirit knowing, feeling, and raging with the fact that it is beyond a big deal.

Okay, then shut it out. Shut it out to survive this pain.

I stay in bed for three days, saying I'm sick, because I am. Sick inside my soul.

Sam can't visit me over the weekend; I'm glad. I need more time. On the fourth day, I get up. I take a shower. I brush my matted hair. I go to the drugstore to fill my prescription. I take the pills, whatever they are. Then I go to the college health clinic to get birth control because I sure as hell can't go through this again. Time to grow up and be smart.

Why was I never on the pill? It's a normal thing sexually active girls do. Sam probably assumed that I was; we never talked about it. Most girls sleep around and pretend like they don't, and then judge other girls who sleep around, especially those who get pregnant. I only slept with the man I love. The end result is the same.

Why didn't Sam or I think to use a condom? Or even discuss it?

Jake and I had never used any protection, either. I guess we got lucky. I guess I thought maybe I couldn't get pregnant because we were so lucky. I guess I just didn't think about it at all. That carried over to when I started being with Sam—like I was immune to any consequences except crabs.

I look in the mirror and gasp. I'm so pale. I have bags under my eyes. I look like death. I feel like it, too. I put on some makeup and force a smile. Nobody can know. Pretend it didn't happen. Forget it. Push it down. Shut it down. My baby… I love you. I'm sorry I let you down.

How could I not know?

*Anguish and despair had penetrated into the core of my heart;
I bore a hell within me, which nothing could extinguish.*

~ Mary Shelley, *Frankenstein*

# Chapter 24

## THE AFTERMATH

### NOVEMBER / DECEMBER 1986

Sam visits a week later, and I cling to him like a drowning soul. I bury my head in his neck and tell myself to cry and let him comfort me, even if he doesn't know why, but no tears come. I've cried so many tears, maybe I'm all out. I'm in a weird state of shock.

When he and Annie ask what's wrong, I don't tell them the truth. I tell them I'm stressed with all I have on my plate, and that winter makes me miss our summer world even more.

I go back to classes, though my grades slip. Back to the pom squad for the end of the season, though I go through the motions without the sizzle. Back to hangouts with Bear and the rest of the gang, though I don't laugh much anymore. Back to phone calls, letters, and visits with Sam, though my smiles are forced. Back to a new, darker reality. No one can ever know.

Fake it till you make it. That's what I do. I pretend that it didn't happen and that it doesn't matter. Hopefully, eventually, it will be true.

As November ushers in the cold, my quiet, sad dazed state turns to a muted, edgy anger. Why exactly, I don't know. Annie asks me what is wrong. So does Sam.

"Stop being so bitchy. That's my job," Annie says.

I don't know why I'm so moody and distant. I just feel angrier as the days go buy. I would rather feel numb—anything to keep these creeping, deeper feelings of rage, hurt, and guilt at bay. Anything to forget. But how? I sleep a lot—a reprieve from it all.

One day I stop by the college health clinic to look into counseling, but I'm not ready to talk about the miscarriage. How can I talk about it when I'm trying to forget it? I decide therapy is not for me. Besides, nobody in my family ever gets counseling. Just bear it and get on with it.

I'm thankful pom pom duties wind down by the end of November. Papers are due as the holidays approach, and finals are around the corner. I'm tense and sullen; I can't help it.

On Sam's weekend visits, I don't rush into his arms anymore. I'm snippy at him for no good reason. I don't want to be, but I am. I don't smile as much or want to make love as much. When we do, I don't melt into him like I used to. I feel too empty inside. I don't know what's broken or how to fix it; I've checked out, and I don't know how to check back in.

Sometimes, it hurts to look at Sam. When I see him, I see our baby, and it makes me remember what happened. I don't want to remember. I love him, but it's painful in a weird way to see our child in his beautiful eyes. They're intertwined. My heart breaks on repeat.

Sam's eyes start to hold worry and confusion. "Are you mad at me about something?"

"No," I say. "I have a lot going on. Classes and work and papers and—it's just a lot."

One Sunday, as we're sitting at the dining room table at my place eating lunch, he starts talking again about moving near me. He says that he's set up a meeting with someone about an assistant coaching job with the swim team at my college. He's also going to see some-one about a room for rent in town just two streets away from me.

"No." I say it too quickly. A fast and firm response.

He looks up at me in surprise and dismay.

"No?" His voice is thick with hurt. "Why not?

I stop chewing, and gulp too big of a bite of my sandwich. I sit silently for a minute to let my food and feelings digest. Did I say that out loud? Why did I say no so quickly?

"I, I just think it's too soon, and I don't think you'll be happy here," I say.

It's true. I know how much he loves the ocean; he'd feel like a fish out of water here, and I don't want him to feel that way. Plus, now that he's taking steps to move here, I'm not so sure anymore if it's the right time. I just turned twenty. I'm in college. It feels like pressure.

Plus, I just lost our baby that he doesn't know about. Flushed down the toilet. I didn't know. I should've known. I don't deserve him. I don't deserve happiness.

*How could I not know?*

"Too soon? It's all we've talked about. And I'd be happy anywhere with you," he says.

He takes my hand. I want to jerk it away, but I force myself not to. I don't understand wanting to pull away from him; it's always been so natural to gravitate to him, to hunger for him, to desire his touch. I feel mad and empty inside: I just want to be left alone.

I don't want to hurt him. I love him, but I feel myself cooling toward him. I don't understand it. I don't know how to love him like I used to, and that scares me.

He and Annie are right, I'm bitchy; I try not to be, but I don't know how to stop it or why it's happening. I'm this way with everybody. I'm not as friendly anymore. I prefer staying at the house reading or sleep-ing rather than hanging out with friends or joining campus activities like I used to. Bear can't even make me laugh as usual with his corny jokes. If I could, I'd crawl in my closet, curl up in a dark corner, and disappear back to the invisible world of my childhood.

Instead, I crawl into bed at every chance. Sleep is the only escape from the anger, gloom, and sadness simmering inside of me. Sometimes agonizing despair grips me. My grades on tests and papers plummet. My tan skin turns pale, like my spirit. I lose my appetite.

Sam and Annie do their best to be patient with me, but I start to withdraw even further from them, and snap at them even more. I'm like a restless, seething, caged tiger.

"You can be mean with me; I can handle it," Annie says. "I promise you I can, even if I don't understand it. But why are you being that way with Sam? He for sure doesn't deserve it."

"I know that! I'm sorry. I'm just stressed."

"We all are. You're beyond that. Please tell me what's wrong."

"Annie, really, I'm sorry. I don't know why I'm in such a funk."

I really don't. I've put the miscarriage behind me, or I've tried to, so why do I still feel like I'm sinking? I want to tell Annie what happened, but what does it matter anymore?

"I've tried to be patient with you, and so has Sam, but you better figure this out before you lose him. I wouldn't take that shitty attitude from you, that's for sure."

I try to pull myself out of whatever dark hole I'm in, but I don't know how. I try to be warm and loving with this great man, and not just pretend, but my heart is too numb.

I hope the holidays will help, but they don't. Sam and I spend Thanksgiving at my parents' house. After the big turkey dinner, Mom pulls me aside and asks what was wrong. I see love and concern in her pretty eyes. At that moment, I don't care if she'd be mad at me or judge me; I just want to sink into her arms, cry about my baby, and let her comfort me. But I don't. I can't. I don't want her to be dismissive or disappointed in me. I'm mad that I'm even thinking about it again. I need to shut it out.

"I'm just having a hard time balancing everything," I say.

Christmas is at Sam's parents' house. Sam gets me a Swatch and perfume, and I give him a navy pea coat from Annapolis that looks striking on him. I fake a smile, but none of it penetrates the wall that has been building within and around me.

I'm with Sam New Year's Eve and New Year's Day at his place in Annapolis. We have good moments, but mostly I'm in a fog. I can't climb out of my own hopelessness and emptiness.

"I feel like you're slipping away from me," Sam says. We're in his bed and he tries to hold me; I stiffen in his embrace. "You're like a different person."

I am. The old me has been flushed away like my baby. I don't want anyone to touch me, even him; I want to sink into the darkness and let it swallow me. I don't know why, but that's how I feel. I've become a sullen, prickly cactus. Why does anyone love me?

*Just leave me alone, leave me alone*, I want to tell everybody. I don't deserve everyone's damn patience with me. I don't deserve their love.

I didn't know my own baby was in me. I didn't protect her. I flushed her down the toilet.

Shut it out. Bury it. Forget it. That's all I know now.

*I am ashes where once I was fire...*
~ Lord Byron, *To the Countess of Blessington*

# Chapter 25

## THE TURNING POINT

### JANUARY 1987

I think, pray, and hope the new year will bring a new beginning. I vow to be a better person for the people who love me. Still, it all feels like pretend. I don't love myself much anymore, and I seem set on punishing anyone who does love me. *How could I not know?*

I'm sullen, moody, and full of fury. I can't be appeased. I can't find the sweetness I held before, no matter how hard I try. I can't understand it or stop the train wreck I'm creating for anyone who loves me, or tries to. My roommates steer clear of me. Annie is kind but distant, having tried everything to reach me. She finally succumbs to the space she promises to give to me until whatever this is passes.

Sam has stopped pursuing a move to be near me, since I basically shut it down, so he starts talking about us both returning to Ocean City in the summer. He doesn't like the dreariness of winter, so he needs some hope. I don't give it to him. I want to, but I can't. I don't have it in me. I can't think about anything other than surviving another day. He makes plans; I'm silent.

There's a turning point when I go from cold to him to dead to him. One weekend in January when I visit him in Annapolis, I wait for him in his bedroom while he takes a shower. I reach on the end table for the remote to watch television. When I lift it, a folded cocktail napkin falls to the floor. I pick it up to return it to the table; I see the stain of red lipstick where a girl has pressed her lips like a kiss. Beneath it is a handwritten note with a phone number and a message.


*Shayne,*
*Tonight was fun. Call me.*
*Tiff*


The heart that I didn't think existed anymore within me flinches in shock and fresh pain. This is something that, once upon a time, I would've found in Jake's room. Not Sam's.

By the time he comes back to the room from his shower, I'm seething.

"What's wrong?" he asks.

I toss the napkin at him. He picks it up and reads it.

"It's not what you think," he says.

"There's not a lot of room for interpretation," I say. I'm shrinking inside of myself even further than before, surprised that there's even more depth of darkness possible within me. This intimate napkin note, and the implications it carries, has turned my icy heart to stone.

He doesn't deserve any of the indifference I've served him lately, but this comes close. Despite my past trust issues, I trusted Sam. Does this break that trust, or is it an excuse to flee because my heart has hardened? I don't know. He deserves everything good from me, and I can't find anything good to give him anymore. Any goodness I have left is dying on the vine.

"She's a regular at the bar," he says. "She likes me. She sits at the bar most of the night with her girlfriends, and I guess she had a good time talking with me and Bill. That's it."

Bill is the other bartender on his shift.

"Just talking?"

"Yes."

"And the lipstick kiss, and her phone number?"

I feel like I'm with Jake, catching him in infidelities, watching him try to squirm his way out of it. It's a familiar, terrible feeling. Sam isn't like Jake, though. Is he?  He wouldn't cheat on me. Would he? That would mean the deep, faithful love he has for me isn't real. That the truest thing I've ever experienced is a lie. That he isn't the devoted man, lover, or friend I think he is. That he's as flawed as I am.

My warped thinking on my one kiss with Jake is that it was a final goodbye, not a desire, so it wasn't so bad. I love Sam and want to be with him, and only him. I even wrote that in the damn diary. Still, I realize that the Jake kiss was a betrayal. It didn't need to be sex.

For Sam to casually cheat on me, though, if he did, with someone who he doesn't even have a history with or feelings for, cheapens what we have. It makes a mockery of our love, and of me. Sam is loyal. Isn't he? Has he ever been? Have I been naïve? I don't know anymore.

"She keeps giving me her number," he says. "I haven't called her. I'm a bartender. Girls like to flirt with us. You never minded when girls hit on me at the beach all the time."

I don't know what to think. I thought I was dead inside, but I'm mad. Sad. Jealous. Hurt.

"That's different," I say. "I never found a girl's phone number and lipstick stain by your bed at the beach. But it's all here: her number, her lipstick, her invitation in your bedroom. You kept it. Didn't throw it away. Tiff. Not even Tiffany. You know her well."

He sits down on the bed beside me and tries to touch my arm. I jerk away from him.

"Like I said, she's a regular. That's it. I didn't call her. I didn't sleep with her. I've never cheated on you, Kit. You know I'm only yours."

I shake my head. "I thought that was true. Now I'm not so sure."

His jaw flexes in anger. "I'm not the one who kissed my ex and then didn't tell you about it, just days after professing unending love to you. If anyone shouldn't be sure, it's me."

"You're trying to divert this to something we already resolved."

"But you actually kissed him. I didn't do anything. You found a napkin from a girl who likes me. Lots of girls have crushes on bartenders. And on guards. I get lots of numbers and propositions. So do you. Since I met you, I haven't given any of them a thought. But lately—"

"Lately, what?" I'm angry, but not sure if I want to know the answer to that question.

"Lately I like how nice these girls are to me, because my own girlfriend is not. You've become cold and hard and, sometimes, even mean to me. You're like a different person. The girl I fell in love with is warm, funny, playful, and loves me on all levels. I could feel it from miles away. Now I can't feel it at all, even being right next to you."

"So, you want to give up on me the minute it gets hard? The minute I'm having a tough time and not quite myself? Is that your reason to want to be with other girls?"

"I don't want to be with other girls. I want you. And I'm still here, right? Despite how distant you are with me. Despite how hurt I am that you don't seem to love or even like me anymore. I'm here, Kit, and I want to know what's wrong. I love you. Only you."

I don't know if he's telling the truth or not. I don't know if I want the truth. I'm terrified of it. I'm already in a dark place, like a pond in winter freezing degree by degree, trying but failing to thaw against a dropping temperature. If the truth is that he cheated on me, it would shatter me completely. The line between my sanity and madness is too thin right now.

The only truth I've ever known is with him, and now I wonder if that was ever real at all. I've put my trust issues aside for him, but seeing what Tiff wrote on the cocktail napkin brings them all back. He says he didn't cheat on me. But what if he did? I can't bear it.

Instead, I tell myself that I don't care. My heart and soul repeat it: I don't care, I don't care. If I hit the replay button enough times, it'll be true so nothing can hurt me more, including this. Especially this. I can't take any more pain. It's too much, too much.

Sam and I may be able to survive if I can trust him and our love like I always did. If I believe what he says like I always did. If I want to make things work like he does. But I don't have it in me. This has turned my pain and hurt up a notch, over the line to nothingness, like an invisible light switch. Not feeling anything at all is awful, but much more manageable.

"I need to go to sleep," I say. Sleep is a relief, a needed escape.

He looks hurt. He wants me to say that I love him, too, but I can't. I do still love him, but from a distance. When we go to bed and he reaches for me, I turn my back on him.

I should break up with him. It isn't fair that he's still trying and I'm too cold inside to do the same. Instead, I'm a coward. I don't want to be the one to break up what has been such a beautiful love story. If I behave badly enough, maybe he'll break up with me. He can save face, and I won't feel so guilty about it. I'm already drowning in guilt.

I return to college. We continue down the path I've taken us. If I was a bitch before, I'm even more insufferable after reading Tiff's napkin note.

Sam still expresses love to me. He still talks about our future. He still writes love letters and drives hours to see me. When he comes through my door, exhausted from working and then driving, I turn my back to him and walk away. I ignore him when he's there, and I barely say goodbye when he leaves. I don't write letters back to him, and I stop taking his calls. I stop agreeing to see him. The hurt in his eyes doesn't crush me anymore. I'm too shut down inside to feel much of anything.

It's the beginning of the end, or maybe the middle. I'm just waiting for him to pull the trigger. He has no choice but to break up with me. It's just a matter of time.

~ Lord Byron, *When We Two Parted*

# Chapter 26

## THE BREAKUP

FEBRUARY 1987

Some Valentine's Day. Some month of love.

Toward the end of February, Sam sends me a love letter—one of many that I don't answer anymore. It's full of tenderness, love, confusion, sadness, and pleading to see me again.

He calls the next day; I finally answer. When he tries to make plans to come and see me, I tell him I'm busy. When he asks when he can come, I say I don't know. He pauses, and then he lights into me, full of hurt. He asks why I don't want him anymore. I don't have an answer.

He doesn't deserve how I'm treating him. I feel like part of the frozen winter landscape that surrounds me, my softness buried deep beneath the stiff ground.

He says he can't do this anymore, and then breaks up with me as he cries. I hastily agree that it's for the best, and then hang up the phone.

I feel relieved. I don't have to pretend to have a heart anymore, and he is free of this version of me that I don't even like. I don't deserve his love. He deserves better.

I'm proud of him. He has the dignity to let go when being disrespected, even though he doesn't want to. He doesn't stay and take it for years, like I did with Jake. Sam tried as much as he could—but didn't hold on to the corpse of the me that was nothing like the woman that he had known and loved last summer. I respect him for that. I know I'll always love him, and he will own a big piece of my heart—it's just that I can't find it anymore. It's buried too deeply.

A week later, I get a letter from him in the mail.

*Dear Kit,*

*I'm sorry I was hard on you on the phone last week. I don't want to let go, but you're already gone. I can't be the only one in this relationship. I've tried, and I can't bear to see the emptiness in your eyes where there was such love before.*

*What happened? You won't say, but I don't want to be another Jake. I don't want to hang on, nor do I want to be abusive or cutthroat.*

*I suppose it all comes down to me needing more from you than you're prepared to give. And timing. You're still so young and have so much to do. Right girl, wrong time. I don't understand what went wrong, when we were so right together. Now I only wish to remember us the way we were. What I wouldn't pay to relive those memories.*

*I'm so sorry, Kit. I will always have you in my heart. I will always be in love with you. I will always want to love you. I only hope for the best for you. May your life always be an endless summer.*

*Yours always,*

*Sam*

*P.s. If you are not too long, I will wait here for you all my life.*
*~ Oscar Wilde*

I want to cry, but I can't. I only read the letter once, and then I stuff it down to the bottom of the box where I keep special things, just like I stuffed thoughts of our baby in a place at the bottom of my heart in a dark place that I can't bear to revisit. I don't write him back. I just need to forget, forget, forget. It isn't the good goodbye our love deserves, but it's the one we get.

I bury myself in schoolwork and sleeping, and pretend like none of it ever happened. I'm polite and aloof instead of warm and friendly. I blow off any guys who try to approach me and ask me out. I rarely go out with friends, and I don't laugh much anymore. I've become someone I don't know, a hollow version of my former self.

When I ache for Sam, and when my love for him cries out from somewhere deep within, I keep the mantra of the miscarriage. Shut it down. Shut it down. Move on.

Annie tries to get me to open up. She expresses sorrow at my breakup with Sam, and at the loss of my joy. She tries to hug me, but I turn away. She looks at me with sad eyes that don't understand. How can she? I don't understand, either.

"I don't know what's happened with you," she says, "but I'm here for you when you want to talk about it. I love you." She means it and gives me space.

Part of me wants to tell her everything, but I can't bear to speak of it. Part of me wants to go to Sam, throw myself at his mercy, tell him everything, and beg him to come back to me. The new, dark me won't allow it. I pretend it all doesn't hurt, until it eventually it's true, or is at least buried deep enough to be silenced. So that's what I do. I bury the love and thoughts of Sam and our baby deep in the tomb of my newly armored heart.

I don't look back. I can't. I know I'll never have a summer like that again, or a love like that again. I had everything, and then lost it all at my own hand. I lost my family: Sam, the baby, and me. It's all my fault. I will pay the price.

All I can do is move forward to a future that just months ago would have been unthinkable: a future without Sam.

*Don't be afraid. There are exquisite things in store for you.*
*This is merely the beginning.*

~ Oscar Wilde, *The Picture of Dorian Gray*

# Epilogue

YES

SEPTEMBER 2024

I look out over the tranquil bay from my back deck and am grateful for the deep sense of peace I now have, and for the new life I have built in my later years. The sun is about to set over the horizon and light the sky with shades of red, orange, and violet. It never gets old. I'm happy.

I think about how far I've come, the journey that brought me here, and that pivotal evening two years ago when I met Sam in Ocean City to tell him about the miscarriage that happened long ago. To explain what he deserved to know before the article came out.

Looking back, I had been so nervous to tell him. He had been stunned and hurt to hear about the miscarriage, but also empathetic.

"I'm so sorry you went through that alone," he had said. "I wish you would've told me back then. Why didn't you?"

"I still don't fully understand it myself," I'd said. "I only recently started therapy about it. In hindsight, I can see that the way I acted after the miscarriage was from trauma, grief, and depression. I didn't recognize it then. I was just so emotionally unequipped for it all. I couldn't process it, so I just shut down. I guess it was psychological survival. I'm so sorry."

He had taken my hand and kissed it. "So am I. That had to be so painful for you."

"I wish I would've told you. You would've helped me. I had so much anger toward myself. So much guilt for losing the baby. I pushed everyone away. I should've seen a counselor back then, but I didn't know how much I needed it."

"In your message to me, you said that all this resurfaced because some people you love died and the grief from that stirred up everything from the past. Who died?"

"My dad, my sister, and my friend Bear all died of cancer in the span of two years, just before the pandemic."

"I'm so sorry, Kit. I know how much you loved them."

"The grief was so strong; I couldn't stuff it down like I did everything else before. Instead, it broke me open. It's like everything bottled up inside of me spilled out, including pain from the miscarriage, and my love for you. I had to finally face it. Process it. Grieve it. Part of that was done in therapy, part of it was writing about it. And telling you, Annie, and Mom."

"How did they take it?"

"They were both shocked I didn't tell them back then when it happened. Hurt. But mostly heartbroken for me, for losing the baby—and for losing you. And that I went through it alone. I didn't give Mom enough credit; she's always been there for me, just in ways I didn't recognize."

Sam had listened and taken it all in. I'd explained how writing and talking about the miscarriage had been healing and liberating, like releasing an anchor holding me down.

"It awakened me, Sam. Like a rebirth. And it inspired me to clear the cobwebs from my life. Seeing a therapist helped. I left my unhealthy marriage, got a place of my own in Austin, and talked about the baby instead of pretending she never existed."

"Thank you for telling me all this. It answers a lot of questions."

We had both sat there in that beautiful restaurant, each drinking each other in as we had decades before. In 1986, we'd fallen in love. In 2022, we still spoke a silent language that had been there from the start. Time and heartbreak hadn't broken our bond.

There had been a question in the air. I needed to ask it.

"Can you forgive me?" My throat was thick with sorrow. "For not telling you, for turning cold, for all we lost and could have been. I know you've moved on, but to the man who loved me back then, thank you—and I'm so very sorry."

He'd squeezed my hand. Wiped the tear falling down my cheek.

"I forgave you long ago. I never understood what happened to shut you down, but I never stopped loving you."

"I didn't stop loving you, either," I'd said. "I just buried it because it hurt too much. I wish I had been able to manage it differently. So many regrets. Losing you, above all."

We had sat in easy, comfortable silence for a while.

"This is a lot." He hadn't let go of my hand.

"It is. What are you feeling?"

He took a deep breath. "I came here tonight because I was curious about you. About what you had to tell me. And because I still can't say no to you." We both laughed at that.

"I was guarded," he continued. "I told myself I'd never let you hurt me again. But from the moment I saw you, none of that mattered. If I wasn't in my current situation, I'd ask you on a date. See where it goes. Take one day at a time, like we used to."

My heart leapt. I wasn't expecting that. I was only expecting to share the secret.

"I'd say yes," I'd said. "But what current situation? Aren't you separated?"

"Not for much longer."

"What do you mean?"

"My son came home on leave from the Navy last week. My wife got nostalgic that we were all together again as a family. She asked if we could try to make our marriage work one more time. She's a good woman; I owe that to her. To myself. To our son. So, I agreed. But first, I had to see you again. It seemed important."

I took a minute to let this sink in. I understood. I had stayed too long in my own marriage for my husband, for my kids, for everyone but myself when I knew it was no longer right for me.

"Like I said, I wasn't expecting to rekindle anything," I'd said. "But I admit that when I saw you across the room, hope did make an appearance."

"Same here," he'd agreed. "I didn't expect to feel so comfortable with you right away. Like all these years—decades— haven't passed. Right girl, wrong time. Again."

"That's okay," I'd said. "Seeing you again is a gift. It's shown me that I'm still capable of feeling deeply. That the love I had for you never left me, after all. I'm glad about that."

I had felt a sense of calm and closure. He said that he did, too, knowing the truth of what led to our breakup. We cried, we laughed, we remembered.

The realist in me knew I wouldn't get the fairytale. I'm grateful for what I did get, though. I got to look into Sam's eyes again and see love and warmth in them one more time. I got to hold his hand, tell him our full story, and receive his forgiveness.

"I won't contact you again," I'd said. "I respect that you're giving your marriage another try, and I wish you all the best. Know that I carry you with me always, and I love you."

He had leaned over and kissed me on the cheek. "I love you, too, Kit."

We embraced and went our separate ways. My heart was broken

and full at the same time. Seeing him again had been a confirmation of lasting love. It was also a good goodbye.

❦

That meeting with Sam in 2022 changed me. I had felt like myself with him—the me from long ago—playful, fun, flirty, confident, and completely authentic. It was mixed with the new me who was more experienced and self-assured, with the lessons of life and therapy.

I was so relieved that part of me wasn't dead; it just needed to be resuscitated. I vowed to do that. Three hours with him tapped into a life energy within me that I wanted to nurture. He always had brought out the best in me, but I needed to find that best on my own.

I knew I needed to make more changes in my life. I vowed to live life fully awake and to feel again, even when painful. When I flew back to Austin, I asked myself tough questions, and dug deep for honest answers. What did I want? What could I give to myself and to others? Where was home? I knew that was by the water, in Ocean City, Maryland or close to it.

I thought about the people I loved and who loved me. My kids. Annie and her husband, Chuck. Aunt Sue and Uncle Al. Mom, who had become a friend over the years. My kids were at the center, but were forging their own paths; a flight could take me to them any-where. I knew that I wanted to be within driving distance to Mom and Annie, so I put my Austin condo up for sale in late September of 2022 and started looking online at Ocean City condos.

My article about grief and pregnancy loss was published that October, during Pregnancy and Infant Loss Awareness Month. I squealed in delight at seeing my name in the byline. I received a flood of feedback from people all over the world sharing their sto-ries, including men. I hoped the article was an inspiration for them to start a healing process.

"I'm proud of you," Mom had said during a call. That meant the world to me.

I also started an online pregnancy loss support group and joined an online grief healing group to further process all the losses I've experienced. It was the beginning of the end of a lot of stuck sadness inside of me, and a new beginning of hope and renewal.

When my Austin condo sold in November 2022, I bought a townhouse in Ocean City with a back deck overlooking the bay and a prime view of the sunsets I remembered. I got permission to work remotely from the healthcare company where I worked as a marketing manager, bought a Mustang, and moved to the beach in December—just in time to ring in 2023 alone overlooking the water with sweet wine, chocolate, and spectacular fireworks.

Ever since, I've been collecting the pieces of myself that were scattered through the years and adding new pieces. I formed new friendships and have even been on a few dates that made for amusing stories for Mom and Annie. I began to eat better, exercise more, and create sea glass art. I continued to write, joined a book club, and started swimming beyond the breakers, always with a lifeguard present. I said yes to life and joy again.

Today, two years after that face-to-face with Sam, I feel more like my true self than ever. I've forgiven myself. I feel compassion for my mistakes, and for the young woman I was back then who didn't know—couldn't have known—how to handle such a heavy burden alone.

My foster dog, Sadie, saunters onto the deck and nudges my hand for affection. I gladly give it to her. She's a sweet, senior lab full of love and hope, despite the neglect she's endured. She appreciates a second chance at happiness, like I do. I'm pretty sure this will be a foster fail; we've both found our forever home.

She takes the treat I give to her and plops down in her bed. I plug my iPhone into the deck speaker, choose a playlist of my favorite songs, and press play. I sit down at the table and write in my journal, which is apparently the new word for diary. I've taken up the practice again.

*Looking back, my life between that summer with Sam and now has been full, and it has been empty without the healing I had needed to fully enjoy it and grow. I'm experiencing that healing now, and what a difference it makes.*

*Life is too short for regrets, but I have a few. I wish I had told Sam about the miscarriage when it happened, when we may have been saved. I wish I had gotten counseling right away for it; I may have forgiven myself and healed so much sooner.*

*Not doing all that affected all aspects of my life. I lost Sam. I lost myself. I had a sadness about me ever since then. If I had asked for help earlier, I could've been a more fully present mom and wife. I could've lived my life with more joy and felicity.*

*That night in 2022 when I met up with Sam, I was surprised by the power of the love I still felt for him. It flowed out of me, despite how much time had passed. It was painful that he wasn't still mine.*

*I had to look at it all as part of my healing process, a starting place to bloom again. Much has changed since then. If I'd known where my path would lead from there, I wouldn't have believed it. I'm right where I need to be, wide awake, in a place I love, with people I love. I am blessed beyond measure. I'm home.*

I put down my pen and take in the stunning vista. My reality is better than a fairytale. I feel whole again. As the summer breeze blows through my hair, and the sky starts to blaze with the brilliant colors of the sunset show, I sigh a grateful breath of deep contentment.

∾

The sliding glass door opens; I turn to feast my eyes upon him. I can never get enough.

Sam holds a Stoli Gimlet in one hand and a cherry cola in the other. He steps out on the deck, puts the drinks on the table, and kisses me. Amos Lee's "With You" plays through the speaker. Sam sits and we hold hands as we watch the sunset.

Inside, on the bookshelf in the living room, is a framed card I got in the mail from him back in May. There is a crab on the front with the words, You Crack Me Up. Inside are his handwritten words:

*Dear Kit,*

*Can we meet? Can I see your sunny smile again? That is, if you are still single, if you want to, and if there are still miracles in this world. Right girl, right time? Third time's supposed to be a charm, you know.*

*Stacy and I made a good effort, but within months agreed that what we had was lost long ago. We've been divorced for over a year now.*

*My heart keeps calling for you. You aren't on social media anymore, so I called your mom. She gave me your address and her blessing. I think she still likes me.*

*What a nice surprise that you now live in OCMD, but I would've come to Texas or the moon for you. Would you like to go to a crab feast with me next Saturday? Kurt and his wife, Pam, will be up from Florida. Another double date. I promise I won't lie about any spiked punch. My number is on the back of the card. Hoping for a yes.*

*Yours then, now, and always,*
*Sam*

*p.s.  I will come back to you, I swear I will; and you will know me still.*
   *~ Edna St Vincent Millay*

*p.s.s.  Grow old along with me! The best is yet to be..."*
   *~ Robert Browning*


# THE END

# Acknowledgments

Writing a book is not for the faint of heart. Many people say they're writing a book, and some start. Few finish. Even fewer publish one. I now know why. The creative part is just the beginning. The rest is an *Alice in Wonderland* adventure, a journey with unpredictable twists and turns around every corner, along with peculiar happenings, unexpected nonsense, quirky characters, and hard-earned lessons along the way.

I'm not special to have labored through this; I'm just more stubborn than most. A writer must have tenacity, curiosity, and a headstrong story that demands to be told—one that endures above weariness, frustration, and discouragement. A strong support system is essential. Mine sustained me through this writing journey; this story wouldn't have taken flight without them. This book belongs to them, and to the readers. Cheers to my tribe, with a heart of deep gratitude.

**To God**

Thank You for Your comprehensive, consuming love, full of grace. Thank You for Your many blessings. Thank You for loving me despite my failings. Thank You for life and for You.

**To My Family**

Scott; Kolten and Jordan; Karina and David; Alex; Mom (Jane) and Dad (Terry); my brother Damon; and Angie, Paula, Jordan, Kaitlin, Jared, Caleb, Koa, Sevy, Jameson, Aliyah, Jim, and Brenda. You are my family, my heart, my tribe. Thank you for your love and support.

**To Mom**

When I was a little girl, I heard you play your guitar and sing songs you wrote from your heart after long days working nine to five in our small hometown. One week, you traveled to Nashville to make a record. Months after you returned, I noticed how your eyes lit up when we saw it at the local record store. You shared your voice with the world. The artist and dreamer in you inspired the same in me. You are more beautiful than beautiful. I love you.

**To the Editor**

Marie Beswick-Arthur, you are more than an immensely talented editor and writer; you are a beautiful human being and now a treasured friend. You believed in me and this story when I did not, and made this all possible when I didn't think it was. Special thanks to Erin Staley for introducing us, and for her sunny smile.

**To the Contributing Editor / Fact Checker**

Scott McIntire, painting a verbal picture of Ocean City, Maryland, and the life of a beach guard in the 1980s would've been impossible without you. You brought this outsider behind the curtain to share the magic there. You and your stories, fact-checking, encouragement, and inspiration are integral to this story. Thank you from the bottom of my heart.

**To the Book Designers**

*Cover:* Kaitlin Goss of Joy Media Designs, you are a talented artist and a beloved niece. Your partnership and vision visually brought this story to life. I'm so proud of you and of us; I know your dad is, too. I can feel his smile from heaven—I really can.

*Interior:* Paul Baillie-Lane, I'm so honored that you have taken the words from my heart and turned them into something beautiful on these pages. Your talent is golden. I've also immensely enjoyed your British accent. I feel fancy.

**To the Beta Readers / My Friends**

Mary Ellen Anderson, Caitlin Bijon, and John Wisse, you are my friends, story advisors, first critics—and oh-so-kind error-catchers before this story went to editing. John, you also provided patient proofreading and steady encouragement. You each gave my first draft a spanking in the nicest of ways, sprinkled the project with encouragement, and made it so much better. I trusted your judgment, voices, and heart; I felt safe there. This is your story, too.

**To My Mentors**

Bob Adamov, gifted author and friend, your smile lights up every room, as does the beauty and essence of your wife Cathy. Your guidance and friendship are priceless.

Christine Kohler, accomplished author and friend, you are generous and wise. You shared your time, knowledge, wisdom, and talent after reading my first three chapters, raw from my heart, and gave me sage advice that changed the book's trajectory. Many thanks.

### To My Feedback Friends

To my friends who shared their feedback on my book and cover options, who are patient with my indecisiveness, and who make my life brighter: Mom (Jane Goss), Mary Ellen Anderson, Lori Rose Centi, Lori Wood, Jennifer Landry, Pat Daly, Debbie Herman, Devlin Smith, William Swanger, Maya Echols, and Barbara Doty.

### To Heavenly Friends

Jackie Rager and Cathy Hanzelik, you were angels on earth and now in heaven. Both gone too soon, and loved deeply, always. My forever friends. You are with me still.

### To Game Night Friends

Jim and Joanne Miller, and Stacey and Rob Dunn, your friendship, laughter, and beautiful spirits helped carry me through stressful times of creating this book. Our game nights are priceless.

### To the Henrys

Kim, you paused during your church sermon one day to give me a word from God to finish my book. You didn't even know I was writing one, but He did. I'm thankful for the faithfulness and friendship of you and John. Caleb, you inspire me with your authentic music, your good heart, and your sincere friendship. You are each a treasure.

### To My Favorite Teacher

Elsie Straub, my high school English teacher, you are foundational to my career as a writer and editor. Your lessons about English, theater, and how to be both strong and kind are baked into me. Thank you.

# About the Author

Andrea K. Goss is a writer, editor, and creative consultant for businesses, the education sector, advertising agencies, and production companies. She also has edited books, adapted a book into a screenplay, produced videos and a podcast, written and produced songs, and written and edited articles for magazines such as *Preferred Travel Magazine* and *Screen Actor*.

Born and raised in Pennsylvania, Andrea earned her Master's Degree in Communications from Regent University, and her common sense from her mom and dad. She lives in Southern California with her family, including her weird but lovable rescue dog, Quiggy.

*The Summer You Were Mine* is her first novel. Visit **andreakgoss.com** to find out more, and to sign up for exclusive emails about events, new releases, and book discussions.